Friends

G·K Hall &C°.

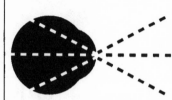

This Large Print Book carries the
Seal of Approval of N.A.V.H.

Friends

Charles Hackenberry

G.K. Hall & Co. • Thorndike, Maine

Published in 2000 by arrangement with M. Evans & Company, Inc.

G.K. Hall Large Print Western Series.

The text of this Large Print edition is unabridged.
Other aspects of the book may vary from the original edition.

Set in 16 pt. Plantin by Al Chase.

Printed in the United States on permanent paper.

Library of Congress Cataloging-in-Publication Data

Hackenberry, Charles, 1939–
   Friends / Charles Hackenberry.
     p.   cm.
   ISBN 0-7838-8945-3 (lg. print : hc : alk. paper)
   1. Large type books. I. Title.
PS3558.A276 F75 2000
 813'.54—dc21   99-059540

This book is dedicated to
Ray Matthews
former collaborator
and lifelong friend.

Chapter One

Back in the winter of '77 I was deputying up in Two Scalp, Dakota Territory, waiting for my friend Clete Shannon — who was the Sheriff there at the time — to say the word for us to quit our jobs and head south. The reason I remember the date so well, come the new year they had strung up a banner behind the bar at Clooney's with 1877 wrote out in big numbers, and we drunk a few more than we usually did. At least I did. Every year I get surprised at how high the numbers of the years is getting, and it makes me just thirstier than hell.

Along about April I noticed Clete'd started riding out in the mornings, scouting around, even before the bad weather was all gone, when fog still hung over the snow and made staying in bed real tempting.

At first, I thought him riding around like that was just restlessness. I was that way a little too. I used to be a lot more that way myself when I was a younger man. Then for a few days I believed he was trying to find the gold Palmer Wilson and that bunch stole from the bank — either for himself or for the reward of it. But then it hit me — he had gotten pretty friendly with one of the young gals from around there, Mary McLeod her name was. I worried he might be planning on settling down, off looking for a spot for a ranch, and to hell with our plans for Texas.

Being Clete's deputy give me mighty little to do but think things over, morning or night. Two Scalp's deader'n a sucker in a sandstorm. Not that there wasn't plenty of trouble before me and Clete broke it up that fall — but when Whitey DuShane and Tom Nace took up residence in the bone yard, things got a lot quieter.

What Clete would get all cold and wet for, riding around those hills, was eatin' at me while I stood at the bar sipping whiskey after sundown one evening. And when I heard him ride back into town, I stepped out on the walk and waited. After a while I seen him lumbering up the street.

"Come in here and buy me a drink," I told him. "Unless you start taking on more whiskey, you're blood's gonna freeze out on them long rides."

I wasn't sure he would without an argument, but he followed me inside and we settled into my regular spot at the bar. *After* he'd tipped his hat to all the folks that said hello to him, that is, which was nearly everone in the place, even the whores. He took a long, careful look around.

"Somebody trying to shoot you that I don't know about?" I ask him.

"Just habit," he said, looking at me. Them deep green eyes of his always made me think of wolves I seen on the trail once. "You notice too damn much, Willie."

Tubbs the barkeep brought us our liquor and wouldn't take Clete's money for it, though he'd

8

had the conscience to pick mine up earlier.

"I just try to keep my eyes open, but I'm surprised I didn't notice 'til recent how much you've been spooking around out there — must be a couple times a week. Still, early morning ain't my most alert time of day. What I can't figure out is why you're doing it. Is it the reward or what?"

That surprised him a little. "Well, I don't know either, but I suspect it's the *what*. You'll be the first to know, after me."

"And when'll I know about when we're leaving this damn town and going someplace where it's warmer and friendlier?" I asked him.

Clete rubbed his squared-off chin and then put back his whiskey. "More than I can tell you right now," he said. "I've got some figuring to do, and some other business. It's still too cold, anyway."

"Sure," I told him. "That McLeod girl ain't the other business you had in mind, though, is it?"

"You could start off by yourself if you're in such a damned hurry to get out of here," he said, a little sharper than was called for. "I could catch up to you later."

I put back the bottom half of my rye before I answered. "Well, I guess I'll wait around a little longer, but I ain't waiting forever, you understand."

Clete just nodded.

After a while Tubbs came over and we got us

9

two more whiskeys.

"Anybody new come in today?" Clete ask the round-bellied barman while he was pouring them.

"A drummer came in on the early stage, but that's all. You could ask your deputy, though. He's here almost as much as I am." The sonofabitch give me a big grin and then went down the bar to tend to the rest of his customers. I never liked that damn Tubbs anyway.

Clete killed his whiskey in a belt. Lots of men and more than a few of the gals came and patted him on the back or said a word or two of praise to him, about bringing law and order to Dakota Territory and the like, but he didn't let it swell him up much. I started to order another round, but Clete shook his head.

"Count me out," he said and started toward the door. "I gotta get up early tomorrow, and I believe you know where I'm going."

"I expect I do, but where're you going now? They let out your room upstairs here to someone who pays his bills regular?"

"No, I sleep here most nights. But old Nell keeps a room for me out at her place, you know. And she's been spooked lately. Thinks some-body's fussing with her cattle, though she hasn't missed any." He walked back to the bar. "I almost forgot. Nell asked me to invite you out for supper Sunday after next. Me and Mary are going to be there and some other people. Nell said to be sure to mention she was roasting a chicken. She said she never seen a Texan that wouldn't walk five miles for a chicken dinner, especially a free one." He slapped me on the shoulder and walked out the door.

"Well, maybe I'll be there and maybe I won't!" I yelled after him. Clete, he just kept on going.

A hollow-cheeked man in a high-peaked hat lay with his long legs splayed out on an oiled scrap of canvas just below the brow of a hill half a mile from Nell Larson's ranch house, watching. He took three deep swallows of cold coffee from his canteen and then replaced the cork. His skeletal hands rolled a cigarette. He licked it and stuck it between his thin lips. He would wait to light it. He would wait.

Of course I had to go. Come the Sunday after next, I rode out to Nell's place listening to the prairie larks nearly the whole way. When I got there, I saw a lot more people than I thought there was going to be. The preacher, Mary McLeod and her father Jesse, old Jim Talfer, some of Nell's family from down Yankton way, and other folks I didn't know.

The women all helped Nell in the kitchen, cooking lots of different things, it smelled like — and it sure smelled good. Ermaline Doughty and her girl were fussing with the big table that Nell had set up in her parlor — all sorts of fancy forks and spoons and such. First I come up here, it was all hardtack and salt pork and sittin' on the ground.

The men were out beside the barn and I lit my

11

pipe when I got there. The talk was of gold strikes and Indian attacks and cattle ailments and the like. I noticed Clete wasn't saying much, just looking out at the hills.

"Something interesting out there?" I asked, moving over to the fence beside him.

"No, not that I can find," he said kind of slow. "Someone was out there, though, but I think Nell's wrong. He wasn't fooling with the steers. He camped right where we did that night we went after Whitey DuShane at the Haney ranch."

"Yes, indeed, I remember —"

"So do I," Clete butted in, "but I need you to help me with *this.*" He looked close at that rolling land. "From out where he camped you can see Nell's house through the break between those ridges. You figure that's what he's doing, spying on Nell?"

"Beats me," I offered. "She got any enemies 'round here?"

"I don't think so, but I'll ask her."

"She seems a little old for it to be tomcats sniffing at the dooryard," I told him. "Ain't Indians is it?"

"No. They're raiding over to the west of here, but it don't smell like an Indian camp. One man by himself — I'm pretty sure of that." He set his jaw and looked at his boots. "How would you feel about riding up there and taking a look around tomorrow?"

"You asking or telling?"

12

"Well, I'm asking because this isn't in town, you know. Just be a favor for Nell."

Well, that was different. Clete and me hadn't been there a whole year, but she treated him and me both like family right from the start — him especially. My guess always was that Nell sort of saw Clete as the son she'd wished she'd had. "Be happy to," I said. "How old's the sign?"

"Two, maybe three days. Think you can see anything I didn't, you old fart?"

"Jest you wait," I said, laying hold of his arm and leading him back to the rest of the fellows, for I seen that Jim Talfer had pulled out a pint.

After a while someone rung the dinner bell and all the men started down to the house.

Well, the table looked just grand, I guess you'd say. Nell had these plates with gold leaves in the middle, and cups to match and little plates and finger bowls and I don't know what-all. She said later, while we was eating one of the best chicken dinners north of the Mason Dixie line, that her momma had brought all this fine stuff west in a wagon. And that her momma's grandma had lugged it all the way from Scotland! One of the ladies had gathered a bouquet of purple and white pasqueflowers and had set them on the white tablecloth too.

The preacher give a short blessing before we all started in. After the soup we had some fish and some vegetables Nell had put up. I had never drunk wine before, and it was curious stuff. Probably had a kick to it if you drank enough. Mashed potatoes and filling too, and plenty of gravy to smother everything.

Later, Clete asked me, louder than he needed to, if the chicken in Dakota Territory was as tasty as it was in Texas, and I had to make up some windy about it being better up here. Everbody laughed, I guess they saw clear through me.

Clete and Mary looked like they was having a good time. She's a mighty pretty girl, is Mary McLeod. Dark hair, and skin like one of them little china ladies setting on Nell's parlor organ. I wondered how much younger she was than Clete. A good bit, it looked like that day.

Everbody was all talking at the same time, and after we ate our cake, Nell stood up like she was going to give a speech. "Come up here with me, Jesse," she said. "We have some work to do." So he did. "Seeing as how Mary's momma ain't here with us this day, God rest her soul, Mary asked me if I'd stand in her stead," Nell Larson declared.

"That's a fact," Jesse McLeod said. He didn't look no more comfortable than I felt.

"Clete Shannon, don't you have something to say?" Nell ask, looking down the table at him.

"I do," Clete answered getting to his feet. "Though I may be saying those words just a little too early." Right then I knowed what this party was all about. He smiled at Mary, took her hand, and she stood up beside him, all perky and bright-eyed. There was almost as many people

14

standing at that fancy dinner table as there was left sitting. "About a week ago," Clete said, "I asked Mary to marry me, and she was fool enough to say she would, come June."

"I'm sure Mary's momma would have been real proud," Nell said. "And Jesse is too, ain't that so, Jesse?"

"That's a fact," Jesse said. Well, everbody clapped their hands, so I did too. But after I had clapped myself dry, I got to thinking the situation over more careful.

Not more than two weeks ago the plans was that him and me were going to start south as soon as the weather cleared. Now here he had went and done this. Still, Clete looked happier than a well laid out corpse.

Chapter Two

Well, I wasn't going to wait 'til next morning to see what I could see out in them hills up behind Nell's house. And I wasn't going to tell Clete, either. I determined right then to help out with this business at Nell's and then head south whether Clete was going or no. But I'd swing west first and take another look at them Rocky Mountains. Maybe go down through the Grand River country. Wasn't as warm as I'd have liked it to be, but it'd be warm enough soon.

Just before midnight I got a whiff of Nell's damned old pigpen, so I knowed I was about where I wanted to be. Now, it would make a better tale, I know, to say right here that I seen someone that night, but the truth is I didn't. Fact is, I rode around out there and almost froze to death. Was darker than a cypress swamp, and I didn't see a thing except a thin slice of the moon for a while and about a million stars. I sat there on my horse, getting what heat from him I could, and waited for more than an hour for the sun to climb up out of his nice warm bed.

That section of Dakota Territory always reminds me a lot of my part of Texas when the weather's right. Big, billowy swells of land far as you can see, which is pretty far. Once the snow quits the land, as it mostly had last week, the air gets nice and dry. Soon the grass greens out and springs up to the top of your boots. Then stays just that tall, 'til it withers from the drought or dies in the frost, either one. Course, it hadn't sprung to life yet this year much, but it would. Least it had every year since God'd planted it.

West of here are the Black Hills, where miners were tearing up the streams to get the color out. I seen the Hills once, and it didn't surprise me to hear that the Sioux were killing whites to keep it for themselves. West of that come the Bighorns and wester still, the Rockies. I wouldn't say this to just anyone, but there are no sights in Texas to compare to them peaks and river valleys over in the Rockies.

The land tilts up from here all the way to the mountains. You couldn't see it, but if you walked west all day your legs'd let you know you had been going uphill when you laid down to sleep that night. Not that I can see any reason for walking all day — since horses have been invented for some time now. Pretty country, damn pretty country, even here. I watched the sun stick his nose over the hill to the east and wondered what I was going to do now that Clete was getting married.

I had first throwed my lot in with Clete over that Wilson mess. About the time we agreed to take the sheriff and deputy jobs, we also agreed to take off come spring. It would do all right to hole up here for the winter, we decided, but come reasonable weather, we'd ride downward on the map 'til we found us some strong drink and willing señoritas and prop our feet up in some place where the sun shines strong enough to blister your scalp right through your hat, so you stay in the shade. We didn't work out all the details, but that's what we had spoke about.

Now, Mr. Cletus Shannon had went and proposed marriage to Miss Mary McLeod. Which looked like it was going to go and change everthing we decided on. I believe I have lost more friends to marriage than to snakes and Indians combined. Course, he had a right to do what suited him, and I had as good a right to hold it against him, going back on his word like he did.

Soon as I said that to myself, I saw something white in the grass. I dismounted and picked it up. It was some kind of cartridge, but it was nothing like none I ever seen before. Not more than a foot from it, there was its twin. They were shells of some kind, all right. The slugs were real soft and they were about the thickness of minié balls, shaped like them too. But instead of brass they had little white cloth sacks fastened where the brass ought to go.

I stuck the pair of them in my vest pocket and got down on my hands and knees and just looked. Sometimes it takes a while to see what you're seeing. I learned a long time ago that most folks'll see what they're looking for, not what they're looking at, and it takes more than a minute or two to take in what's there instead of what you expected you'd find. I crawled around some and finally noticed how the grass was sort of laid down in one spot. Oh, it'd almost all sprung back up, even half dead like it was, but enough of it was still bent over to see where somebody'd laid out a piece of canvas, or a rubber sheet, or something like that. After I had it square in my mind where the corners was, I crawled around the outside and found some little black holes burnt into the matted-down grass.

Whoever'd laid out here had faced Nell's place from this little rise and spent a good piece of time looking at her house or something around where she lives. Reason I knowed that was from the little burn holes. There was a lot of them along the edge of the blanket-sized square that faced toward the buildings, and they was made from grinding out cigarette butts — lots of them, no question. Little rise like this, the snow would leave here first, though the ground would be froze hard, wet and cold as hell turned inside out.

Clete was right, too. One man by himself, I would bet, because the holes made by the burning cigarette butts was in the center of the side toward Nell's house. Two men laying on a tarp looking down there would be more toward each side, even if one didn't smoke. Course there might of been three men, with one in the middle, but I doubted that. Fellow might talk one fool into laying out here in freezing weather spying on an old woman with him, but I doubted if he could find a second. Craziness to do a thing like that stays bottled up in one man by himself, mostly. And he was careful not to be discovered, too, because he'd gathered up his butts and taken them with him.

It surprised me, then, that he'd been so careless with his shells. But maybe he was in a hurry to get out of here. Maybe he fired and run, or maybe somebody run him off, I don't know. I crawled around some more and out in front of where he laid, on the side toward Nell's place, I found a little scrap of cloth that looked a lot like the stuff holding the powder to the whole shells I found, only burned some. Well, he had fired at something — or someone. I checked all over for heel holes or boot tracks and fresh horse droppings, but there was none I could see.

About the time I was thinking of riding down to Nell's and then to town, here she comes riding up toward me with Clete beside her, both of them going slow and looking for sign. Soon they saw me and waved and I mounted and headed down that way.

"How do, Willie," Nell called. "You're about pretty early." She didn't seem to be jabbing me about sleeping late so I didn't take no offense. Clete smiled some, but he didn't say nothing.

"Yeah, I saw the sun come up but not a lot more," I told her. "Been out here all night and I'm stiffer than a badger's tail. Got any coffee down there?"

Clete raised his eyebrows. "How come you did

that? I didn't ask you to do that."

"Thought I might catch someone if he was out prowlin' with the coyotes," I answered. "Mighty hungry up here now, though."

"You asking me to fix you something?" Nell ask me.

"Would you mind, Nell?"

"No, not a bit. Come down in a while and I'll have something ready," she said, and kicked her old mare around. She stopped a little distance away and looked back at us over her shoulder, suspicious. "You men have your private talk, if you must, but don't you keep me in the dark about nothing. I mean it!" Then she dug her heels into that mare's ribs and cantered on home. Wasn't an entirely bad rider either, for a woman.

"You found something, huh?" Clete asked after we watched Nell for a minute.

"I guess so," I said, and showed him the square spot where the grass was laid over a little and the burnt holes. Then I took the cartridges out of my pocket and handed them to him. "She say anything about hearing a shot?"

That set him back on his boot heels pretty good. He turned them over in his hands and ended up smelling them, just like I did earlier. "Nice piece of looking, Willie," he said, kind of like he was congratulating me and kind of surprised that I done it, too. "What do you make of this?"

"Well, I don't know. Ain't nothing I'm familiar with, but I sure as hell know I wouldn't want to be hit with a piece of lead that size."

"Me, either," he said. "You know, I've seen something like this before, but damned if I can remember where. Seems like I ought to, though."

"I'm surprised she didn't say nothing to you about hearing a shot. Something that big would sound like a cannon between these hills."

"How do you know he fired?" Clete ask.

I fished out the little scrap of cloth and handed him that, too. Buckshot scared up and Clete took a minute to settle him. "Well, she didn't hear it, but Jesse McLeod did. He was around her place day before yesterday — Saturday that'd make it — and someone took a shot at him. Nell was in town buying things for the shindig, I understand." He took off his hat and wiped his brow, though it wasn't warm enough to work up a sweat. "Jesse didn't want to worry her about it. Sorry I didn't mention that to you, Partner. Just forgot to." He looked kind of hang-dogged after he said it.

"Well, I didn't get no bullet hole in me over it so it don't matter . . . Pard. Though it don't look like I'll be calling you that much longer, does it?"

He knowed what I was about. "Meant to tell you that, too, but it just came on before I had a chance."

"Sure," I told him. "I'll bet you didn't even ask her yet that day in Clooney's when you invited me to them high old times at Nell's, huh?" I guess I could have been a little easier on him about it, but, damn, a man desertin' his friends like that!

He waved me off and shook his head. "Shit, we didn't sign any contract about going south, just talked about it, as I recall. Things change, you know that."

He was right, of course. I'd seen it plenty of times, had even talked about doing something myself with a fellow or two and then went and done the opposite. After a minute or so it was pretty clear neither of us had nothing more to say on the subject.

"C'mon," Clete said, mounting Buckshot and heading toward Nell's. "I could use some more coffee while you're filling your gut."

We rode quiet for a while. I guessed if I'd ever caught a bad case of the calico fever I might act the same way. "What'd McLeod tell you about gettin' shot at?" I ask him.

"Not much," he said. "Jesse was off his horse and walking toward the door and saw the dirt fly in front of him, like a big geyser, so he said. At first he thought somebody'd thrown something at him for a joke. But then he heard it and ducked for cover. Didn't figure out what direction it came from for a while, and by then it was too late to go after whoever fired at him. Probably a good thing he didn't anyway.

"Mind if I hang on to these?" he asked, still fingering one of the cartridges. "I'd like John Tate to have a look at 'em."

"Well, I wasn't plannin' on startin' a collection of unusual shells," I told him.

"Wouldn't surprise me if you did do that. 'Willie Goodwin's Mementos of the Wild and Wooly West,' you might call it. Travel with one of those rough-riding shows and get rich telling lies to greenhorns. Ready for a belt-stretchin' breakfast?"

Clete put away his share of flapjacks and eggs, too, but there was no shortage, I can guarantee. After we ate, Clete looked around the dooryard to see if he could spot where the bullet had hit, but he couldn't and neither could I. Been too many people tramping around after the big engagement dinner was my guess. He didn't say no more about me going out to look around again. Guess maybe he was afraid I would get myself killed, but I woulda bet that the old boy who laid out there watching was long gone by then.

I'd a lost that bet, surely.

Chapter Three

Clooney's was still pretty empty when I sat sipping my first beer the next day. Truth is, I was hoping one of the girls might be trying to pick up a little extra money, but none of 'em was. Clete come in and looked around and saw me.

"C'mon," he said, walking up to my table, his eyes full of some annoyance or other. "Let's go ask John Tate about these cartridges."

"Sit down and have a beer, and let me finish this one and we'll go do 'er," I told him. It was still nice and quiet in Clooney's.

"No, it's too early for me," he said. "C'mon. Let that stuff alone. Let's go." He started for the door taking strides like he wanted to get somewhere.

I couldn't see the sense of letting a nice, cool half drunk beer go to waste, but I picked up just the same and followed him outside, where he was lighting a smoke.

We walked down toward Tate's store but neither of us said anything. It was a fine spring day, though. Sun had a little heat to it already, and you could tell the cold weather didn't have a chance no more.

Nice town, Two Scalp — mostly a one streeter, but you can't help but notice that there's houses going up pretty regular. They had started another one over in the east end, and you could hear them banging away at it from all over town. Mabel's whorehouse was the oldest building in Two Scalp, I guess, but it certainly wasn't the handsomest. The bank would carry off that prize, for it was made of stone and higher than any other thing in town, except the water tank. Pictures of lion's faces and leaves carved into it, all around the top. The bank, I mean, not the damn water tank. Course, most places were like Jones' Barber Shop, pretty rough and small, showing all the saw-cuts, but at least the barber shop didn't try to look like more than it was with a squared-off false front like a lot of the businesses did.

"What's on your mind, anyway?" I asked Clete after we'd walked for a while. "You worried about Nell or are them new pants too tight for ye?"

"No," he said after a minute. "I was just trying to figure out how to tell you you've been drinking too damn much without making you mad." He kept walking while he said this to me, sounding like he was just commenting on the weather. "Of course, it's your business, but it seems every time I need you I've got to go to Clooney's."

Well, I stopped right there and just waited for him to turn around, which he did after a few steps.

"Now just a minute," I said. "You're the sheriff here and I do what you tell me, but I don't remember bein' asked to sign no damn temperance card when you offered me the deputy job. Besides, there's nothing for me to stay sober for, anyhow. Biggest problem in this town, outside of a few drunks firing off their pistols, is the dust settlin' on people's furniture."

"Shit, Willie, I'm not against a man taking some whiskey, but not at the rate you're going. When was the last time you went all day without a drink? Or two or three?"

"Why, I don't know *when* that was and I don't care to try and recollect it, either."

Clete just stood there with a flat expression on his face expecting me to confess the error of my ways, I suppose, but I wasn't about to do that. "You want this badge, that what you want?" I ask.

Well, he screwed his face up and glanced at the sky and finally walked back to me. "No, I don't want the damn badge," he said, letting a little mad show through his voice. "But you're wrong about there being nothing for you to do." He lowered his tone some then. "I don't like whatever's goin' on out at Nell's. I talked to Jesse McLeod again last night and he came damn close to being killed." He took those funny-looking cloth-backed things out of his coat pocket and held them under my nose. "Whoever threw one of these at old Jesse meant to kill him. He lay in ambush and shot from more than half a mile off, you realize that? Now that doesn't sound like the work of anyone we know here in Two Scalp, does it?"

27

He waited a minute for me to answer. "No, it don't."

"You're damn right it don't," he said before the words was hardly out of my mouth. "Look, I'm going to need your help here, Willie. I rode around out where you did at Nell's and *I* didn't see a damn thing. But you didn't have anything to drink that day except a swig from Talfer's pint. You were probably more sober than you've been in two months."

He took a minute and hitched up his pants, likely waiting for me to cut myself a nice big wedge of humble pie, but I didn't.

"It's your business, true," Clete said, looking at me a little sideways. "But if you're gonna keep trying to pickle your brain in alcohol, I'm gonna *have* to get a new deputy, and I'd rather have you backing me up, when you're sober, that is, than anybody else I can think of — even though you can't shoot worth a dog's asshole."

Again he waited for me to declare myself a reformed man, but I'd already decided against that. A man's drinking is his own affair and nobody else's.

"Well, come on," he said. "Unless you intend to stand there all day like a damn statue. Doesn't seem right, two men standing in the street squabbling like schoolkids. I'm going to talk to Tate." He turned and walked off down the street, but I wasn't sure I was going. If he looked back, I didn't see him.

After a time I started down that way too.

Truth is, I couldn't think of nothing else to do. Clete was already inside by the time I got there, but he was waiting for Tate to finish up with a customer, a lady who was buying some lamp wicks and yard goods, and I don't know what else.

John Tate sold dry goods and hardware, but mainly he sold guns. Everyone around bought guns and ammunition from John Tate, because if there was anything worth knowing about firearms, he knew 'er. Had all kinds of catalogs and announcements from the companies that made them, too. I watched him helping the lady out the door with her packages, and I never would have guessed that someone as gentle and polite as him would spend all his free minutes studying on the tools that men use to shoot one another.

After he said goodbye to the woman, Tate turned to Clete and me. "Can I help you gentlemen?"

"I hope you can, John," Clete answered. "Would you mind closing your shop for a few minutes? I'd rather not have everyone in Two Scalp gossiping about what I have to ask you. I'll ask you to keep this to yourself, too."

Tate's eyebrows sprung up. The spectacles on his nose slid down a notch or two, but he pushed them back up quick, locked his door, and then went behind the counter. "Of course, Sheriff, of course. What can I do for you?"

Clete dug the two shells out of his coat pocket. "Ever see anything like this?" He laid them on the counter real careful. Well sir, Tate picked one up and turned it around in his hands, eyeing it as careful as most men do a good-looking woman.

"Yes, indeed, I know what this is. Haven't seen one in a while but I know it. Let me check my lists, just to be sure." He went into the back part of his store and Clete and I followed him. The place smelled of gun oil and turpentine, and I didn't see a cobweb anywhere. There were more revolvers and rifles back there than I ever seen in one place before, blued ones and browned ones and silver ones, enough to outfit all the Rangers and then some. After a minute he located the book he was after and flipped the pages quick. "Yes, indeed! Just as I thought, Sheriff. This is for the old breech-loading Sharps — fifty-two caliber!"

He smiled at Clete and me like he had just found a double eagle in the mud of the street.

Clete looked at me and I shrugged. Hell, I don't know nothing about firearms. "What can you tell me about the Sharps, Mr. Tate?" Clete ask.

"Well, I don't think I can get you one, if that's what you mean, not a new one anyway," John Tate answered, looking pretty sorry about it. "I'm almost sure they don't make them anymore, but you can still buy the cartridges."

"No, I don't want one," Shannon said. "Just tell me whatever you can about it."

"Oh, I see," Tate said, kind of lit up again.

30

"This has to do with the law, doesn't it?"

"Yes, it does," Clete told him, trying to be patient, I could tell, even though he didn't feel like it. "And if you could just —"

"Yes, sir, I understand." He checked his book again. "Single shot breech-loader. That's linen there," he said, pointing a stubby finger at the cloth part. "Separately primed, of course — regular percussion caps. Let me see, I think this was the piece issued to Berdan's Sharpshooters."

I could see the hurry-up slide right off Clete's face. "This piece would have a pretty good range, then, wouldn't it?"

"Oh my yes! A thousand yards or more! That's why Berdan's men got them. Of course, you had to have a sharp eye to hit something that far away. They came with good open sights, but I've seen some of them fitted out with telescopes for sights, peep sights too, now that I think of it. Pretty heavy ball, and apparently pretty good rifling, too. And of course it took quite a bit of powder to —" Tate took to examining the shells again and frowning, and for a minute it seemed like he just forgot we were there. "Why, this is peculiar . . ." He took out what I guessed was a little measuring tool with arms and sized up the lead I had sunk my thumbnail into before. "Well, it's the right size, certainly, but this isn't the standard projectile. I'm sure of that. Looks queer . . ."

"What do you make of it?" Clete asked after a time.

"I don't rightly know, Sheriff. Somebody has modified this cartridge. I've never seen that before. The rings are all right, I believe, but this shape is off. If you could spare this one, I could take it apart and tell you more."

"Go ahead," Clete told him.

Tate took the thing over to his work bench and I watched him cut it open. "Thousand yards is more than half a mile, if they haven't changed the numbers since I was in school," I said to Clete.

"Lot longer range than my Henry," Clete allowed.

"My God!" Tate whispered, "will you look at this?!"

Well, we'd have like to, but we couldn't see a damn thing from where we stood. In a minute he brought it back.

"Why, this is an explosive bullet, gentlemen!" Tate said, waiting for us to be as confounded as he was. When we wasn't, he decided he'd have to give us our lessons. "They called them musket shells during the War, but nobody ever made them for the Sharps, as far as I know. Judging from the look of this, somebody turned these out for himself. See the remains of the file marks here?"

Clete picked the lead up off the counter and looked it over good. "What's this?" he ask.

"That's the fuse," Tate told him. "Set for just a little over a second, judging by the length of it. The explosion in the barrel lights it and then the fuse ignites the fulminate. Same principle as the exploding cannon shell." He fussed with the lead a minute and then laid out a chunk of stuff smaller than the end of your little finger. "This is what explodes it. If it's in your body by then, well, you're a dead man. If it's still in the air, it sends sharp little pieces of lead in all directions. Never saw one for the Sharps, though."

Clete tipped back his Montana and then rubbed his jaw. "Anyone around here gunsmith enough to fashion these for himself, except you, of course?"

"No, sir," Tate answered right away. "And I wouldn't do it either. You could easily blow a hand off with this stuff," he said, picking up the little core of fulminate. "And if you didn't form the lead properly, it could blow up in your rifle. No, I'd not try anything like that. Why, it's not even safe to carry these around in a standard cartridge box. I remember stories of some exploding under cannon fire. The man that happened to would never tell the tale, you can be sure."

Clete thanked the short, stubby storekeeper for his help and asked him again not to mention this to nobody else. Tate promised twice he wouldn't. Clete unlocked the door and we went back up the street the way we'd come down. "Willie, I don't like this, not one damn bit. Especially since I don't have a single guess as to who these things belong to and why he would want to use one on Jesse McLeod. Why, that old rancher has never harmed anyone. Nell says he never got around to making an enemy in all the time he's lived here, and he was one of the first ones in. Beats the hell out of me."

We got to Clooney's and I stopped. "You have anything you want me to do?" I ask him.

"No, I don't even know what I'm going to do." He looked at me hard but he didn't say nothing further.

"Well, I'm going in here and continue where I was," I told him. "You want a drink, I'm buying."

"No, I'm going over to the office and read the posters. May be something there. Keep a lookout over your shoulder," he said, and started across the street. Course, I knowed nothing about what was going to happen later when I spotted Corrie Sue by herself at the bar in Clooney's and walked over in my best strutting walk and told her how damn pretty she looked in that pink dress.

A few days later, I remembered him saying that to me, warning me to be careful about myself. The remembering brought tears to my eyes, I confess, for I believed then that they were the last words I'd ever hear him say.

The man in the high-peaked hat looked down on the town through his glass, a leather and brass model he had pried from the fingers of a dead Yankee officer on Horseshoe Ridge after Chickamauga. He had spotted his prey twice already today but could not get the shot he wanted. He would wait. He was good at waiting.

Chapter Four

I *could* blame it all on Corrie Sue, I suppose. But I can't do that. Fact is, she was everthing a man could of wanted that afternoon. Sweet and willing and just like a lady sometimes. No, I could not blame what happened on Corrie Sue, for it wasn't her fault I drank like I did.

She took me upstairs after a few whiskeys, and we brung a bottle with us, of course. Maybe we had two, I'm not sure. I don't remember as much as I'd like to about that afternoon. We come downstairs after a couple of hours to find something to eat, I think, but Corrie Sue's younger sister Jenny was there, and we had a drink with her. Jenny was going on about me being a deputy and how she always favored lawmen. It come out she was only seventeen and I didn't feel right about a girl so young drinking whiskey, but her sister could of said something, I didn't see it was my place. Matter of fact, Corrie Sue got so quiet I thought for a minute she was mad at me, but I didn't see how that could be, friendly as we was just a little while before. She had a pretty smile, had Jenny. True, her jaw hung out toward the front, and she was awful broad in the sitter, but a young girl's smiles and a young girl's attentions takes twenty years off a man's age. Yessir, I was standing there at the bar with this pair of pretty ladies and feeling like a big bug when two shots was fired in the street. At least that's what I thought at the time.

I winked and showed young Jenny my deputy badge again, tipped my hat, and stepped out in the street to quiet things down. Walking steady was a chore, I remember. Most times, just a word would settle whatever the trouble was, but I admit that I often let things quiet themselves.

A few people was gathered down close to the livery and I knowed that's where I'd find the fire-works. After pushing inside the crowd, there was the boy from the livery bent over my pardner. Clete's face was all blood and he didn't seem to he breathing much. Dark blood was flowing too fast from a deep gash that run from in front of his ear to beneath his jaw. I got my handkerchief on it and pressed it as hard as I dared. It wasn't a gunshot wound, that was plain, and it looked like nothing else I had ever seen done to a man, except by an axe or maybe grizzly claws. His gun was still holstered, so he hadn't even fired at whoever'd done this.

"You there, Clete?" I yelled at him.

His eyes didn't open, but he mumbled something or maybe he just moaned, I don't know which. At least he wasn't dead.

I can't decide now if I'd a done things any different if I'd a been sober. I told the Lowrey boys to take Clete to Doc Plummer's and get the sawbones there right away if he was somewheres else. I asked the men standing there, but nobody'd saw it happen, and I convinced most

36

of them to go inside so that I could have a quick look around to see if I could catch whoever done this. I also asked Bill James if he'd heard two shots, like I thought I had. He said, no, but he thought he heard the shot echo, which was strange in town, he said. No one had rode in or out of Two Scalp since the shots, that much was clear to me. Janey's boy Lyle come over, and I got him and his friend Bob to walk down the other side of the street to see if we could find someone moving around, but we couldn't.

"You look kinda peaked, Mr. Goodwin," Lyle said after we had holstered our guns and was walking back up the street. "You all right?"

"Yeah," I answered, but I wasn't. Everything was spinning so and I didn't know what to do next. Why in the *hell* had I ever let Clete talk me into being his deputy, anyway? I couldn't hit an elk with a shotgun if I was riding it. Never could, drunk or sober. And I sure as the devil didn't know what to do — there was no one at all to shoot at or punch. And I could feel everyone's eyes on me, everyone in town expecting me to go somewheres or do something right away, but damned if I knowed what it was.

After a few minutes of just standing around, I told Lyle and Bob to ask the people I hadn't spoke to if they saw what'd happened. I went over to the office, where I kept a bottle, and flopped down on my ass.

I thought about it being in the drawer, but I didn't have none. I knowed I was already too drunk to walk around anymore, and I didn't have an idea in my head about who might of done this. Maybe I should have went over to Doc Plummer's to see how Clete was doing, but I didn't want to know, if it was as bad as I thought it was. And, besides, I wanted to figure out what to do next, if I could.

After a while, I walked down to the livery to look again at where Clete'd been hit. Blood marked the spot, the blood of my friend, where a foul deed was done against him. I looked and stood and looked some more, but I couldn't see nothing that helped me understand what'd happened there.

I went in the livery and the boy was the only one there. "You want me to saddle your horse for you, Mr. Goodwin?" he ask me. He saw how drunk I was and was only trying to help, I see now.

"Hell, no!" I yelled at him. "The day comes I can't saddle my own horse, you can bet that'll be the day I'm dead!" That's another bet I would of lost.

I was trying to throw up a saddle — and it wasn't even mine — on my gelding and it went over the other side. Last thing I remember, I was sliding down that horse's flank and heading for the floor.

A hammer was smacking the back of my brain when I woke up the next morning. The livery boy or someone had throwed an overripe horse blanket on me and put my horse in another stall.

Rolled me onto some fresher straw too, I discovered. I stood up as best I could and got outside before I threw up the first time. Fresh air cleared my head some and after a while my legs would work nearly right.

By the time I got to Doc Plummer's I was feeling as good as I was going to that day. Plummer was by himself in his office, a square little room with whitewashed boards at the back sectioning off the room where he had a couple of beds.

"You look sick," that lanky old man growled as soon as I was in the door. "Are you sick?"

"Never mind me," I told him. "How's Clete?"

He shook his head and then scratched it good where it was bald in the middle. "I can't tell. He's still out and that's bad. Quite a concussion, I should think, but I could tell a lot more if he was to come around. He caught whatever hit him about seven last evening." Standing up slow, he stretched and then pulled out his egg-shaped pocket watch. "And it's almost eleven now — nearly, oh, fifteen hours. He don't come out of it soon, chances are he isn't going to."

I pushed the door to the other room open a little and saw Clete lying there with his head all wrapped up in a bandage. "What hit him, anyway?"

Plummer had a sneaky little smile that settled over his face once in a while. "Why, I thought you were the law after Clete. Suppose you tell me!"

"Well, it wasn't my fault," I told him. "I'm not hired to be on his hind pockets all the time, am I?"

"Not what I meant," he said, sitting again. "I never saw anything like it, that's all, and I don't like not knowing what happened to a patient. Makes me look stupid and it lowers the fee I can charge."

I saw he was trying to help me out with the way I was feeling for letting Clete get hurt, and I appreciated it and reminded myself to try to do a good turn for that peppery old sawbones when I could. "Don't you have any idea, Doc?"

"Well, it's not a gunshot wound, that much I know. There's nothing left inside, I probed it twice clear to the bone. Looks more like a tear a cannon ball would make than anything else, but that can't be. Gave him one hell of a whack on both his jaw and his skull, too, whatever it was."

Right then I knew what had done this to Clete. "Like a cannon ball, Doc? You mean like a solid ball or like an exploding shell?"

"Why, like pieces of iron thrown out when one explodes, of course!" he hollered at me. "Solid ball would've taken his damn head clean off. Weren't you in the War?" he ask.

"Well, I was, but I never saw a man hit by cannon fire. I have got to go look at something now," I told him. "You sure he ain't awake in there maybe?"

"I doubt it, but you can go see for yourself if

you want to," he grumbled, picking up his newspaper.

Clete was a sorry sight. He had bled a little through the bandage that was wrapped all the way around his head and down under his jaw. Both his eyes and most of his cheek on the side he was hit was swelled up tight and bruised nearly black. He was breathing, I could see, but real slow and not deep enough to suit me. I touched his hand and called his name a time or two, but his eyelids didn't even twitch.

Doc had nothing to say when I left the sick room, didn't even look up from his paper, so I went over to Clooney's. While I was standing there trying to figure it out, Tubbs come down and set a shot of rye on the bar in front of me.

I had started to reach for it before I thought. "What's this?" I ask him.

"Why, that's what you always have!" he said. "I can't give you nothing stronger, if that's what you're looking for."

"No, it ain't," I told him squarely. "Take this away and bring me a couple hard-cooked eggs — and a cup of tea, I guess." That's what my grandma'd always give me to settle my stomach.

I thought for a minute he was going to fall over. "Tea? We don't serve tea in here!" After he picked up the shot and drank it himself, he looked me in the eye while he wiped the bar with his rag. "I'll get you the eggs, but we got no tea." He started into the back and then turned around. "I got a pot of coffee I made for myself.

41

You can have some of that if you want."

I nodded and he went to get it.

The coffee helped some, but I could only get one of the eggs down. I knowed if I ate the other one I'd lose them both. After going up to my room and washing my face and putting on a cleaner shirt, I went back to where Clete'd been hit, blood all over the place. That piece of lead that'd hit him had to be somewheres, but after an hour or more I still couldn't find it. I don't know what made me drift toward the livery, about three rods off. There, half of it wedged into one of the weathered boards, stuck in about as high as your chest, was a bright shiny sliver of metal so sharp I cut my finger trying to pull it loose. It was a little more than an inch long and as wide as your thumb nail. Thicker than a slice of bacon and sharp as a razor on three sides.

I took it straight down the street to John Tate's store.

"This here's a piece of one of those musket shells, ain't it?" I ask him right off, plunking it down on his counter.

He looked it over real careful before he spoke. "Looks like lead," he answered, "but I can't be sure. I never saw one before you and the sheriff brought those in the other day. Where'd you find this?"

"Stuck in the side of the livery," I said. "About fifty feet from where Clete was hit. Ain't likely this is the piece that hit him, but I'm betting it's a piece *like* the one that did. Now, I need an answer. And if you can't give me one you're a hundred percent sure of, at least give me your best guess. Is or ain't this a piece of one of them exploding things?"

John Tate picked it up again and studied on it 'til I wanted to hit him, he took so long. He carried it over to his bench and filed on it and bit it and I don't know what else.

Finally, he come back. "If I must say yes or no, I'll have to say yes. You see here where —"

I didn't listen to the rest of what he said. I saddled my horse and was out in the hills beyond the livery pretty quick. After looking down at that stable a long time, I got it fixed in my mind where Clete must of been standing when he got shot. I walked back and forth and up and down, and I was about ready to give it up 'til I had better light, when I saw where someone'd laid on his rubber sheet or whatever. And he wasn't so careful about picking up his butts this time, but there were no more exploding shells to be found.

About thirty yards off, down in a shallow ravine, is where he had tethered his horse to some sage, and judging from the piles of horseshit, he'd stayed here some time. Two days, it looked like. I could see the rings where he'd set a bucket, a canvas one likely, so I guess he'd brought feed and water along. This boy knowed what he was about. I followed his trail north and east but it come night pretty fast and I stopped. I wasn't prepared for no chase through the countryside and I didn't know if I ought to go anyway.

I sat my horse for a while and just listened to the night sounds. Those two shots I heard while I was in the bar with Jenny and Corrie Sue, they was really only one shot, I saw, after thinking on it there in the peace and quiet of the evening. The loud one, the one I heard first, that would of been that damn shell exploding. I knew then why Bill James thought he'd heard an echo. The second shot, that would of been his rifle — *whose* rifle? Who in the hell would be trying to kill Jesse McLeod and Clete Shannon both?

Some bird I didn't know the name of was finishing his sundown song and before he was done, a poor-will started in. I got to pitying myself some, I admit, over how my friend lay hurt and how everyone was waiting for me to do something about it, and I didn't know what to do. My, the world seemed a dark and lonely place. Like standing in a hole where you could barely see the rim up above. In a minute I seen how unmanly that kind of thinking was and put those thoughts aside. A coyote commenced to howl a time or two. I reined my horse around, kicked him good in the flanks and headed back to Two Scalp.

Chapter Five

Next morning, Doc Plummer said Clete had come out of it a little, late in the night. Mary was sitting there beside him when I went in the back room, and I wisht then that Doc had told me she was there. I don't like busting in on a man and his intended bride, even if they was only holding hands, which they was. More truthful, she was holding his hand, but it didn't seem like he was holding hers much, because he was still out.

"He's going to be all right," Mary whispered to me, her face one big smile and runny with tears. I stood there just hanging on to my hat for a while. I couldn't see any difference in him, but I guessed Mary knowed what she was talking about. After a minute, I went out to see Doc.

"Is Mary right? Is he going to be okay now?" I asked, pretty quiet.

"More than I can say," Plummer told me, fiddling with the tools of his trade. "He comes in and he goes out, but he doesn't seem to get fully awake before he slides out again." The frown on his face worried me. "And he doesn't seem to hear me when I talk, even when he is a little awake. Oh, she's happy, but that's more than I am."

I asked him some more things, but I didn't understand much of what he told me. A bad bang on the head scrambles your brains like eggs, I understood that. My brother Lewis was kicked in the head by a horse once and the whole time 'til he died he kept asking whether Pa was all right, and he'd been dead for more than a year by then. Doc said they call it concussion, but beyond that I could make nothing out of what he said. Before I left, Doc asked if I could stay the night with Clete. Mary'd stayed last night, and he hated to ask her again. Doc done the night before, and that tall old buzzard looked like he needed more sleep.

I went back out to where I'd followed the track of that sonofabitch who'd sent them exploding shells at Clete and Jesse McLeod. Mostly, I had to remember which way the trail was, for the sign had almost all been blowed away since yesterday. In one place, though, where he'd cut between some hills where water ran, there was some clear prints in the mud. Well, his horse was shod irregular, but I couldn't tell what it was, exactly. They was shaped strange or something, I just couldn't put my finger on it.

I stooped and studied those shoeprints for a long time, burning them into my brain. The foreleg shoes was pretty much a match, but the hindleg two was both different. Now, I figured this man for a traveler, someone who didn't stay in the same place very long. Man works on a ranch or lives in town, his horse's shoes all look pretty much the same, because it's likely the same farrier does the work, though maybe at different times. But a man who's moving on, he takes what he gets depending on where he is, 'specially if his mind is on something else.

I studied and studied, but I wasn't sure I'd remember the shape of them, much as I wanted to. Sometimes, the face of a shoe will be as different as one man's face from another's, but sometimes not. And as unregular as these were, as big or shaped funny or something, there was nothing, no detail I could latch on to, so's I could be sure to remember them later.

After I got back to town I sat in the office for a while trying to figure things out. Towards eight o'clock I went over to Doc's.

"Glad you're here, Willie," he said. Doc didn't have to say how tired he was, his face showed that. Not a young man, Doc Plummer. Older than me by ten years, I'd guess.

After he left, I took the lantern and went in back and stretched out on the narrow bed he said I could sleep on, right beside Clete, who looked about the same as he did that afternoon. If he was coming out of his concussion, I couldn't see it. Ever once in a while, though, he would move around some and make sounds that seemed like he was trying to say something, but it was more like a man talking in his sleep than anything else. I read the paper and looked at the pictures in one of Doc's doctoring books. The things that can go wrong with a man's skin! Before long I was itching and scratching and feeling miserable from scalp to toes.

About the time I decided to throw that damn

book in the corner, Clete let out a yell that would have woke a winter-sleeping bear. I jumped a foot off that bed, got over to him quick and took hold of his shoulders, he was twisting around so.

"Hold still!" I told him, but he paid me no mind. After a while I figured out what he was saying.

"Where am I, where am I?" he kept asking over and over.

Well, I told him several times he was at Doc Plummer's, but it seemed like he didn't understand me. His eyes were open, but it didn't look like he knowed who I was. He was thrashing around so bad at one point I had to hold him down, I thought he would hurt himself. I could see fresh blood coming through his bandages, especially on his jaw. Also, he seemed like he was trying to get up off his bed. And I knowed he oughtn't to do that. For a while we had as much of a tussle as I wanted and then some. I was about to call out for someone to come help me when he just stopped.

"Willie?" he asked. "Willie?"

"Yes, damnit, it's me!" I said to him.

But he just kept asking, "Willie? Willie?"

He moved his hands to my arms and then to my face. I admit it felt strange to have a man running his hands over my nose and chin and everywhere and poking his fingers in my mouth and eyes, but then I seen how things was. He couldn't see. My, his eyes looked wild, I put his hand on top of my head and shook it yes about as big as a man can.

"Willie," he said, not asking now. "Willie . . ." he laid back, all out of breath and looking as played out as a newborn calf. He said something and I leaned close to catch it.

". . . see. I can't see. I can't see anything and I can't hear." His voice got real loud then: "I can't hear!"

Damned if I knew what to do but pat his shoulder, and that seemed to quiet him some.

He said my name a time or two and from the way he was squinting up his eyes, I could tell he was trying his damnedest to see, but he could not do it. "Where am I? Where am I?" He repeated everthing that way.

I told him again, of course, but it did him no good, for he was as deaf as an adobe wall. After a while, he sniffed the air. "Doc's — Doc Plummer's office," he said. And then he said it again and again and again until I thought he had maybe lost his mind. Pretty soon he started to go off, asleep or into his concussion I didn't know which. Whichever it was, he kept saying "Doc Plummer's office" all the way out.

I went back to that other bed in there and after a while I blew out the lantern. Sleep didn't come easy that night, but I guess I did drop off after a while, for the next thing I knowed it was starting to gray up in the room and Clete was calling my name.

It was still pretty dark, so I lit the lantern and sat on the bed beside him. His face was as white as the belly of a fish and the sweat was running off his forehead in streams, though it was pretty cool. Mostly, it was his eyes that looked so strange — open as wide as the doors to hell. He was scared, I could see it plain, and that made me feel scared myself, for I never seen him afraid before. Why, we had stood against more than twice our number in that shootout at the old Haney place, and Clete never showed a sign that he even considered that he could be killed, though I surely did. And he'd faced down Whitey DuShane all by himself that snowy afternoon last year without a trace of being afraid, and he knowed as certain as a skunk will piss on you if you give him the chance, that DuShane was faster than he was by a long shot.

"Move closer," he said, all out of breath.

I picked up the lantern and did as he wanted.

His eyes straining hard. "I-I think I can see you a little. Move closer," he said again, his voice like an iron rasp on an old oak board.

"Take it easy on yourself, Pard," I told him, but it was clear he didn't know what I was saying.

He grabbed my shoulder and I thought for a minute he was mad at me, he gripped me so hard. "Closer, damnit!"

Well, I was only a hand's breadth from his face when he stopped yanking at me.

"I *can* see you!" he yelled. "Not very plain, but it's you, it's you!" And with that he lay back and closed his eyes. Pretty soon he was out.

50

I laid back down, but sleep was gone for that night. Before long I heard Doc Plummer coming in the outer door and I sneaked out so as to let Clete rest. I told Doc what'd happened, and he smiled. When he did that, I felt better than I did in a week.

The tall, scrawny man sat his horse where Medicine Creek flows into the Missouri and pondered deep and long. He had hit him, he was sure, for he had watched him go down in the street. But was he dead? Did the ball pierce his body or didn't it? He had been sure when he rode away. He was not sure now, though. He would have to be sure.

Over the next week Clete found himself. His sight come back gradual and then his hearing too, but he said things was faint still. He complained about his ears ringing all the time and of having a headache that never left him, but I figured he was lucky to have a head at all.

The next week, he was sitting up in a chair. Looked to me like he was tired as a canal boat mule, though. We spent some afternoons playing poker for match sticks, but he was pretty quiet. Mary visited him every day, sometimes twice a day. Doc said Clete was fighting him all the time to let him go, but Doc didn't want to because Clete was talking about taking off after whoever'd shot him. It would be all right for Clete to get out of the sick room, Doc thought, but Clete had to take it easy for some time — and wouldn't I talk to him about staying out at Nell's for a while, please?

I said I would, but I didn't look forward to it. Shortly after Doc talked to me, I went over to the office and rounded up Clete's gun and holster and took them with me when I went back.

"Here, strap this on," I said going in. " 'Bout time you earned some of that fortune the town's paying you for strutting around and talking big."

Well, that got a laugh from him. He stood up, a little slower than he usually done, and took his gun. "I've been thinking the same thing myself," he said, buckling the belt. "Only Doc's been telling me to stay here. You clear this with him?"

"Damn right," I told him. "Only you're going to have to do your sheriffing out at Nell's for a while, boss her chickens and milk cow around for starters. Better to get some practice before you start pretending you're a real lawman in front of everone in town again."

He looked at me a minute. "What I had in mind was to start after the bastard who shot me."

"That's what I thought you'd say, you damn fool. Got any idea which way to go? Cause I don't!" That was a lie, of course, but he didn't suspect it — not from me. "He's lit out of here more'n two weeks ago, and his trail's colder'n a Missouri whore's heart."

About that time Mary McLeod come in, and I didn't know whether she'd heard me or not. I could tell she'd sized things up about Clete

52

leaving Doc's place and wasn't very happy about it. "Where do you think you're going, Mr. Shannon?" she asked, real smart and sassy.

"Well, I'm not exactly sure about later, but Willie here has sprung me from this sick man's jail and I'm getting out. Now, you can go along over to Taylor's while I eat the biggest damn steak he's got, or you can stay here and play some checkers with Doc when he comes back, take your pick. But if you're interested in what I'd like you to do, you'll come along and eat with me. And you too, Willie."

"As long as you're paying," I said.

Chapter Six

That next week it took a lot of doin' to talk Clete out of going after the bastard who'd shot him. Once he was well enough to ride, we went up to where the bushwhacker'd laid out in ambush. I told Clete the direction the man took off in, north by east, though there was no trail left at all by that time.

Clete remembered the lie I told him that day I sprung him from Doc's — that I didn't know which way that backshooter went. He got over it quick enough, but still, he was mad as the devil at first. Truth is, I was catching hell all around. Mary thought it was my fault that Clete wasn't resting any more than he was, and Doc bawled me out a couple of times for not seeing to it that his star patient wasn't living out at Nell's like he oughta be.

I had just collected me the latest of Doc's tongue-lashings on that subject one evening when I spied the lamp lit in the office.

My hand wasn't even off of the knob before I started ordering him around. "C'mon, get your things together. I'm taking you out to Nell's. I've heard enough bitching from both your intended and old man Plummer to last me. Whatcha doing here, anyhow?"

"Just going through the posters again," he said, sounding weary. "Seems like there should be something here on him." He wiped his eyes and stretched his arms, but then he went back to leafing through them. I seen the dark color was almost gone from the lines beneath his eyes, but he had recently stopped wearing the bandage by his ear. The gash there looked just terrible, all red and raw. You could still see the string marks where Doc'd sewed back together, too.

"Now I mean it, damnit," I told him, taking the posters out of his hands and putting them away. "I'm delivering you to Nell's if I have to tie you up to do it. Weak as you are, I don't think you'd be no trouble."

He smiled and stood up then. "Well, all right, but my guess is she's asleep by now."

"Don't matter," I told him. "Won't be the first time we woke her up and probably not the last."

I had a drink at Clooney's while he gathered up his things from upstairs, and before very long we was on the way out to her place.

The man in the high-peaked hat lay where he had lain before and watched the old woman's house through his glass. He saw when she lit her lamp and he saw when a man rode up on a dark horse and took his animal into the barn. The woman didn't come outside. A minute later, the rider led his unsaddled horse into the corral, took the bit from its mouth, and turned it loose. When the old woman's caller went inside without knocking, the scraggly man on the hill smiled a thin-lipped, flinty smile. Half an hour later, the lamp went out and half an hour after that, the bony man picked up a satchel and a can and walked silently down the long hill toward the house.

We didn't talk much, I remember, but it was a real nice night to be out. The moon full as a pumpkin and it'd got warm enough to be comfortable riding after dark.

Clete seen the glow in the sky before I did. As we topped one of them big hills south of Nell's, he said something I didn't catch and then pointed. The sky to the east was lit up like someone'd lifted the lid off of hell. Clete kicked that big black of his hard enough to make him grunt and I took off after him. Most times I can outride him, but that night I couldn't keep up. I think he'd figured out what that glow in the sky meant long before we crested the rise where you can see down on Nell's ranch good. My God, her whole place was a sheet of flames, licking out most of the windows and even coming through the roof close to the back door. I'd stopped for a second, so surprised I was, but Clete was going flat-out down the last few yards by then. He was off his horse and kicking in a front window before I was even there.

By the time I got up on the porch, he was handing Nell out the window to me wrapped up in something. I hate to admit it, but the smell of burned flesh and hair nearly made me vomit right there. We got her out in the dooryard a ways and I went a few rods off so I could throw up by myself. I come back soon as I could and I

56

seen she was burned as bad as I was afraid she was. By the light of the flames that was eating away her house, I seen that her hair was mostly all gone except for a little patch in front and I didn't even want to think about her legs and feet.

She coughed real weak, and Clete sat her up a little so's she could breathe better, but she winced at the least touch.

Nell said something, but we had to lean close to catch it. After a minute, we figured out what she was saying. "Jesse?" she was asking.

"No, it's me, Clete," he said, kind of surprised she didn't know him.

"Clete?" she ask. "Clete?"

"Yes, it's me," he said. "You just take it easy and you'll be all right."

"Where's Jesse?" she ask. "Did Jesse get out safe?"

"Who?" Clete ask.

"Jesse! Jesse McLeod! He was in there with me." She turned her head a little and looked at her home as the fire burst out the window we had just dragged her through. Already it was catching the overhang of the roof in front. "Oh, God, if Jesse's still in there, he's dead." She cried real quiet after she said that, and then she started coughing again.

"Jesse McLeod? Mary's father?" Clete asked. He was as taken back as I was. I figured she was maybe hit on the head or something.

"Yes, Jesse McLeod. We . . ." That old gal just

stopped talking and watched her home burn down.

A big black scorched place on her cheek and neck was oozing clear stuff down onto the checkered tablecloth that Clete'd wrapped her in, probably to smother out the flames that'd been on her. Pain grabbed at her then and she screwed up her face worse than I could stand to watch. When I looked back, I thought for a while she had died, but after a minute her breathing told me that wasn't so.

"We got to get her in a wagon and over to Doc Plummer's fast as we can," I told Clete.

He looked at her while she was sleeping there or whatever a good long minute. Then he shook his head slow and turned them wolfish eyes on me. "She'd never make it, Willie," he said. That was the closest to crying I ever seen him.

"Yes," Nell whispered. "I'd never last the trip."

Well, if Clete Shannon wasn't the sorriest looking man I ever saw then, I don't know what. "I didn't mean — Nell, I —"

" 'Tell the truth and shame the Devil,' my Elmer always said." She gripped Clete's hand real tight and said something that was hard to hear. ". . . figure it. I just . . ."

"What's that, Nell?" Clete asked after a while.

"What started it?" she said, louder than before. "What started that fire! The stove was banked off good, and it was practically new, no trouble with it at all!" Her eyes looked crazy at him, and I was glad it wasn't me she was looking to for answers.

The roof fell in about that time, and a million sparks flew up into that moonlit sky. I walked over and lay my hand on the side of the barn. It was hot, all right, but it was in no danger of catching fire, so I figured the animals in there was better off than they'd be outside. I went in and looked around and then checked the corral. Sure enough, there stood Jesse McLeod's big old chestnut standing right by the door. I penned him in the barn and then went back out and walked around the burning house, looking to see whatever I could. Well, I didn't see nothing worth talking about, but around back, where the smoke was going, I smelled it. I saw my buckskin out at the edge of the firelight and he let me catch him easy enough, though Clete's horse was still jumpy as hell.

After I tied them both in the barn beside Jesse's, I come around front to where Clete was still bent over Nell. I sat down close to them, for I couldn't see what else to do. I could of used a drink.

Nell stirred some and squeezed Clete's hand. I could hear most of what she was saying if I listened real close. "There's something you can do, if you're able to, son. Find out who did this to Jesse and me. And when you do, string him up from the highest tree you can find. Somebody must have set it, fire around both doors like that.

Somebody *must* have set that fire, there's no other way. Poor Jesse . . .Tell Mary . . ." Her voice faded and I saw her go limp against Clete. He held her up while the walls fell in and after some time the fire burned lower and lower. Nell's breathing got real coarse and unregular and finally so faint that we wasn't sure exactly when it was she slipped away from us.

It's peculiar how a man can both know something and yet not know that same thing at the same time. I seen it before, of course, but that night it was as clear to me as the moon and just as natural. We sat there with Nell propped up and the fire in the house dying away to embers all night long. We knowed she was dead, both Clete and me, though neither one of us said so. And at the same time, it was like if we didn't say it, she wasn't entirely gone either. And that's how we were 'til first light.

When daylight comes on, Clete stood up and brushed off his pants. "She's dead, Willie."

"I know."

It was pitiful to see the look on his face then. "First time I laid eyes on Nell, she was pointing her old Winchester at my heart," he said, his voice full of catches and burrs from sitting there all night and not saying anything, I guess. "I slept the night in her barn, uninvited. After we talked that morning, she fed me and then threw Wilson's men off my trail. I still owe her for that."

"Some gal, was Nell," I said. "I'll miss her."

"So will I, and I'm going to pay her back by getting the bastard who did this to her. You smell the coal oil?" he ask me.

"Yes, I did. Around back."

"It smelled strong inside where I found her," he said. "You see any tracks?"

"No, it was too dark to look, but we can look now."

We walked around the north side and there was the boot tracks coming in and going back out, right up toward that notch in the hills that looks like a rifle sight. About a hundred yards out was a five gallon can on its side.

After Clete smelled it he nodded his head. "Coal oil. I'm going now."

"Where?" I ask him.

He spun around on me so fast I thought he was going to poke me. "Where!? Why, after that sonofabitch, is where, and don't you try and stop me!"

"You can't do that," I told him. "Not now."

"What in hell do you mean, I can't? You heard what that woman asked me to do, almost with her dying breath. You think I'll walk away from that?"

I took a minute before I answered him, hoping he would cool off some, but it was plain he wasn't going to.

"Clete, I want the same thing you do. We *got* to catch that murdering bushwhacker." Then I just waited.

"No, I'm going alone, and I'm leaving right

now." He strided off toward the barn and I followed him.

"Will you just stop a minute and listen to me?" I asked. He was trying to get Buckshot's reins untied and was having a time with them, it still being pretty dark in the barn.

"No!" he yelled back over his shoulder.

"And I suppose you're just going to let her lie out there for the vultures and coyotes?" That was a low thing to say to him, I know.

He run over to me and I thought for the second time that morning he was going to take me apart. But he didn't. Instead, he calmed way down. "Take Nell's body into town, to Biezmier's. And then get word to her family. After that, take —"

"You can stop giving orders any time now," I told him, " 'cause I just quit working for the dumbest goddamn sheriff north of Sweetwater!"

He was so surprised he didn't know what to say.

I had plenty more to say. "I was willing to help you with Wilson's bunch because I owed that to you. But I don't owe you this, lettin' you get yourself killed." I got myself settled some before I said any more. "Seems to me, the last thing Nell asked of you was to tell Mary. Have you thought about that?"

He was still lost for words.

"You're going at this all wrong," I told him plain. "Just listen to me for a minute." I sat down on the barrel there and after a time Clete leaned against a stall. "Let me start after him," I said. "I'll go slow and easy 'cause there's no way in hell I can shoot him myself. You take Nell into town, and maybe whatever you can find of Jesse, and then go out and tell Mary. You know, you might lose her if you don't."

He was quiet for a minute before he spoke. "I might at that," he said.

"Maybe you can see about Nell's being buried. Might be able to get it done by this afternoon or tomorrow morning at the latest — probably tomorrow would be better anyway. That way you could get yourself some sleep and us some supplies and a pack animal. And I need a better horse. That buckskin of mine's too old for much hard riding. Take the money for it — a good one, now, don't matter how much it costs — take it out of my pack at the Dakota House and bring my trail things. Speak to someone about keeping an eye on the town 'til we get back, too, maybe John Tate. I'll leave a track broad enough for a blind man to follow, and we might have him in a couple days. What do you say?"

Clete stood up straight. "Maybe we could catch him a couple of *miles* from here if we left right now," he said.

"You think he slept around here last night?" I asked him. "Just burned down a ranch with two people inside and then took his rest? Would you have, if you was him?"

Clete took a deep breath, but he didn't have to

63

think on it very long. "No, I wouldn't. And I'd still be riding now, and probably this time tomorrow, too."

"Well, come along up the trail with me a few miles so we can both be sure I'm not dead wrong and then come back and do like I said, all right?" I didn't know for sure if he would.

"I thought the deputy was supposed to stay and take care of the town when the sheriff was out chasing killers?" he asked, and I saw his eyes soften under the brim of his hat.

"Maybe so," I answered real smart. "But I ain't the deputy of Two Scalp no more, remember?"

"You are if you're riding after that sonofabitch. Otherwise, you're just a damn vigilante, and I don't ride with vigilantes."

I had to laugh at that one. "Well, all right, have it your own way," I said. "But I'm getting on his trail now and you'll catch up to me in two or three days, right?"

"Willie, damn you," he said, but he wasn't mad no more.

We tied Nell's body in a heavy piece of canvas and put her in the wagon she kept in the barn. Clete give me his jacket and for my bedding I took a big piece of canvas from the same roll we had used for Nell.

I knowed where the trail would start, up close to where I'd found them shells before. Clete rode more than a couple miles with me, and then he saw how it was. Our man had lit out, and he was traveling light and fast — without even a pack horse.

We got to the top of a little rise and he reined Buckshot in. We sat and watched the smoke from Nell's place curl up into the blue sky.

"Willie, are you up to this?" he ask.

"Wasn't me that got shot a couple weeks ago," I told him.

"No, I meant following his trail and living rough for a while. Risking your life in this business, I guess I mean to say."

"Shoot, I'm not new to this game," I said. "Fact is, I earned my daily bread doing this very thing for a time. Not so awful long ago, either."

He looked at me real curious after I said that. "Is that so? Where'd you do that?"

"Down in Texas and the Indian Territory. Tracked into Missouri once, too."

Well, he waited for me to tell the tale, but I didn't feel in no storytelling mood just then, but after a minute I seen he felt he needed to know. "I ain't real proud of it, but I worked for Pinkerton's awhile. Don't you fret over me. I know what I'm doin' — well enough, anyway, long as I don't get in a shooting match with this boy."

He took off his hat and scratched his head. "I never knew you were a Pinkerton," he said.

"Lots you don't know about me, young son," I told him.

Clete pulled his Henry from the boot and handed it to me. "Here. You may need this before I see you again."

"Yeah, maybe I can club him with it, if I get close enough," I said. "Bring me one of them scatterguns from the office when you come back."

"All right, I'll do that," he said, and then turned his black around. "Watch out for yourself, old timer!" he yelled back, ridin' down that hill fast enough to break his neck. For a minute I wished he would.

Chapter Seven

By midday I got to know the tracks of that horse real good. He swung wide around Two Scalp and then headed east by north, the way I figured he would. That was the direction he'd headed before, when I'd followed him a ways out of town after he'd bushwacked Clete. In some dried mud, I found the tracks we both'd made then.

He was still traveling fast, though not as fast as he was when he lit out of Nell's like a demon out of hell. I saw where the right rear shoe of his horse had come off. And not too long after, the hoof split pretty bad, and the animal started to favor that foot. A good ten miles beyond where I'd trailed him earlier he led me to where a prairie stream flowed into a river I guessed to be the Missouri. I cursed myself then for not carrying a map. I hoped that Clete would think to bring one when he come along, which I hoped would be soon.

I guessed the Big Muddy instead of the Cheyenne, which I knowed was in these parts somewheres, because I'd heard different people speak big of the Missouri breaks. And damned if that river I sat my horse beside didn't fling its banks wilder than any I had saw before. His tracks led across the stream and come out in a rock bank on the other side, and it looked like he was going to follow the Missouri upstream for a piece.

Only his sign didn't come *out* upstream of the rocks. I searched in the first good river soil I hit, back and forth for three rods or more, but I seen no tracks at all. I went on upstream for the better part of a mile before I convinced myself he didn't go that way.

When I got back to where he'd crossed the stream, I rode in circles that I kept widening at each loop. I knowed I'd have to cross that damn freezin' river and look over there too, so I did. But seeing no tracks on the east bank either, I swum my horse back to the west side, widened out the circles some more, and rode as fast as I could. Well, it took me two hours, but I found them. Heading due west. He'd swept a good long piece of his backtrail clean with a cotton-wood branch, which I found close to where the tracks started sudden.

I went back to where the hoofprints'd left me in the rocks beside the creek and dug out the pencil and the old Bible I always carry. I hated to keep tearing pages out of the back, the part called Revelations, but it was the only paper I had, and it would save Clete a lot of time if he didn't have to follow me all around searching for that boy's trail like I did.

I could of tore pages out of the front, of course — that Genesis part — but there was a lot of good stuff there I wanted to think over some more. Like always, when I had to tear a page out of the back, I read it before I wrote on it. I sup-posed I'd never live long enough to get to the end. Still, I hated to lose a part that I didn't get to yet. But like most of what I'd read this way before, that page made little sense to me. Maybe it suffered some from reading it out of place, I don't know. Something about locusts that looked like horses wearing crowns, and with people's faces and lion's teeth and woman's hair. I guess the horses was a whole lot different back in them days.

I wrote a note crossways on the Bible page telling Clete which way to go and tied it to a rock and put it in a place he'd be sure to see.

Back where my man's track started again, it looked like he'd just dropped out of the sky. Close to there was where I saw his boot tracks for the first time since he'd left Nell's. He'd taken himself a good long piss before he mounted his horse again.

I knelt down looking at that boot track and trying to picture him in my mind, but I couldn't do it clear as I wanted to. He was a tall man, I could see that just by the size of his boots and the length of his stride. But he didn't weigh as much as me, and I'm not too heavy, never was. From the way he dragged his toe, leaving a little furrow in the sign, you could tell he had hurt his back or his left leg some time ago and it pained him still. More than that, he'd been chased a time or two, for his trick almost worked on me. This whole little jog up to where this stream emptied into the Missouri was just apurpose to throw me off the track. Yes, this boy had run before.

The man in the high-peaked hat slowed his pace to spare his horse. She had thrown a shoe and was getting sore-footed. The bony man knew she had only a few good hours left, and though he had covered his tracks back at Medicine Creek, he felt someone following him. An uncomfortable tickle on the back of his neck like the twiddling legs of an ant. He waited and watched the horizon with his glass for a while, but no rider appeared. About noon, he crested a rise and saw someone chopping wood in front of a soddy. In the corral, beside a stable made of willow poles, stood a fine-looking paint.

I had been looking for a place to camp by some water for more than an hour. The tracks was getting damn hard to see. Just as the sun was starting to set, I drew up on the top of a slope where the yeller Prairie Mustard was just coming into bud. Below, someone was trying to prove up on a claim. Whoever he was had dug himself into the bank and throwed up side walls of sod. The front was logs, and from where I sat my buckskin, I seen where he had cut them from beside the little stream that edged the valley on the far side. There was a pole shed, but there were no horses or mules. He'd started on another outbuilding, too. Neat little place, with what looked like real glass windows and whitewashed window frames. They'd had their troubles, though. A little patch of crosses was clustered on a low hill close to the stream. Probably some of their babies. Somebody was home, too, for feathers of smoke was lifting from the chimney, though I couldn't see no one out around the place.

My man had spent some time here watching. I found where he laid in the sandy soil — hadn't bothered with his ground cloth this time, though. I stretched out beside where he did and put my toes even with where his'd been. Where his elbows rested was a good eight inches ahead of mine, so he was about as tall as I figured from his boot tracks — close to six and a half feet. He'd burned enough time to smoke two cigarettes, so he was being careful about riding in. The tracks led right down to the house, though, so whoever lived there'd seen him, maybe even talked to him.

He could still be there, I told myself, but then I argued against that notion — no horses. I mounted and rode down slow so as not to alarm nobody.

I had just stopped in front of the place when the door flew open and a rifle barrel poked out at me through the opening.

"Go away!" a voice warned.

I tried to spot the face behind the gun, but the shadows was too deep. "I'm just traveling through," I said. "Don't mean no harm." I just sat and waited after that.

"Ride in closer but don't get down!" It sounded like a boy.

Well, I did that, and in a minute the person who had the drop on me stepped out. But she certainly wasn't no boy. "You are not with that other man?" she ask.

"No, ma'm," I answered her right off, shaking my head. "But I'd sure like to catch him. Could you tell me which way he went, please, and how long ago he passed through?"

She studied on that and then lowered the rifle to her hip, but she still kept it on me. I was wishing I could see her face, so's I could figure out what was going through her head, but she had on a broad-brimmed black hat and I couldn't see nothing of her features. "What did he do to you?" she ask.

"He kin of yours?" I asked her back.

"No!" she yelled. "He stole our last horse!"

"Well, he shot my friend, the sheriff of Two Scalp, whose deputy I am, ma'm." I held out my badge for her to see, and I was glad then Clete'd made me keep it. "Also, he killed two people while they laid asleep in their bed, a man and a woman. Burned them up, set fire to the house."

"I'm not surprised, the way he acted." I could tell she had eased off some.

"Would you mind not pointing that rifle at me no more?" I ask her. "I'll be happy to drop this here Henry if it'd make you feel any safer."

"There is no need of that," she said, lowering the lever-action. "And you can step down if you please."

Well, I felt a whole lot better then. She come forward and took off her hat, and I dismounted.

I had no time to be prepared for the face that I

72

saw then, and it made me feel more uneasy than having her rifle pointed at my chest. To tell the truth, she was the prettiest damn woman I ever seen. A gal I knowed once in Texas would come close, but not real close. Now, I must stop and explain myself here, for when men speak of a beautiful woman, it brings up a picture of blue eyes and fair hair and skin, maybe dainty little hands and whatnot, at least to me it does. But she was not like that at all. To begin with, she wasn't even a white woman.

Not entirely, anyway, though you could tell some of her was. She was dark, not like Spanish women, but dark like some slave women who had their owner for a daddy. Her cheekbones was set high in her face. We stood in her dooryard, looking at each other. Her eyes was on a level with mine, maybe even a shade higher, so she was a tall woman, not one of those little things. Once you got over the slant of her eyes and how clear they was, they made you think of that half-wild look you see in the eyes of an Indian. Like varnished walnut they was. The white in her come out mostly in her nose, I guess you could say, for it was straight and thin and a little pointy.

A breeze'd been blowing all day and it moved a lot of her hair across her face. That big gal's hair hung in ropes and rings around her shoulders and down her back a long ways. Not wooly like a slave's or straight as an arrer like an Indian woman's, but shinier and blacker than both, like new-mined coal.

It wasn't 'til then that I noticed how young she was, not more than a year or two older than Corrie Sue's sister Jenny. I guess she saw how taken back I was, for she blushed a little, making her face glow even more than it was before, there in that orangy sunset light. But it didn't bother her long, for she stuck out her hand and without thinking I took it.

"I'm Amanda Boudoin," she said. "My folks called me Mandy." Her smile was so pretty I felt uncomfortable.

"Well, I'm Willie Goodwin, the deputy sheriff of Two Scalp, as I said before, I guess. And I'm pleased to make your acquaintance." I must have held on to her hand a little too long because she started to blush again. Of course, I let go soon as I noticed.

"I was just about to have dinner when you rode up," she said. "Will you join me, Mr. Goodwin? It's the least I can do after welcoming you that way." She laughed such a musical laugh then that I thought of a New Orleans cathouse, though I was secretly ashamed of myself for thinking it.

Of course, I needed some food, no question, and I had already thought of stopping for the day, since I could no more follow tracks in that light than I could dance. "I would be pleased to take dinner with your family, Miss Amanda, ma'm. If you could just show me where to clean up?"

She pointed out a bucket of water and a basin by the door. "You can wash there, but I have no family, Mr. Goodwin," she said, and then went into her house. I used the little piece of soap she had there and thought things over while I washed myself.

Then I stepped into the doorway to talk to her. "I'm going to ride across the valley a piece to make sure my man isn't still around here," I told her. "I'll find a place to camp over by your stream while I'm at it — if you don't mind, of course. Then I'll come back and eat."

"As you please," she said, bent over a pot that hung just out of the fireplace from a chimney crane. "But I don't think he is still close to here."

Well, I rode across the valley and across the stream and went to the top of the far rise, and because of it getting dark, that was as far as I could follow his tracks. He was still headed west, riding the girl's horse by now and trailing his own and making good time once again. *Damn* but I was tired, all day in the saddle and no sleep the night before. It was near dark 'til I started back toward the soddy, the evening star up pretty, and I fed myself a story about coming in from the fields to my new bride waiting for me. Eating supper with her in our own snug little house. Did no harm, far as I could see, to amuse myself so.

She had the table pulled up in front of the fireplace when I got back and apologized for being out of lamp oil and candles, but I said it didn't matter. It was a tidy place for a soddy, even with the dirt floor. Whoever'd made it had dug it down far enough so you didn't have to stoop over all the time, like you did in most I've been in. All one room, of course, with the bed to one side and the fireplace dug into the back wall and dry-masoned with cut stone. Whitewash over the sod walls and the back made it cheerful and bright, even in the little light we had. Curtains at the windows, just like in town.

What was different about it was the roof. Not a shed roof, either. The big timbers was bowed, just the crooked way they growed, I suppose, and they humped up a place there in the middle. From the ladder that went up, I guessed it was a sleeping loft for children. Course, a lot of dirt would fall on them from the sod roof when they slept up there, but it would have anyway if they'd laid on a pallet on the floor, like most sodbusters' young ones did.

She'd baked a big pile of biscuits in her Dutch oven and got me started on them while she fussed with plates and spoons and the like. In a few minutes she brought a pot of something with beans and carrots and some kind of meat, though it wasn't beef or pork.

"This is mighty good," I said. "What kind of meat is this in here, anyway?"

"Rabbit," she said. "I shot it this morning. Is it all right?"

"It's fine." And it was, too. She had spiced it up a lot, made it nearly as hot as my mother's chili, but it had something else in it that made me think of Cathay or India or some other far away place, though it make me think of the smell of fresh dirt, too, but it was good, bad as that sounds.

"Would you mind telling me what you can remember about the man who stole your horse, Miss Mandy?" I ask after we started eating. "Did you talk to him?"

She looked kind of sheepish then. "Yes I did. I was chopping wood when he rode down the hill." She fiddled with her fork.

"Tall man?" I ask. "Walked with a limp?"

"Yes," she said after a minute. I could see she was trying to fix him good in her mind. "Almost a head taller than me. 'Tall as an asparagus,' my father would have said, which means that he was also very thin. I didn't notice his limp then, but I believe he had one. He was the first person I've seen in months, and I wasn't being very careful, I'm afraid. Not as careful as I should have been."

"You live out here all by yourself? All winter?"

"Since January, I have been alone. My father and my brother died in November. My mother I buried in January."

She said that so flat, like she could have been talking about making cheese. I didn't know what to say.

"He was strange looking. Ugly, you know? But I was glad enough to see him. He asked me if I had coffee, and when I came inside to make him some, he took Suzie. I heard the horses and ran out, but he was nearly to the stream by then. I shot at him once, but I knew it was too far. He stopped and looked back, but then he kept going."

"You're lucky," I told her. "He could have killed you — or worse."

It took a minute for her to catch my meaning, but when she did she surprised me. She throwed back her pretty head and laughed. "*Or worse,* Mr. Goodwin? You think a woman would rather be murdered than raped?" She got up and got a jar of jam out of the cupboard and opened it. "If I had my choice, I would take neither. But if it had to be one or the other, I would not take the death, I can tell you. I watched my mother and my father and my little brother die, and nothing could be as bad as that." She was quiet then for a time, and I thought she might cry, but she didn't. "Besides, it means nothing, the sex, not if you don't want it to. Just a natural thing, like eating a meal. Would you like to taste the jam, Mr. Goodwin?" she ask, sticking her finger into the pot and then offering it to me.

I guess I looked pretty bewildered, for she laughed again and then sucked it off herself, smacking her lips over it. I had a feeling for a minute there that she was a lot older than I'd figured her for, but her face was smooth like only a young girl's is. "How was he dressed?" I ask.

"A tall, soft hat — black. His rifle had a tube on it, but I didn't see his pistol. He wore one of those long riding coats, only it was dark. Brown, I think. A lean, scrawny man. His teeth were bad and he stunk, but I had already decided to ride away from here with him if he would take me. As soon as I saw him riding down the hill I knew I would ask him."

I spread some jam on a biscuit and ate it, but I don't remember what it tasted like.

I'd mostly gotten over the way she looked and her boldness, I guess, while we sat having our dinner together and talking, but afterwards I couldn't help myself from staring at her. She was dressed more like a man than a girl, but it didn't do her appearance no harm. The firelight twinkling off her black hair and shining in her eyes. I looked at her young body when she bent and moved the pot of coffee closer to the flames, and I cursed myself for doing it.

We each had a cup and then I stood. "I'll be going now," I said. "Thank you for my dinner and for what you've told me about the man I'm chasing. I've never seen him, but now, thanks to you, I have a pretty good idea of what he looks like."

"You knew about his limp just from following him?" she ask, doubt in her dark eyes.

"I'll stop back in the morning, if you like," I told her.

"I would feel better if you would stay here to-night, Mr. Goodwin. You can sleep in Mother's and Daddy's bed there, and I could sleep up in the loft, where I used to." She read the look on

79

my face. "It would be all right. Who is to know but us, eh?"

I didn't see how she could say that right out that way. *I'd rather spend a night in a regular bed any time,* I told myself, but even as I thought that I knowed it wasn't just comfort on my mind.

Anyway, I unsaddled my horse and brought my trap inside and barred the door. She'd cleared the table and put things away by the time I went back in. The fire was burned low.

"I'm up here, Mr. Goodwin," she said after I'd looked around and not seen her. "Goodnight."

"Goodnight," I told her. I pulled her rocker up close to the embers of the fire, lit my pipe, and helped myself to the last of the coffee. It wouldn't keep me awake tonight. Nothing would, tired as I was.

I'd just got into bed when I heard her stirring in the loft. "Are you awake, Mr. Goodwin?"

"Just about."

"Can I come down with you? I'm awfully cold up here."

Well, I didn't say nothing and a minute later I heard her climb down the ladder. Then she slipped under the quilts beside me. After a while she put her hand on my shoulder, and I could feel her loose breasts against my back.

"You wear your clothes to bed?" she asked.

"Just my longjohns," I said.

She laughed then, that warm throaty laugh. "That is a strange way to sleep." She slid one of her long legs over against mine and I could tell she wasn't wearing nothing at all.

I determined I would just wait and see what happened next. I don't know how long I laid and waited there in that big old featherbed, but after a while her breathing got slow and regular. I rolled over and put my hand on her hair. My, it was smooth and soft! But she was asleep. Fast asleep. I rolled back over and called myself a fool. My baby-fetcher was as hard and as long as a rake handle, and I don't think I slept at all that night.

Chapter Eight

I woke with a start, not knowing where I was for the longest minute, 'til it come to me. A fire burned in the fireplace and you could smell coffee brewing. The front door stood wide open and my bedfellow was gone.

I dressed quick and from the doorway I seen her working at my horse. It was warm and sunny, later than I wisht I had slept. She had made a pile of her things in the dooryard, and from that I knowed what she was up to.

I walked out and leaned over the top rail, just watching her for a minute, a beautiful sight of a spring morning. But then she saw me, though she didn't say nothing at first. You could tell she knowed what she was doing — with the curry comb. "Did you sleep well, Mr. Goodwin?"

"Not as good as I would have on the ground out by the stream there," I told her.

She had a good laugh on me then. "I think perhaps you are not used to having a woman in your bed."

"What are you doing?" I asked.

"Making ready your horse, can't you see?" She went back to combing for a minute and then begun to whistle a tune. Well, she could whistle a whole lot better than me, but that didn't take much. "You *do* plan to leave today, no? And if the horse must carry two riders, he should at least be as comfortable as we can make him, don't you think?"

I tried to come up with some gentle way to tell her, but the only way I could think of was to say it straight out. "Miss Mandy, I can't take you along, much as I'd like to oblige you."

She stopped brushing and turned them big dark eyes on me in the most mournful way. Two tears commenced to roll down her cheeks.

"Now, I wish you'd stop that," I said, feeling lower than a lizard's belly. "I'd take you along if I could, I truly would. It's just that I'm following a killer and I have got to —" I seen her shoulders start to shake, but she was doing all she could to keep from crying. "Riding double would slow me way down, Mandy, and I might lose him. Hell, he probably gained a couple hours on me already this morning."

She come over to the rail and stood on the other side, just looking at me. Tears dripped off the sides of her chin and I felt awful.

"Besides, you might get killed. He's going to lay in ambush somewheres and watch his backtrail. That rifle of his —"

"I can't remain here, Mr. Goodwin," she said, lifting her arms out wide and then letting them drop to her sides. Two new rivers poured down her cheeks. "I will take my risks with you, for I will surely die if I stay by myself any longer."

Well, I didn't see how that could be, since she'd already come through the winter out here, but then maybe that entered into it. I'd heard of women dying of loneliness by themselves out on the prairie, nothing wrong with them. Just shrunk up and died from being all alone, so I heard tell. Still, she didn't appear in no danger of being shriveled to death, fresh as she looked standing there with the wind blowing the black rings of her hair across that pretty face.

"You can leave me wherever you find some people, and I will ask them to take me further. Please, Mr. Goodwin, do not leave me here!" She reached over that top rail and squeezed me so tight my hat fell off.

That was the fix I was in, and I argued it both ways with myself standing there awkward as the devil, bent partly over the rail and with her arms still around me. After a while I nodded my head.

She laughed through her tears then, and I could feel her jumping up and down like a youngster will do.

I took her shoulders and moved her off so I could see her good. "Now, if we're going down the trail a piece together, you must do just as I tell you, no two ways about it."

She kissed me. I didn't even see it coming. Oh, nothing big, you understand, but it *was* on the lips. She had such a funny look on her face then it puzzled me. "Of course, Mr. Goodwin. I will do just as you require."

In a minute I seen what she thought I meant. Well, she had got me all wrong there. "It's not like that, Miss Mandy," I said. "I didn't mean —"

But she just smiled like she knowed some

84

secret and went to sorting her things.

It was a fight getting her to pare down that pile of goods she wanted to take along — some of her mamma's silver, her brother's cradle, and a big old Spanish guitar. Instead, I let her take just a quilt, some heavy clothes, a frying pan, and her Remington. Which I stuffed in the saddle boot along with Clete's Henry. Sure, we could of left her rifle, but I preferred she have it if we had to gun for that old boy. Truth is, she could probably shoot better than me.

After we ate, I got a piece of paper from her and tacked Clete a message on the door telling him the day and the time we'd left and which direction. When she come back from the little cemetery on the hill by the stream, she stood by the low corral and looked at the house. Though she didn't cry none, I knowed she was saying goodbye to her home.

Of course she talked me into letting her take the guitar, which she strapped across her back before she climbed up behind me. We had fixed my canvas and her quilt into a kind of seat for her. It softened the bumps some, but it wasn't much good for staying on. So she clung to me with her arms and tighter still with her knees and thighs.

My buckskin took the extra weight well. Better than I took her legs around me so. I lost his tracks twice before midmorning and it was clear I wasn't gaining on him, like I done yesterday. By noon the horse needed rest if we was to go on much further and so did Mandy. She would probably have been all right in a saddle, but riding the rump of a walking horse is a different thing entirely.

Beside a river I guessed was the Cheyenne, she slid off and unpacked some food she'd brought. Then she unrolled her quilt and we had us a picnic on the bank.

She chewed a bite of jerked antelope and laid out biscuits and jam. "How far will we follow this man, do you suppose, Willie?" she ask.

"Well, *you'll* be following him 'til we get someplace I can leave you," I told her. "And don't forget that's part of our deal. I'll trail him 'til I find him, or lose his tracks, which is what will happen if it rains. Don't rain up here much, but springtime is still the wettest."

"Did he hurt you, too?"

"No," I said. "Killed some people I cared about, though. And he shot my friend, the sheriff of Two Scalp. You'll meet him. He should be along in about a day." I drank some water, though I wisht it was whiskey.

"But this man, *le meurtrier*, if he did not try to kill you, why do you search for him?"

It was plain she didn't understand the responsibilities of the peace-keeping trade nor the way of things between men. And if she didn't know that, I figgered she was mighty poorly equipped to understand how your friend's trouble is yours too, and how his fights are your fights. How, at the same time, you could fight with your pardner

86

over *how* to fight his fights. And I could also see no way to explain to her how being the sheriff or the deputy of some damn little town was just something you did because you couldn't see nothing better to do, or how else to sit out a Northern winter. But, still, if someone raised hell in your town, or killed someone, why, he must pay for it, and you are the one hired on to make sure that he does. You must see that the laws are obeyed and the rules of people living together are followed to the letter.

I decided against even *trying* to explain all that to her. "He'll be laying for us up here somewheres, and he'll be shootin' to kill, you as well as me, since you're along."

She lost the smile her teasing me had put on her pretty face, and it begun to cloud over. "How do you know that?" she ask.

"Because he's done this before and so have I," I told her. "Been chased like him, I mean. And I've chased others as well. Comes a time when you got to be sure no one's after you. It wears on you, running does, bears down on you like a heavy stone, crushing the wind out of you so's you can't hardly draw a full breath. He'll stay put soon, wait for whoever's following to come along behind him. He almost done it yesterday, before he reached your place, but then he changed his mind for some reason. I seen the tracks where he waited an hour or more, and he'll do it again. Only next time he'll wait 'til he's sure."

When the scrawny man saw the eroded pile of clay in the distance rising above the rolling plain, he knew he had found what he had been looking for all day. He was careful to take his horses in close to the base and then some distance around the rilled and fluted butte before he circled and came back from the other side. He hobbled the horses in a bare gully which had cut itself into the clay, where the heat stuck his shirt fast to his narrow, sweaty back, and he scrabbled up the side with his gear.

Down from the top he found a notch. It was not as level as he would have liked, but it was level enough. He could stay there all night if he had to, and to-morrow too if need be. He could see miles through his glass; miles and miles back across the dusty green flatland toward the distant river, a ribbon of blue and luster. He spread his oiled canvas on the ground and sucked a mouthful of cold coffee from his bottle, then checked the primer on his Sharps and lay down. Someone was still after him. He knew it. He didn't know who it was or how he knew it, but he did. Sure as the South had lost the war. Sure as he knew that he had finally killed the murderer who had gunned down his brother.

We took a little longer with our picnic lunch beside the river there than I was happy about, but I could tell from the fresh look of his tracks after we started again that we weren't slipping no further behind. He stayed on the southern bank of the river, moving upstream at a good, regular pace, and easy as anything to follow in both sand

and gravel. He was still riding the girl's horse and leading his own, but he wouldn't be much longer, lame as it was getting.

My, it was a pretty day, getting warm unto summer almost, no danger of rain and losing the trail.

Mandy, she was happy as sunshine. Pointing out wildflowers and getting me to name them, after she knowed I could. Singing songs almost all afternoon, she was. French words to most of them, so I had no idea what they was about. Someone'd taught her to sing like a songbird and you could tell she liked doing it. One, she got me to learn and sing with her while we rode, but I made her teach me in English. Something about some young pullet waiting for her rooster in the moonlight, I don't know what else. Young girl takes twenty years off a man's age, maybe more.

Midafternoon rolls around, she pesters me to stop for a while where a little stream tumbling in from the left formed a good-size pool in the river, a low bluff on the other side. I'd already noticed that his tracks cut away from the bank here and headed more south, along the stream, and I wanted to fill our canteens anyway before heading in that direction.

Soon as she slid off, she laid down her hat, slipped that guitar strap over her head, and her shirt followed it. And she had nothing on underneath, like women usually wear.

"What do you think you're doin'?" I ask.

"I am going to get clean, go swimming," she

said. "Come swim with me." She was already unbuttoning her pants so I turned around.

"Doesn't seem like a proper thing to do," I said.

She just laughed and soon I heard her walking into the water. Well, that was too much for me. I turned around and she was standing up to her knees, bent over and splashing water on her arms and breasts and looking at me so level and bold.

I wish I had the words to tell what a sight she was standing there. I saw a white tailed deer standing in a stream once, and I thought of that then, of how right it was for a young thing like her to be enjoyin' the water. Strange, I didn't think before of how her whole body would be the color of her face and hands, but I didn't. Not that I didn't picture her that way, though, I confess. Like coffee with cream that'd turned to wet silk she looked standing there in the slow-moving river. She had got her hair wet by then too, and the drops run off the rings in a shower that the sun caught and sparkled.

It was entirely too much for me. I took off my hat, which I almost never do unless I'm going to sleep, and then my shirt and boots. I did turn back around to take off my pants and longjohns, and I could feel my face redden when I faced her again.

She'd waded out to where the water was up to her belly, and she held out her arms toward me. "Come on, Willie!"

So I did. I guess the water must of still been pretty cold, but I didn't notice much. When I was up beside her, she put her hands on my chest. "How white you are!" she said, laughing the while. I couldn't deny it, next to her.

She sat her smooth bottom down on the sandy river bed and I did too. Just our heads sticking out.

When the sun started to slide down toward the west, the lean man dozed and snored, awoke, and nodded off again, dribbling saliva down his hollow cheek. He woke up suddenly and knew someone was there, but when he looked, he saw they were still far out on the plain, riding slow. And they were trailing him, like he knew they would be, following his tracks with their faces down. He put his glass aside and picked up the Sharps, then slid the bead onto the first rider's head. He would wait 'til they got a few yards closer, give himself an easy shot. Two easy shots.

"You do this with all the fellows?" I ask her, making it a joke, thinking I could get her to blush.

Mandy splashed water in my face with her hand. "Only one," she said, laughing at me. "Last summer. His family, they were white people, all white. But after they saw him with me, they fought with him and then went on to Oregon. He took me to St. Louis. Do you know that place, Willie?"

"I been there."

"I loved it there. I loved Robert, too, my first love. We were so happy! But then he gambled and owed a lot of money. He sold me to the man he owed most of the money to."

I couldn't believe I heard her right and I guess my face showed it.

"Oh yes, he sold me! Just as if I were a slave, like my mother had been. The man said so after Robert left, but I did not want to sleep with him, so he beat me and then I ran away from him and came back home. St. Louis is not such a nice place if you have no money and no man to protect you." She looked down into the water and wiggled her toes and watched them for a minute before she looked up and smiled at me. "But that is long over, eh?"

"It's a wonder you can see it that way," I told her. "Best to forget and move on forward, but most folks —"

She took my hands and stood up then, so I stood up too. She was leaning close to kiss me, like I was towards her, but she stopped sudden and turned her head. "Did you hear that?" she asked.

"What?"

"A gun shot! There, again!"

I couldn't decide if I did or not. For a minute, I thought maybe she'd changed her mind about kissing me and all, but when I looked at her face close I seen that wasn't so. She was *scared*. We waded out of the water pretty quick and got into our clothes.

I was hoping it was Clete firing to let me know he was close. "Could you tell which way it come from?" I ask.

"That way," she said. "The way the stream goes. Toward the little mountain." I looked where she was pointing, the way his tracks led, and far out was a butte.

I was mighty uneasy heading out there, I can tell you. Not far from the river two more sets of hoofprints joined those made by the girl's paint and my man's limping animal. The new tracks was those of unshod horses, and around here that could only mean Indians. Lots of Sioux still running wild. Some'd settled on the reservations, Red Cloud's tribe, mostly. But I'd heard Crazy Horse and his people was still killing whites over the Black Hills trouble. Just what I needed on this ride.

When we got closer to the butte, every hundred yards or so I stopped and stood in the stirrups, seeing what I could see up there on top. Not much. Once, when Mandy thought she heard something close, we jumped off and took cover behind a little clump of sage. But nothing happened, so after a while we led the horse a piece — after I got us our rifles. A few yards further on I seen two bodies sprawled in the short squirreltail grass.

From their dress and the way they was painted up, I believed they was Sioux, though maybe Cheyenne. No question about it being the work of the man I was following. I saw where he come

93

down after he'd shot them, done his knife work, and then climbed back up. I didn't need to see his tracks to know who done this. He'd be gone now, or Mandy and me would be dead too. One of the Indians had his whole head gone — blowed off, it looked like. The other with a hole in his chest big enough to set a bucket in. And he'd been scalped, though the hair was just tossed beside him, so I knowed double sure it couldn't of been other Indians.

I looked at Mandy's face about the same time she first seen them braves, and I wisht I'd thought to keep her away from this. It was too late by then, though, and the best I could do was take her back to the horse.

Before we left, I scratched Clete a note on another leaf I tore from the back of my Bible, tucking it under the one Indian's breechclout, but I didn't take the time to read the pages that time. I climbed on and pulled her up, and we walked the buckskin slow around the butte. I found where he had put his horses, but I didn't want to leave her while I climbed up to see where he'd waited, and he'd already lit out besides.

She didn't say nothing while we rode out of there, but once I felt her crying some. I could think of nothing to do or say to make things any easier for her. Funny how being with someone who's Indian or part Indian will make you think different about the dead ones. Like they was regular people.

We made an early camp under some cottonwoods beside a free-running spring I was lucky enough to find. I asked her to unsaddle the horse and make camp while I gathered buffalo chips and a little wood from a big dead branch in one of the trees.

I got the fire going good, though I kept it low, and we ate some beans and more jerked antelope. Neither of us talked much, but I did tease her into playing her guitar when it started getting dark, and she sung for me in a voice as sad as burying a friend. Her face shone like copper there in the flickering firelight.

After a while she stopped and just stared into the flames. "What happened to those men, those Indians, that could have been us, couldn't it, Willie?"

There was nothing to tell her but the truth. "Yes, it could have."

"That was what you were trying to warn me about, I see now, about being killed. I didn't think of how it could be when you told me. To lie dead out there in the night with the body torn apart."

"Best not to dwell on it," I said. "Death comes to all of us soon or late, and they suffered less than most."

She sighed a big sigh and leaned her head against my shoulder. "I hope I die in my own bed, like my mother." She stayed that way awhile and then put her hands behind her on the ground, looking up at the early stars. "My mother loved this land," she said. "She said it was the only place she ever felt really free."

"I think I know how she felt," I said.

"Perhaps, but perhaps not, too. My mother was a black woman, Willie, blacker than me. And she was part Indian as well. My father was white, a Frenchman. His ways were strange in Carolina, for he loved my mother. But he did not begin by loving her."

I didn't know what to say, so I just waited.

"He began by owning her. He bought her to work in his business."

"What was his trade," I ask, hoping to lead her away from the sadness that had overtook her.

"He was an undertaker," she said. "You know. He prepared bodies to —"

"Yes, I know that business."

"But after she worked with him for a while and was carrying his child — me, Willie — he took her north. To Philadelphia. I was a little girl in Philadelphia. But his business did not do well there either, and Mamma hated the city. She had grown up on a big cotton farm and loved living things — flowers, vegetables of all kinds, animals. Papa said he was going to buy her chickens and a goat this summer. . . ."

A coyote yipped and howled a time or two, and after a while we watched the moon come up.

"Time for some sleep," I said, starting to spread my canvas so's I could pull a piece of it over me.

She got her quilt and dropped it on my bedding.

"We'll get more rest if we sleep separate," I told her. "At least I will."

She plopped down on her quilt. "But I thought —"

"I know what you thought," I said. "Even though I told you different. When I said you had to mind what I told you, I said it because I knowed you could do something that would get you killed, nothing more. And I meant it about getting more rest, too. Last night, what with your hair and the smell of you —"

"You wanted me, then, as you did in the river today?" she ask, leaning close.

"Why, hell yes! Who wouldn't, sweet as you are and the way you look. And I'm not ashamed of it, neither!"

She put her arm around me. "Of course not. Why should anyone take shame of that?"

Well, she asked me a question there I could not answer, and I just sat and looked at the way the firelight played on her pretty face.

"Is it that I am . . . not a white women?" she ask, her eyes full of questions. I thought for a minute she was playing a game with me, that she would get me to say I wanted her now or I would make a move towards her, and then she would laugh at me. But looking into her eyes so close, I seen she was just trying to understand how things was with me.

"Has nothing to do with it," I said, speaking low.

She waited for me to go on.

"Mostly, it's how young you are. Hell, I'm fifty, Mandy! And how old are you?"

"I am nineteen," she said, shrugging a shoulder. "My father was more old than that above my mother. She was seventeen when I was born. And my father, he was *more* than fifty, I am sure."

Why, them damn randy Frenchmen! "Most people would say that that's too much difference. And besides, it's more than just age, girl. You have no one to look out for you. No one to see that . . . well, you are not took advantage of. Like that boy done when he sold you to that other man."

She took off my hat then and put both her arms around my neck. It's the rich, warm scent of her I remember most. "I have you, Willie, to take care of me. I know you will not take the advantage."

She kissed me then and it would be a lie if I said that I didn't kiss her back. Only thing I could think of then was that beautiful girl there beside the campfire, a million miles out from nowhere on the rolling prairie.

I started to unbutton her shirt and she started on mine, but after a minute of fussing with our clothes and kissing at the same time, she started to giggle and I guess I laughed too. "It would be faster if we each removed our own garments," she said, all out of breath but not a hint of being ashamed in her voice.

"Yes, it would," I told her, breathing just like

she was. "But speed is not too important to me right now. I would as soon take mine off, like you said. But I'd like to take your *garments* off too, if you wouldn't mind."

"All right, Mr. Goodwin, I will do just as you tell me," she teased. But I didn't care.

Her breasts was the sweetest things, though of course there was no taste to them, only softness. But so hard was her nipples they felt like stones on my tongue. She pulled my head in so hard to her breast I feared I had hurt her when her body writhed so, but it was not pain that moved her around on the canvas like she done.

The skin on her belly was like no other woman's that I have ever touched. It was smooth and taut, but it was . . . I don't know . . . it was like stream-worn sandstone, too, the gritty way it dragged at your palm. She said my name over and over while I touched her.

It was a shock how firm her legs was. And they stretched down from her rounded hips a long, long ways. The fur under her arms was curled tight, wirier than buffalo grass after a frost. That between her legs was more wicked than that. And her smell! It rolled over me in waves so, I thought I would drown, and I caught the scent of wolf or bear in it. And ginseng root and fresh-caught trout and cedar shavings and spices, too, all mixed and mingled together 'til I thought my head would burst.

She grabbed my hair then and pulled my face up, looking at me so direct. "Do you enjoy yourself, Willie?" she ask, moonlight glinting in her eyes.

"Why yes, yes I do," I said, "but I enjoy you more."

She sat up some and kissed me, then turned and looked at the fire. I pulled the quilt over her, thinking she felt a chill, but she kicked it right off.

"No," she said, turning back to me sharp. She spread her legs and tried to pull me between them. "Please, I want you now. And I want to see your face as you enter me."

Well, no woman had ever said anything at all like that to me before.

"Slowly!" she cried out, pulling her hips back away from me. "Go very slowly, Willie, for I want to feel all of you enter me."

I looked into her deep eyes the whole long time, and the pleasure glowed there like coals.

She begun to cry and make noises in her throat, and then I thought something was the matter, but when I ask her, she only laughed and squeezed me tighter with her legs, wrapped around my middle like they was, like when we was riding, only from the front this time. She commenced to move under me, and first it was a trot and then a canter that turned into a hell-bent-for-leather gallop. My word, that girl was strong, and more stamina than the best horse I ever had. And I had some good ones. Well, it was way too much for me, and I went off like a cheap gun, but she wasn't ready to stop yet, and after a short slow-down I was ready to run again too. She hit the top of the hill before I did the second time, but I wasn't far behind.

I collapsed right on top of her, not a drop of gumption left. But she didn't seem to mind.

"Sonofabitch," I said, after a time, raising up on my arms.

She laughed at that. "And you said you were an old man," she teased.

"Not too old yet, I guess," I told her. "Shall I go out as slow as I come in?" I ask.

"As you please," she said. But before I started, she begun moving her hips sideways in some kind of a half circle. I thought I would stay around a while and see what this was all about, and the closest I can come to it is to say it was like a lying-down dance, one I was willing to try. Dance we did, once I caught the rhythm of it.

But she rolled me off too soon and climbed on top, mostly sitting up. "Relax, now," she whispered, pulling the quilt up over her shoulders. She come forward some, so the rings of her dark hair made a kind of tent around our faces. "No, don't move at all," she told me. "Let me do that. Just look at the moon, *Monsieur* Rooster, and let your Pullet do the movement. Let your body go to sleep."

I took a deep breath and done as she said and right then the world changed all around me. The air smelled sweet and new and the moon looked right at me with the most satisfied look I ever seen on his face, before or after, and I've looked for it a hundred times since. The sounds of the prairie night filled up my ears and my brain so they could hold no more.

She was moving slow and easy, but I barely noticed the gait any more. Mostly, I was aware of her body, I think. Of her breath and the feel of her skin, and of the rich scent of her, the most female part of her, of its silk and wetness and warmth.

I don't know how long she had been making the cries she was making, but I knowed I had been hearing them without hearing them for some time, impossible as that sounds. And then I heard the cries I was making, and they was almost screams. I never felt closer to heaven or dying than I did right then. After a while we lay still, catching our breath.

"You learned all that from the young fellow who took you away from here?" I ask her.

She giggled like a schoolgirl. "No, that last I learned from watching Mamma and Papa, after I came back from St. Louis. Perhaps I should not have watched, but what is a girl to do out here?" The fire was out by then and she took a good look around her. "Are we in danger here, Willie? Will the man we are chasing come back in the night?"

"No, ma'm," I told her. "He's bedded down, just like we are."

She give me a funny look then, and finally I saw what she was thinking. "Well, not *just* like we are, I suppose, but you know what I mean."

She laughed a little and I suppose I did too. "After killing them Sioux, he thinks his backtrail is clean. I figure them braves done us a favor." She breathed easier for a minute. "But there is the wolves," I said.

She looked around again. "Are they . . . *dangereuse?*" she ask, saying it peculiar.

"Sometimes they are and sometimes they ain't."

"Would they attack us as we slept?" She wasn't smiling no more.

"Well, let me tell you," I began. "I was camping with a lady up beyond the Yallerstone, a Paiute lady, in the dead of winter. And we was running from her husband and his brother — but that's another story. It'd snowed hard, like it does up there, and we had a nice fire going. Past midnight I woke up and saw a big white wolf, tall at the ears as my friend Clete Shannon. Well, almost, anyways. He was sitting beside that died down fire, right next to us, keeping warm like a dog on a hearthstone. I figured, if he was content there, so was I — and went back to sleep. Come morning, I discovered that damn critter had eat a dozen eggs and a large slab a bacon. That wasn't what bothered me, though." I settled in on my piller, Clete's jacket rolled up. It felt strange being out of my longjohns.

Took her a minute 'til she ask. "What *did* bother you, Willie?"

I rolled over and looked her in the eye. "Why, that big wolf had made himself breakfast of our last food there beside our campfire and didn't even think to wash out the frying pan." I give her a little goodnight kiss. "Don't you worry, Mandy."

My, that girl had a pretty laugh. "Goodnight, Willie."

Chapter Nine

A gunshot. Right beside my face. I rolled for my pistol, but a hundred hooves was right on top of me. Mandy screamed. Horses stamping and turning all around the quilt and kicking up the canvas. Mandy fired her rifle again, sitting up, and someone hollering at the horses.

I yelled, pushing the barrel of her Winchester toward the ground. But she got off another shot anyway, making the horses even wilder. I throwed myself over her, partly to protect her from the hooves flying all around and partly to keep her from shooting.

It took a while, but they started to move away. I laid still as I could, trying to hold her, squirming as she was. The dust settled some and things got quieter. That big strong girl finally laid still beneath me.

"Morning, Deputy," Clete called from a little distance off. "Looks like you've caught somebody, but I thought this was a *man* hunt."

I rolled off of her and sat up, mustering as much of my dignity as I could. "About time you showed up. What kept you?" It wasn't 'til then that I remembered I was in my birthday suit, bare as a new-hatched magpie. When I reached for the quilt to cover myself, I found Mandy had wrapped it around her. There was nothing else to do but stand up, put on my hat and then my longjohns. Clete, he watched the show still sitting his horse and smiling like the devil does when a Baptist gets drunk.

"This is your friend?" Mandy asked.

"That's right," I told her, buttoning my shirt. "This here's Clete Shannon. You almost put a hole through the sheriff of Two Scalp, Dakota Territory." I sat back down to put on my boots. "And if he's anything at all like he usually is, he won't let you fergit this 'til the day you die."

I went over to where he was. He looked tired and kind of smirky, but I was glad to see him. "Clete, this here's Miss Amanda Bowden, or something Frenchy like that."

"Boudoin," she corrected me, and then said it slow for both of us. "Boo-dwanh. I call myself Mandy." She pushed at her hair and reached for her boots. "You will excuse me if I do not stand up to curtsy, Mr. Sheriff."

"Of course, Miss Amanda," he said, that grin still on his face. You could tell he was taking her in and liked what he saw. When he looked back at me, he was surprised that I caught what was on his mind. "I'm sorry, you two. I didn't figure on finding anyone asleep, seeing as how the sun's already up."

"It is I who must apologize for shooting at you," Mandy said. "I thought you were the other man, the man we follow, Mr. Sheriff."

"Call me Clete, ma'm," he said, touching the brim of his Montana. "When you fired, those two horses I've been leading busted loose and yours got mixed in with them. I'll go round them up now and let you get yourself dressed. We got a long day on the trail ahead of us and need to get started right away."

Mandy sat and looked back and forth from Clete to me 'til he rode off a ways. I tied on my bandanna, grabbed my saddle, and walked out after him. Before long he caught my horse and brought him in. Clete stayed on Buckshot while I saddled mine. "Why in hell'd you bring her?" he ask.

"Had no choice," I told him. "Her parents died and no one else lived around there. She didn't slow me down, though."

"Except maybe at night," Clete said.

"I can't see as that's any of your damn business, just like my drinkin'," I told him flat. "Long as I do my job."

"Didn't know you liked them quite so fresh out of their swaddles."

I was about to tell him I was no older than her pappy was compared to her ma when I seen that damn grin back on his face. He was just hoorahing me was all, so I gave him a good wink and let 'er go at that. I looked back toward where Mandy and me had camped, and she was gettin' dressed, putting a clean shirt on.

"Where's her horse?" Clete asked, watching her too.

"Our man took it. Ridin' it now, 'cause his is about lame."

"Damned inconvenient, Willie," he said. "And dangerous for her, but I suppose you know that."

I mounted up. "Yessir it is. And I told her so, too, but she still decided she had to come. I'm sorry, Clete, but I saw no other way for it."

"Well, I'm sorry too for actin' like a jackass back there at Nell's. If we catch him, it'll be to your credit, for I'd a never done it, starting out by myself like I had a mind to. I'd have lost him back at Medicine Creek where he covered his tracks. I've been thinking on it, following behind, and I was wrong as shit, so I guess we're even again, huh?"

"Suits me," I said. "Now, are we going to go catch them other horses and get after that hardcase, or are we going to sit here and just apologize all over each other for the rest of the morning?"

Well, it took no time at all to catch them other two and bring them back. He had brought me a fine-looking bay gelding, almost short enough in the barrel to be an Indian pony and long enough in the legs not to be. Sounds like an awkward sort of horse, I know, but he was smooth as the seat of a banker's britches. But what surprised me even more was that the citizens of Two Scalp had sprung for him. The pack horse carried more provisions than we could eat in a month, even with an extra mouth to feed. Clete got out the shotgun he'd brought from the office and I gave him back his Henry.

108

"I found this with your trail clothes," Clete said, handing me the tied-up skin I kept my pistol and powder and balls in. "Is that a Navy .36?"

"Yes it is," I said. "Stopped wearing it a few years ago when I finally saw I'd never learn to hit anything with it. Don't know why I ever bought it in the first place."

"Pretty old piece and not the best gun for the job we've got here, but I'd appreciate it if you'd strap it on anyway," he said.

"All right, only don't expect much."

"I know better than that," he said, starting out.

He'd brought ammunition enough for a regiment on patrol and even a tent. But of course he didn't bring another saddle for the horse he brought me, so Mandy had to go bareback on the buckskin. She didn't seem to mind.

I rode beside Clete, leading the pack animal, and Mandy followed, keeping well up with us. He looked back every so often to see how she was doing, and then he'd give me that big shit-eating grin. But once when I seen him looking back, I noticed it wasn't just her welfare on his mind, and it was me had the smile on my face after that. While we rode he told me about how everyone in town had gone to Nell's and Jesse's funerals, and thought nothing much about them two old timers sleeping together, though Mary'd been a little funny about it.

"Looky there," I said, after we'd been on the

trail for a while. "He's heading back up to the Cheyenne again," for his sign struck out toward the northwest.

Clete stopped and took out his map. "Looks like he's heading back toward the river, all right, but it ain't the Cheyenne. That's a lot west of here. The one you followed him along, that's the Bad."

"The Bad? I never heard of no Bad River. What's bad about it? Looked pretty peaceful to me."

We dismounted and studied the map he'd brought and soon Mandy joined us. "It is called the Bad River because it begins in the *Mauvaises Terres*," she said, as if that should mean something to us. Clete looked at me and I shrugged. "It means 'bad lands to travel through,' " Mandy explained. "I have heard my father talk of it. 'Where hell comes up to the earth,' Papa said. It would be better not to go there, I think. We should go south 'til we come to a town."

Clete give her a look and then walked over to his horse and snap-mounted him. "If that bastard's going into the Badlands then that's where we're going. At least I am."

I climbed up too. "I didn't sign on for half ways," I said. "Mandy, you're welcome to that old buckskin of mine if you want him. Take my compass, too, and some food. Head south by east and you'll find someone in a few days. Course, there are Sioux and Cheyenne running around. And I'd miss you plenty, especially if you was dead."

She shook her head and I couldn't tell whether she was just refusing my offer or if she thought we were crazy. Maybe both. But she didn't mount. Just stood there looking at the ground and sulking like a kid.

I turned my horse and went over close so I could say a word to her private. "Now look, Mandy. I didn't say nothin' about you not doing what I told you this morning. I yelled at you to stop shooting and you went ahead and did anyway. You was startled and so was I. But this is a whole different thing entirely. Now, either mount up and go along without trying to change our minds or else head off on your own, don't matter to me. If you go with us, I'll look out for you best I can, but you'll have to keep your ideas about going elsewhere to yourself. You promised to do like I told you. If you go on with us, I'll expect you to live up to your side of the bargain."

"Oh, I will go along, Mr. Goodwin," she said, sharp as a spider bite, "for I cannot go by myself. But I see who makes the orders here and who follows them. It is senseless to chase this man! He is a killer and will kill again. Your friend he shot is well now, so why chase him? *Le meurtrier*, he was only trying to kill the man who shot his son!"

I guess Clete heard her, for he rode right over. "What's that? You talked to him?"

"Back at her place, before he took her horse," I told him.

"What'd you say about him killing someone

111

who shot his boy?" Clete ask, and not very gentle.

She stood with her hands on her hips and kept her mouth shut, glaring at us like a rattler in a den.

Clete waited a time before he spoke, and when he did his voice was raspy. "I need to know who I'm chasing, Missy."

She smiled at him but it weren't one of her pretty ones. "I will be happy to tell you what I know, Mr. Shannon, as soon as you take me to a place when I can board a stagecoach." She crossed her arms and looked real pleased with herself after that.

Clete wheeled his horse around, grabbed the reins of my buckskin, and turned to me. "Leave her!" He nudged that big black and headed off with her mount. I seen her face good then, and she looked a whole hell of a lot different than she did a minute before.

"Hold on," I called to Clete. I caught up in a few yards, for he was only walking the horses at a good clip. "You can't do this, leave her out here all alone!"

"Don't think I'll have to," he said kind of soft, though there was no need for it, she being then three or four rods behind. "Just let her think on it."

Well, I didn't know what to do. Before I decided, we heard her call out and we stopped.

She was running after us, her hair streaming out behind. "Wait! I will tell you! Wait for me!"

I glanced at Clete, but I was surprised he seemed to be taking little pleasure from his victory over her, his jaw set so firm as it was. I didn't notice the scar by his ear before, since he caught up, but it was still red and nasty looking. It would be with him the day they lowered him into the ground, too.

When she got there, she looked pretty shamefaced.

"What'd he say?" Clete ask.

She took a minute to catch her breath. "I asked where he was going. He said he was going home. That he had avenged the death of his son and was going back to his home. He did not say where his home was and I did not ask him, so glad I was to be leaving there." She took off her wide-brimmed hat and wiped her brow with her sleeve. "I did not know that it was important, Mr. Goodwin, or I would have told you. He said some other things, too, but I did not understand him very well. He talked, how do you say, peculiar?"

She stopped talking and you could tell she was trying to remember.

"Think more would come back to you if we was to ride on?" I ask.

"I will try to remember all I can," she said, and it sounded like a promise.

"See that you do," Clete told her, tossing her the reins to my old buckskin. "Here. Take this rifle too. It's yours. No reason for me to carry it."

Riding bareback at the pace we was going was

no picnic. It would be worse carrying that Remington — she had no rifle scabbard because she had no saddle. Which also meant she couldn't dolly welter it to the horn either. She'd have to carry it in her hands a long distance and that old piece had some weight to it. Not an easy man is Clete Shannon when he's crossed.

We rode a long ways saying nothing and making time, nearly ten miles before noon and gaining on him, I figured. The sign was easy to follow and getting easier all the time in the thin grass. His trailing horse was about on its last legs then and it slowed him down. The animal avoided putting that split hoof down as much as he could. He'd not be able to run at all soon, and I couldn't figure out why our man still trailed him. Maybe a bad spare horse was better than none at all.

We made damn good time that morning, but it wasn't good enough to suit Clete. Often he ask me couldn't we go no faster, but it was either the pace we was doing or wear out our horses like the man we was following. Midafternoon, we come onto the river again, and that's where he'd camped.

We dismounted and looked around. Still a few warm coals under the thick ash. He'd killed his trailing horse with a knife beside the river, its head under water. Blood all over the bank. Slit the critter's throat, probably while it was drinking its fill. The slope of the bank raised the dead animal's haunches up some, and it was from there that he'd sliced himself off a couple of steaks. His bootprints showed me where he'd stood when he done his butchering. The flies were helping themselves to the leftovers by the time we got there, so he had probably done it last night and then fed himself.

He'd stayed in camp a while this morning from the tramped-down look of things. Arranging his trap and resting some, I supposed.

"What kind of man eats his own horse, Mr. Shannon?" Mandy ask, looking at the dead beast.

"A hungry man," he told her. "Let's ride."

Chapter Ten

Along the river his sign was as clear as a Texan's conscience. We sailed along for several hours at a quick trot and even cantered some. "This fast enough for you," I called back to Clete.

"If it's the best you can do. I *would* like to catch him before you die of old age."

Well, we like to had a horse race then. Mandy kept slipping further and further back, and after about four miles I slowed down.

"C'mon," he yelled, up ahead of me. "That horse has a lot more left than that."

"Yeah, but Mandy don't," I told him, looking back down the river but not seeing her.

"Forget her," Clete yelled. "She'll catch up."

"Like them braves caught up to our man, most likely. No, I'm going to wait here for her. Go on ahead, if you want. You'll not catch him in the two hours of daylight left — nor even see him."

"Damn it, Willie, come on! For a dollar you can buy what she's got in any town."

I took a minute before I answered. "I told you what I was doin'. We'll take him tomorrow, maybe the day after. Soon enough for me. It's not worth risking this girl's life to catch him sooner. Not to me it ain't."

"I'm going on," he called back.

"Watch out for an ambush," I yelled after him.

After a while I seen her. She was coming up

the river in a awkward sideways trot and she was bouncin' three different ways at once, like the dice in a chuck-a-luck cage. I had to laugh despite myself.

I fell into place beside her. "A slow canter would be easier on you. Try it."

My old horse caught the rhythm of the smooth-gaited bay I was ridin', and Mandy nodded her head. And damned if I didn't think of the night before. We kept at it solid 'til the sun set and the stars begun to come out. I was just starting to worry that Clete might try to go on in the dark when I seen a big blazing campfire far upriver.

Half a mile off, we dismounted and led the horses.

Mandy walked with a hitch and she had a time getting her breath back all the way. I felt as tired as she looked.

"How you doin'?" I asked.

"I am all right, Willie," she said, but I didn't believe it entirely, for I had rode beyond my means a time or two myself. "Why did we go so fast and so far today? You and I were not in such a hurry yesterday."

"Well, one reason is we was both on the same horse and I had to go slower. Another is, I didn't entirely want to catch up to him, not by myself."

"Yes," she said. "And another reason is that you are not a crazy man — like Mr. Shannon."

"Aw, Clete's all right. A little impatient now and then is all. You got to remember that this man tried to kill him. You had a little taste today of how he gets when someone goes against him. Just can't abide it. I seen it before. Everbody's like that some. Clete's like that a lot. Makes him a difficult man, I agree, but it don't make him crazy."

She surprised me then. She put her arm across my shoulders like we was old compadres and laughed. "You are a good man, Mr. Goodwin. I hope you will be as good a friend to me as you are to Mr. Shannon."

Damned if I knowed what to say to that. How she could think a man could be just friends with a woman was as addled as her thinking me a big bug because I understood old Clete.

When we got close, I whistled to let him know it was us coming in. He was leaning back against his saddle beside the fire when we got there, and he give us a big wave and a howdy. I was happy to see he'd got over his mad.

Played out as she was, Mandy still offered to take care of both the horses. I got the idea she was trying to prove up on her worth to this outfit so's not to be in danger of being left behind again. I told her I'd rub down the bay, but she wouldn't hear of it, and to tell the truth, I didn't have enough spunk left to argue with her. I went over and sat beside Clete. "Reminds me of the time last fall when I had that big fire built for you. Long day in the saddle then, too, I recall."

"Yeah, I remember," he said. "That coffee should be about ready."

I poured myself some and another cup to cool for Mandy. "We covered a lot of ground today," I said.

"Yes, we did," Clete answered. "Gained almost a day on him. I was hoping to see his fire along the river here."

"Maybe tomorrow, if he's still goin' like he was today. Last time I could see his tracks clear, I'd guess he's about six hours ahead of us now. You know, if he spots us, we're in for it, because there's no chance to check out every place he could be layin' in wait. Along the river here it ain't so bad, but if we get into rough country —"

You could see from his face he knew what I was thinking. "Yeah, well, I'll look out for him. Can't slow down now, can we?"

"No, I guess not," I answered. "I suppose you saw he's been mostly walking that girl's paint, since he's got no spare now, I guess." Mandy joined us at the fire about then, spread her quilt and flopped down like a sack of turnips. I handed her a cup of coffee and got a pretty smile for my trouble. She looked awful sweet in the firelight, but you could see she was played out.

"Willie, where'd you ever learn to track like that?" Clete ask. "I never knew you could do that. Reminds me of an Indian down in Kansas who used to track for me, old Heavy Nose."

"It was an Indian who taught me," I told him. "A full-blooded Jicarilla Apache I spent some time with."

Clete laughed. "How in the *hell* did you ever

119

come to throw in with an Apach?"

"You could say we was thrown together by fate, I suppose. More accurate, you could say we was linked together at the ankles for two years, two months and eleven days. Being a deputy in Abilene and all, I suppose you know what I'm talkin' about." I fired up my old corncob.

He looked at me square then. "Where'd you do time?"

"In Texas — the land of the free and the chained."

"You were chained to an Indian?" Mandy ask.

I nodded. "Good man. One of the most truthful men I ever knowed, too. He'd do exactly what he said he'd do, give you his food or break your arm, either way. But that old *Coyotero* was smart, too. He knowed it would be the white man's country before long, unlike most of his people. He wanted to learn to read the white man's language, and to pay me back for showing him how, he taught me what he knowed best, how to read sign — fair trade. All of what I know of following men and animals I learned from Stalking Bear." I yawned and finished my coffee.

"Did he learn to read English?" Mandy ask.

I tossed two of the branches Clete'd gathered into the fire and sent a passel of sparks up into the night. "He did. But he changed his mind about the worth of it after he could do it good. He learned real quick, and the only thing I had for him to read, once he knowed how, was that old Bible of mine. The first winter, after the

120

work got slow, he read that book straight through, cover to cover, and it had a good many more pages in it then than it does now. Asking me questions the whole way, not that I could explain much of it to him. He liked the stories best. He 'specially liked the part about Noah, I remember. But the way he saw it, if white men said they believed what was in that book and still acted like they did, he wouldn't live among 'em. Either they was crazy or untruthful at heart. After that he never wanted to read nothing more. By the time he died, I don't think he could even remember the alphabet. Not the whole thing, anyway." I stood and brushed off the seat of my pants after I stretched good.

They was both quiet then.

"Shall I prepare some food?" Mandy ask after a time.

"Not for me," I said, gathering up my canvas and the blanket Clete brought me. "I'll eat in the morning. I'm going down by the river there and make a bed in the sand."

"I thought we were going to ask Mandy about —"

"Go ahead, if you want," I said, ambling toward the bank. "I'm done in. Need sleep bad. If you want me in on it, it'll have to wait 'til tomorrow. Suit yourself."

I planned on finding the softest spot I could, roll and wiggle around 'til the sand took my shape, and spend a comfortable night. Truth is, I settled for the first level place I hit and barely got my canvas spread and my blanket around me before I was out. Only thing I saw before leaving this weary world was the clouds rolling in from the northwest.

Come morning, the sky was threatening rain about as much as it can without dripping water, and Clete was in a like mood, anxious to get going. The temperature'd dropped like a stone down a well and the fire felt welcome. Spring in Dakota will do that. One minute it's warm as summer and the next you'll see snow flakes drifting down. I finished all the beans Mandy saved me from the night before, fixed with a big hunk of salt pork. And I ate what was left of the biscuits, though they wasn't what you'd call fresh no more, nearly a dozen, with my coffee.

"Come on, let's go," Clete yelled while I was washing my face in the river. "It's going to rain soon." He'd saddled his horse and mine and'd loaded just about all our gear on the pack animal by then. Lord, I was dragging my tail that morning.

They started without me, but I didn't care, stiff and sore as I was. When I caught up, they was stopped about a half mile from where we'd camped, beside the river, letting their horses drink where his had. Beyond, his tracks led south along a little creek. This boy knew the country by its water, that was clear.

"I'd a never found his fire last night if I'd gone more upriver," Clete said. "I'd a been lost this morning, too. Would have had to come back to here."

"He's a fox, all right," I said. *A fox against a wolf,* I said to myself, but Clete'd never of understood that. "A real careful one. Even when he thinks no one's following him. Probably just his nature by now. How old you guess this fellow is, Mandy?" I ask.

"As old as you, perhaps. Younger than my father." She looked off across the prairie, sulky about something, but damned if I knowed what.

"You talk to her about our man last night?" I ask Clete.

"Not much," he said. "Let's get on him and get done with this."

A few miles up the creek we run into the twin of the butte where he'd shot them bucks. Thick gray clouds draped the sky.

"Careful," I told Clete, who was getting up even with me, off to the side. "Good spot for an ambush." But instead of leading close into the butte, like his tracks done before, they angled west around it, beyond where the stream petered out. Another mile further, another butte, this one wider and higher than the last.

"We can't keep slowing down, Willie," Clete said. "It's going to rain and then we've lost him. Let me go first. I'll take the risk of going faster. You and the girl stay up if you can and follow *his* trail if I go the wrong way. He's still walking his horse, ain't he?"

"My horse," Mandy said.

"Yes, he is," I told him. "We'll keep you in sight if we can. If it rains and we lose your sign, we'll look for a day and then head back to the river. Think you can find it?"

He took off at a gallop without answering. We loped after him, but in less than half an hour, he was just a speck far out in the grass. And what grass there was was getting thinner all the time. Clay mounds and hills was everywhere before long. Some was sliced into peaks by the wind and rain and others looked like the chopped-off feet of dragons and lizards, complete with toes and claws. A few tables of sod stood between the washed-out gullies, but three miles further on, even these give way. In spots there was nothing green at all, only the bare ground — gray and red and pink and sometimes a little thin yeller layer. Humped up and twisted and hillocky and I don't know what-all. Of course we lost sight of Clete in that crazy country.

If Clete hadn't of went first, I doubt if I would of gone through there after the man we was chasing. He could've been hid *anywhere*. I wondered if Clete knew the chance he was taking. Probably he did, but he'd bull it through anyway.

Mandy rode in closer to me than she'd been doing. "I do not like these badlands, Mr. Goodwin. It is not safe here. I know now what my father meant. Nothing grows here, and I have not seen any animals for miles, not even a prairie dog."

124

We went through a flat place, a hundred acres or more, where broken up rocks of all sizes lay on top of the clay or were buried in it a little ways and others loose and in small piles. Some stones the size of your head or more, but most big as your fist. Tough going for the horses. But it was easy following Clete, rough as it was, for he'd traveled through here fast enough to move plenty of rock. Going a lot faster than we was, I can tell you. Ahead, peaks of striped clay lifted higher than those we already passed by — some like rows of fangs and others rounded like molars on top. Evil-looking country. I liked it no better than Mandy did, but I tried not to let her see that.

"The devil must have his ranch around here somewheres," I said to her. The words was no more out of my mouth than we heard shots.

Chapter Eleven

In them hard clay ravines and canyons, the blasts rolled like thunder. Two different rifles, it sounded like.

Mandy squirmed around on that horse's back, and what with the shots, she scared the hell out of it, so I grabbed her reins. "Follow me across. Go the way I go. Head toward them two pointy peaks, but don't go no farther! I'm riding on up ahead to help Clete, but I'll come back. Only *stay* there, 'cause that's where I'll come to when this is over." I let go the reins of her horse and handed her the lead rope of the pack animal.

"All right," she said, looking awful scared.

"Don't risk your horse hurrying through these rocks. This trouble may take some time."

"All right," she said again, taking off her broad-brimmed black hat. She looked me square in the eye then. "You will come back for me, won't you, Willie?"

"I'll be back," I said. "Just wait somewhere between them peaks. Take some shelter. I won't forget about you, girl."

But I risked *my* horse some through them stones. That long-legged bay was as surefooted as he was easy ridin', and I was glad for it that day. I looked back when I got to the far edge of that rocky place, and Mandy was making her way across it slow like I told her to.

I heard more rifle shots then, but I couldn't tell where they was coming from.

It was a regular sort of trail once you got into the mouth of the bigger canyon, though it rose some. The clay was firm and smooth, so I pushed that bay as hard as he would go.

Where it widened out into a little valley, there lay Clete's black horse with his guts blowed out. Saddle still on him, but he was dead. Clete's hat was there, though his rifle was gone from the scabbard. My bay reared and we danced a few circles 'til I calmed him down. I could find nothing to tie him to but Buckshot's reins, and he didn't like that at all.

A rifle exploded above me, up on the peak in front. I hit the dirt. Nothing happened for a minute, and when I looked, there was Clete up there sighting down his rifle — but not in my direction.

After he lowered it, I hollered, "Clete!" He looked and waved and after a while he started down toward me.

"I saw him," he called.

I set and waited 'til he got down.

He was out of breath, and his clothes was in shreds at the knees and elbows. "Mandy's horse, the one that bastard's riding, it's a paint, isn't it?"

"Yep, a paint. That's what she told me," I said.

"He's a tall man, real lean." It was then that Clete seen Buckshot. He stood and stared for a

127

minute, then picked up his hat and smacked it against his leg. "I knew he was hit bad, but not like that. Look at the damage that damn bullet did."

"What happened?" I ask.

Clete brushed at his cut-up elbows. "He jumped me. Waiting up there, where you saw me. Only he hit Bucky instead of me. I took a spill, ate some gravel, and came up shooting. He fired back, almost hit me once, but when I started working my way up there, he took off."

"Did you hit him, when you fired that last?"

"No. That was just pissin' in the wind."

"You all right?" I ask. He was bleeding through the busted-out knees of his pants pretty good.

"Yeah, but I'm stove up."

"You're welcome to the bay if you want to go after him," I offered. "Good horse."

"No, the trail goes up from here and he's got too much of a start on me now, goddamnit." I expected him to say that he *could* have chased him if I'd a been there with him, where I ought to of been, but he didn't. His eyes showed it for a minute, though. But maybe that was just in my head, I don't know. Then he hunkered down by his dead horse. "Sorry to lose this old fellow," he said, patting Buckshot's jaw.

We got Clete's McClellan loose after a time and the rest of his gear we piled beside it. Of course we could do nothing about Buckshot, not even put stones over him, since there was no stones there. Only thing in this place was dried clay, formed into knuckles and lumps the size of eyeballs where it was steep and washed smooth where it was a little flat. I asked him if he wanted to ride back with me or stay there 'til I brought the pack horse, which he would have to ride now — that, or the buckskin. He decided on staying.

I gave him my canteen, since his was nearly empty, so's he could wash out his cuts. He was sitting on the ground beside his gear tending to his knees when I left.

The bay loped easy going back for Mandy. I didn't push him, but I didn't poke, either. All in all, I guess it'd been a little more than an hour from when I'd left her 'til I got to them two peaks where I told her to wait.

The pack horse was tied to a stone that looked like a big old turtle, but both Mandy and my old horse was nowheres to be seen. I took the bay up into the clay draws on both sides, up high as I could get him, thinking maybe she had done like I said and took shelter up there with the horse. I called her name loud as I could, several times, but there was no answer, only the echo of my voice calling back to me.

Gullies and ravines led off in all directions. I searched some of the big ones I could get my horse in, but saw no tracks, though sometimes I wasn't sure. I lost myself for a spell in there too, and though I followed the bay's tracks backwards, I went in a circle for some time. Just by luck I stumbled onto where the pack horse was still tied. If I hadn't, I might still be wandering around in there, so cut up and twisted it was. I had followed sign over all kinds of country, but nothing like that. I tried to think of what Stalking Bear would of done and just did that.

I don't know how long I wandered around looking for that girl, but I knowed I would have to go back to Clete before long. I suspected he had camped without fire or food many a time, but I couldn't just leave him there for the night in this country, not without a horse.

I got the pack animal and headed back to him.

"Where the hell have you been?" he yelled before I even got to where he was sitting on his wrapped-up bedroll.

"I couldn't find her," I told him. "Looked all over, but she's not around."

"Now maybe we can catch that sonofabitch!" he said, standing up. You could see how hard moving around was for him. A good bone-rattling fall will make you remember all your old hurts.

I dismounted and unloaded the pack horse. Clete threw his blanket and saddle up on it. After we stuffed our saddle bags and put some things in our bedrolls, we just left the rest of it there on the ground, including the tent. "I can't just leave her there," I said. "Just like I couldn't leave you here. I'm going back."

"Damned if I am," Clete said. "Come along up the trail a piece with me. It climbs a big ridge and it looks like you can see for quite a ways.

Maybe you can spot her."

"All right. But if I can't, I'm going back."

Took us a while to get to where he had in mind, following our man's tracks the whole way. Where the trail cut through a notch in a red clay spine, you could see miles and miles of this broken-up, washed away country spread out before you.

"Good God," Clete said. "I never saw anything the equal of this before." I knowed what he meant. The sky was gray and dark, spoiling for rain. Beneath us laid a broad, flat valley, grassy in many spots, but those was all a good ways off. Jumbles of clay mountains stuck up in places. Far across, you could see the tree line of a river and beyond that, another jagged ridge like the one we was standing on. Down to our left, maybe fifteen miles, was a large tableland and up to our right, a farrago of spiky peaks and roof-slanted things that looked more like a big story-book castle than anything else. The wind come through with a cold edge on it.

I got Clete's glass and scanned the ridges to both sides and back the way we come. We sat there a long time and Clete looked too.

"Well, I don't see her," he said. "You'd be smart to come with me, Willie — be dark soon."

"I'm going to find Mandy," I told him.

He didn't give me no argument, just nodded his head. "His tracks lead down to where the trees are and that's where I'm going. If he's there, I'll kill him. Or else he'll kill me. If he's not, I'll camp and wait for you 'til morning. But I'll wait no longer."

It was easy to see where he meant to go. Looked like a big part of the ridge we were on had broke off and slid halfway to the valley floor, leaving a mostly level place down there a hundred yards deep and maybe a quarter mile wide. Appeared to be water there, too, for it was covered with juniper and a few patches of high grass.

I turned my horse and offered him my hand. "Good luck, Clete."

He took it and shook it good. "Good luck yourself, you dumb sonofabitch."

The light was starting to go by the time I got back to between them two peaks. As leathery as the clay was there, baked almost like gray bricks, her sign were hard as hell to see. She had been nervous waiting there. Tracks going all different ways, back and forth. I went back to the edge of the rocky place, got off and led my horse so I could get down close to the ground every few yards to unravel the trail. I was about to go back toward them two peaks again when it started to pour rain.

Chapter Twelve

Damn that girl, anyway. There was nothing chased her off. I'd a seen the sign if there was. Indians or wolves or whatever beasts of hell lived in these hills — I knowed I would have. No, she'd just run off scared of the gunfire and of this place, but mostly afraid of being left alone. Showed how much she trusted me. And it couldn't of been our man after her either, for he was well out in front.

Whatever happens to her she deserves, I told myself. And if I could've just believed that, I could've stopped riding and looking and calling for her in that bone-chilling rain. I kept thinking about my slicker, but it was back hanging on a hook at the Dakota House in Two Scalp, for Clete didn't think to bring it. I kept seeing it in my mind and wishin' I could change places with it. As much good as I was doing riding around and getting wet, it would've done as good out here as me, and I could've just went downstairs and got some supper if I was back there. An hour after the downpour started, it was nearly night. I drew my pistol and fired it quick three times, but there was no answering shots. I knowed it was dangerous to be sending out signal shots into a country where you don't know what Indians might be around, but I could think of nothing else.

I believed for a while that I'd found the bay's

weakness at last, that he done poorly at keeping his footing when the way got a mite slippery, but then I stepped down to piss and fell plop on my ass without even thinking about it. Stickiest muck I ever put a boot in, though for some reason it never got very deep. Underneath, two or three inches down, it was as firm as you'd want . . . strange stuff.

I knowed Mandy had brung this on herself, not keeping a tight rein on her fears, but I also knowed it was my fault she was out there, lost and cold and as wet as I was. It was me, no other, who had let her come along and promised to look out for her. And then I'd failed her just when she needed me most. For a while I blamed her for making me think that about myself, and then myself for a time for thinking *that,* and then both together. And if that's not stupid, I don't know what is.

I walked the bay through those slick gullies and slippery ravines for hours, even after I knowed that it was hopeless. She was not to be found that night — or not likely any other, either. To top it off, I got lost again. I knowed also I should stop where I was and wait for daylight, but I couldn't let myself just quit like that.

It was black as the heart of a cave.

Later, long after midnight, I guessed, I slogged through water and muck and rain 'til my legs felt about ready to give out. Leading the horse, I stumbled and fell over something, and when I put my hand down to get back up, I touched slick wet fur. I had come upon Buckshot. I worked my way up through the gouge in the ridge Clete and me rode up earlier. It was slow work, too, that mean and oily ground fightin' me the whole way, but I got to the top before I played out, though I wasn't sure I would for a while.

Down below, but farther off than I hoped it would be, Clete's fire was a heart-warming sight, though I'd a rather it warmed my feet instead. No matter it was late, he still had it built up big. I drew my pistol and snapped off three shots. In a while he answered the same way. Since I was already wet to the skin and muddy as a pig, I sat down and rested. Right there in all that gumbo. Yes indeed, mud right underneath my sitter, cold and clammy, whether I could see it or not. I was thinking I would come around some and then make it down the slope to where Clete was, but twice I dozed off sitting there, wet and shivery as I was, and I knowed this would be it for me this night.

I front-hobbled the bay with an old piece of rope from my saddle bag. It was hard getting my bedroll and canvas off the horse and laid out when I couldn't see a damn thing, 'specially as I was doing my damnedest to keep my bedding dry. When my sogans was as good as I could get them, I took off my clothes, all of them, longjohns too, and just tossed them beside me in the mud. I wouldn't be able to get to sleep wearing them things, and they couldn't get no wetter or muddier than they already was. Naked as a jay bird, I crawled into them wool blankets and pulled the top half of my canvas snug over me. The sound of rain falling on my water-proofing kept me awake for almost a full minute.

Morning come, the rain still fell, though it'd eased up some. First time in memory I'd let a saddle on a beast all night and went to sleep with my horse untended. Bay didn't hold it against me, though, for he hobble-jumped over after he seen my head poke out.

I stood and searched for my dry clothes in the bags, but they weren't there. In with Clete's things, most likely. Right away I wished I'd throwed my clothes over the saddle horn the night before. It was plain I was wrong about them not being able to get any muddier than they was then. I looked down at my sloppy longjohns and shirt there on the ground and knew I couldn't face putting them things on again. After a while, I took my knife and made a slit in the middle of one of my blankets, slipped it over my head and belted it around my middle. With my hat, that would do me 'til I got down below. Not very comfortable sittin' a saddle with no pants on, I can tell you — especially when it's soaked. I thanked the Lord I wasn't on a McClellan, anyway.

Wasn't 'til I walked my horse about half way down that slope to Clete's camp that I thought about Mandy. I promised myself I'd go back and look again after I got some breakfast and dry clothes. Right about then the rain stopped. Clete'd camped in a grove of junipers close by a little pond with cattails clogging it. Probably had slept pretty good under them trees last night. But now he was laying at the rim of this overgrown shelf looking down at the valley floor with his glass. Before I got below the trees, I seen what he was looking at — a man with a horse down there doing something. I tied the bay beside the pack horse, only it was Clete's mount now, and walked up to where he was spying. He motioned me down and went back to looking.

I could see better beside him, peeking through some scrubby junipers right at the edge, than I did from above. The man down below wasn't our man. For one thing, his horse wasn't no paint. And for another, he was way too short.

"What's he doing down there, anyway?"

Clete's eye was glued to the glass. "Digging a stone out of the ground with a shovel. Maybe he's prospecting, but this is a strange place for it." We watched some more before he spoke again. "Couldn't find her, huh?"

"No," I told him. "She cut out, scared to death, I guess, and of course the rain . . ." I didn't have to finish it for him. "But I'm going back again after I'm dressed proper."

He took his eye off the glass and took a good look at me. Well, he started to laugh and then to hold it in, so's not to give us away to the man

137

below. Tears come to his eyes, and about the time he could almost take charge of himself again, he'd start laughing again.

We crawled away from the rim and he let it loose then. He was still chuckling and looking at me from time to time while he dug for my clothes in his bags.

"You look like you're all set to go to Mexico," he said.

"Well, I'm not. I'm going back for Mandy after I get something to eat. You took all the food, as well as my pants."

"You're wasting your time," he said. "No tracks to follow now. You know how long it would take you to cover all these cut-up badlands? You even have any idea what direction to start in?" He handed me my clothes.

Well, I didn't.

Clete put his hand on my shoulder and looked me in the eye. "Let it go, friend. *Let* her go. You did all a man could. She cut out because she thought she'd be better off on her own than she would be with two hardcases chasing a dangerous killer. That's all there is to it. It was her decision, just like coming along. Now let her live with it. Who knows, maybe she was right."

"But, damnit, Clete, I was responsible for her!"

"No, you weren't," he said, packing up his gear. "You just believe a lot of old-fashioned bullshit about the way a man should act in regards to a woman. Maybe you've noticed that this isn't Michigan or Boston. A man takes his chances living here, and so does a woman. And sleeping with her doesn't make you her keeper. Anyone who doesn't like it here is free to go to some more citified place."

"That's just what she was trying to do," I told him.

"Yeah, but who said it was your lookout to see that she did it?" He waited for an answer, but I had none to give him. "Think on it. There are no tracks for you to follow. I'm going down there and talk to that man. Maybe he's seen that lean bastard, maybe not. If he hasn't, I'm traveling southwest, the way we were going before we got into this damned place. Could be we'll see his tracks down that way. If we have no luck in a week, we'll head back to Two Scalp and look for something more profitable. Like that money Wilson stole."

He had his gear all loaded by then. He climbed into the saddle, fixed his hat, and looked at me. "Up to you," he said. "I'd like you along, but I'm riding on now. Got no time to look for that girl further."

After I finished dressing, I mounted and followed him to the edge of the shelf, where a good path led downwards into the valley. I sat the bay and thought on it and looked at him going down and thought on it some more. The man down below must have heard Clete's horse, for he stopped what he was doing and just watched Clete ride down, same as I was doing. In a little while, the short man down there saw me too and took off his hat and waved. I took mine off and waved back before I started down.

Chapter Thirteen

Clete waited for me where the trail reached the valley floor. "That's a fine-looking animal you're riding," he called out. "Wanna sell him?" Clete's old roan scarcely raised his head when the bay and I got there.

"No, not if it means I have to ride that poor creature you're on."

"Didn't think you would. Let's go see what this man knows," he said, turning the roan and spurring him into a fast trot. The fellow we watched before had went back to his digging, but he stopped and stood with his hands on his hips when we come up to him.

"How do, gents?" he said, kind of surly and friendly together. "You're a long ways from nowheres, you know that?"

I'd seen from up above that he was a short man, but I didn't understand exactly how short 'til Clete stepped down. This man had a crookedy sort of smile on his face, but at the same time it looked like a thundercloud too. From a little distance, you might think he was a Mexican, so dark was his skin, but up closer you could see he was all freckles — freckles on top of freckles, too. Like a lot of short men, he was short mostly in the legs. He stood looking up at Clete with his weight on one foot, and, my, was he bowlegged. If someone could of throwed a

141

strap around his knees and pulled them together tight, he would of been about as tall as the next fellow.

"Shannon's my name, and this is Willie Goodwin," Clete said, tilting his head in my direction. I nodded. "Seen anyone ride through this morning or yesterday?"

"Nope," the man said, just standing and looking at us like we was some kind of bugs that'd caught his fancy, but that he would as soon squash. Clete waited for him to say something more, but when it was plain after a while he wasn't going to, Clete walked up closer to him.

"We're from east of here. The law's our business. Man we're looking for killed some people in Two Scalp."

"Never heard of it," the short man said, and went back to scraping at the muddy clay.

"What are you doing there, anyway?" I ask.

"Why, I'm diggin'," he said, spitting the words out of his mouth real fast and sassy, but his tone made it sound like he was explaining something to children. "This here's a shovel," he declared, holding it up and pointing to it with his other stubby hand. "And I use it to dig the dirt. See that pile there? I done that." That man had the queerest ways. He wasn't exactly what you'd call nasty. I'd seen that plenty, a man saying kiss-my-ass with his eyes while his mouth curved up. No, it wasn't that, but you couldn't exactly say he was the kind of fellow you took to right off, either.

"You have a name, you little sawed-off sonofabitch?" Clete asked. "Or didn't your daddy figure you'd ever grow up enough to —"

I seen it in the little man's face before he done it, of course, for his eyes bugged out and the veins at the side of his neck swole up. He swung his shovel at Clete's head, but Clete was ready for that. He grabbed the shaft and yanked it down past his side, though the blade struck his shoulder a glancing blow. With his other hand, he punched the runty man square in the mouth. A short punch with plenty of steam on it. After that, it wasn't no trouble for Shannon to wrestle that shovel away and toss it down. No sooner did it hit the ground than Clete smacked him a backhander that spun him around and landed him on his arse in the dirt, leaning back on his hands. What you saw first when his hat come off was the color of his hair, somewhere between flame and a brand-new penny. I didn't notice 'til then that the man wore no gun, but I figgered my pardner must have. Strange, because short men always have a pistol around somewheres. Often they tote the biggest damn gun they can find, sometimes two.

Clete drew his pistol slow, cocked it, and aimed that big-bore Remington right at this little man's bleeding nose. "Now, I'm going to ask you the same question he did. And if you want to be a full head shorter than you already are, you little shit, just come out with another smart-ass answer. What're you doin here?"

The short man sat up straight and quick, got his hat and stuck it on. "Why, I'm collectin' bones for O. C. Marsh. What the hell you think I was doin, anyway, pannin' gold?"

I feared Clete was going to shoot him. But instead he holstered his Remington, walked over to where the man'd been digging, hunkered down, and brushed some dirt away from the thing that was sticking up. I got out the shotgun, just in case.

"Looks like a bone, all right," Clete said to me. "But it looks like it's turned to stone."

"Well, of course it has," the little man said, standing right up. "It's a fossil bone, not a fresh one. That's what Perfessor Marsh pays me for, collectin' fossils." Then he strutted over to Clete and stuck out his hand like nothing at all had happened, even though there was still a trickle of blood dripping off his chin. "Name's Foote, Thomas Bell Foote, but most everbody calls me Banty. Banty Foote."

Clete looked at me and I had to laugh. "Go on and shake the man's hand," I told him. "Looks like he don't hold nothin' against you, you big bully."

Clete pushed his hat back and looked bewildered for a minute. For a while it appeared he was going to say something sharp to the little man, but then he changed his mind and shook the bowlegged bone-digger's hand. "Glad to meet you, Mr. Foote. I guess."

"Call me Banty. Everbody does. Mr. Marsh,

the students, everbody." All of a sudden he pulled hard on Clete's hand and stuck his face right up into my partner's, and I thought there was going to be more trouble. Clete was trying to draw back some, but they was so close their hatbrims was bumping into each other, and Foote wouldn't let go. "Wasn't no lie. I don't lie. Can't abide a liar, no I can't. Nosiree, Sheriff, I didn't see no one. Not this morning or yest'day either." The little man turned Clete's hand loose and walked straight over to his pony and mounted.

"Where ya goin'?" I asked him.

"You'll want to talk to the Perfessor. He's the one to talk to. C'mon, you two men. Haven't got all mornin'."

"Don't you want to gather up your gear?" Clete ask as he walked back to his horse.

"Naaah," Banty Foote said. "I'll be coming right back here anyhow."

Foote took off on that thick-necked, stubby cayuse of his — couldn't of been more than eleven hands — and Clete and me followed at a good clip. Banty knew the trails, all right. We dodged between them clay mountains and galloped into gullies that twisted and turned through little canyons and big ones, goin' like hell both uphill and down after the short man. I seen there were plenty of sign here, leading every which ways, but our guide wasn't following none of them. Half an hour later we come out into a flat place with scrubby grass between a couple of low sod tables and there we hit a pretty big encampment. Maybe not so large as a trail drive outfit will have, but big enough. Five military tents in a row and as many or more of some other kind in a circle around the blackened stones of a campfire. Looked like they cooked on a stove, though, for they had one — with big pots and pans and kettles and basins scattered around it. A fellow cooking something there or cleaning up turned and watched us ride in. Four wagons — one that looked like it hauled provisions, one with forage, I saw, and two others, big ones, I couldn't tell what they carried. A stack of heavy wooden crates was piled behind the wagons.

They had a good rope corral made, and in it was draft horses and maybe ten riding horses. Beside a bigger tent, off by itself a little ways, someone'd strung some tarps up on poles to cast some shade and keep off the rain, and underneath them were tables and benches and desks and chairs and I don't know what-all. Whoever this was had been here a while and intended on stayin' longer. Banty trotted us right up to where the tarps was rigged, and two men walked out from under them and come toward us, one a wrangler by the look of him, and the other a hefty fellow with a mostly white beard, wearing a rawhide vest and a funny-looking Eastern kind of hat slanting toward the side of his head.

"Hal-ooo, Banty!" the hefty man called before we was there, giving a big friendly wave.

Banty tied up and hurried up to the big man I

guessed was the boss of this outfit. "These here men are lookin' for somebody," he said.

That good-size man bent over some and looked at Banty's face. "Why, Mr. Foote, you're injured. Have you been fighting again?"

Banty looked at the ground and gave it a good kick. "Yes, I was, Perfesser Marsh. I know I said I wouldn't, but I did. It was this man here I fought. Wasn't his fault, though. I ast for it."

The hefty fellow put his hand on Banty's shoulder and looked at us with a long, sad face. "I see you've met our Mr. Foote," he said. "I'm very sorry, for his sake. I hope you will accept his apology."

Clete said nothing so neither did I.

"He's a fine collector, takes great care not to damage the specimens, but he has an odd personality aberration. A peculiar aggressiveness that's associated with his diminutive size, I believe." I would have described Mr. Banty Foote a little different. I'd a said he was a feisty halfpint and let it go at that.

"We're looking for a man who rode through here, maybe last night, maybe this morning," Clete said. "My name's Shannon and I'm the sheriff of Two Scalp, about a hundred or so miles east of here. This's my deputy, Willie Goodwin. We'd appreciate it if you could ask your men if anyone saw the man we're chasing — tall and skinny, riding a paint mare. He's a killer is why we're after him. Been trailing him for several days, but the rain last night washed out the sign we were following."

"I see, I see!" the hefty man said. "I'm Professor Othniel Charles Marsh of Yale College, leading the Summer Paleontology Brigade. I would be happy to —" He walked up close and looked from Clete to me and back to Clete. "Are you men waiting to be asked to dismount?" he ask.

"Folks around here generally wait 'til they're invited," Clete said.

"Yes, of course. Please step down from your horses, gentlemen." He swept his arm in such a way as to welcome us, I guessed.

"Please excuse my rudeness," he said, giving Clete's hand a good pump and then mine. "The customs here are quite different from those I'm used to. I meant no offense."

"None taken," Clete said, touching his hat brim. Marsh touched his hat too, but it looked like he was saluting a Mexican general.

"Will you take tea with us, or is your business too urgent, gentlemen?" the professor ask.

"Thanks, but we'd best ride on," Clete said. "Where are your men, anyhow?"

"The students are in the western field this morning, searching for mammal bones."

"You brought a bunch of boys out here and let them run off by themselves?" I asked.

"The Yale students are young men," Marsh said, kind of uppity. "The youngest is twenty, I believe. And our military escort is with them, eight soldiers."

I felt kind of taken back then. "When you said students, I thought —"

Professor Marsh had a good belly laugh, throwing his head back and roaring, but he didn't seem to be making fun of me by doing it. "Imagine, bringing young boys out here for field work!" He finished up his laugh and shook his head a couple of times, but then he noticed that Clete still had business on his mind. "Come and look at my map," Marsh said. "I'll show you where the students from Yale are digging, and where we are, exactly, and then I'll take you up there to talk to them, if you like."

Banty and the wrangler fellow who hadn't said anything went off together while Clete and me followed Marsh under the main tarp. We stopped at a big map of just this washed-out country, laid out on a table. I seen the way we had come into this place and where Clete's camp of the night before was. These badlands was a lot bigger than I thought, for we'd come only a short ways through them, with better than thirty miles more stretched out to the southwest.

Thin wavy lines connected places of the same level, and you could see the shape of the hills and the steepness of things real plain. "What are these pins for?" I ask.

"Those represent our major digs," the professor explained. "We're working some Jurassic beds for dinosaur fossils here at this red one. This blue one shows where the students are today, recovering the petrified skeletons of

149

Eohippus, the dawn horse."

I took a step back from the table and looked at him. "You mean you come all the way out here from the East to dig up dead horses?" I could tell Clete was itching to move, but I had never heard nothing to beat this.

"Yes, the calcified bones of all sorts of prehistoric species — reptiles, birds, and mammals — one of which is the horse."

"Could we go talk to your men now?" Clete ask. "This is important work for you, I can see, but ours is catching a killer, and it's important to us."

"Of course, Sheriff. If you're sure you won't have tea first, I'll just have a word with my men here and then we'll leave."

"No tea," Clete said.

I shook my head. "No tea for me, neither. I'm feeling all right." Marsh give me a odd look and went out from under the tarp. While he was seeing to whatever he had to see to, I looked around in there. There was leg bones longer than a man, and one skull with three curved horns, a head the size of a boulder off some creature I hoped never to run into. "What do you make of all this?" I ask Clete.

"Reminds me of some bone pickers I came across on the way up from Abilene. Only they were after buffalo bones on top of the ground. These fellows are a whole lot pickier about the bones they want, and more polite, but beyond that, I can't see a lot of difference between the two. Bones are bones, and they don't interest me much right now, unless they're the neck bones of that bastard we're chasing."

Marsh come back wearing a regular hat. "We can go speak to the Paleontology Brigade now, gentlemen."

Clete studied the map. "How far is it to the river from here? Looks nearly three miles."

"Yes, I'd say that's accurate," the professor said.

Clete looked at the map some more. "And about twelve miles up to where the students are working?"

"Perhaps a bit more," Marsh said. "It will take us about two hours to get there. Pretty rough going right here." He pointed to a spot on the map that looked all cut up and steep.

Clete turned to me then. "We could cover more ground if we split up," he said. "How about you go along with the professor here and I'll go scout the river, unless you want to do it the other way." I could see what he was gettin at. If none of them young fellows had seen our man, we'd be burning nearly five hours and getting nowhere for our time. If there was sign along the river, Clete could see them as good as I could, since the rain'd turned this clay into some of the easiest tracking ground there is — fresh mud.

"Makes sense to do it that way. Suit yourself who goes where," I told him.

"I'll take the river, then. If I find his sign, I'll follow them and leave a broad trail — like you did coming up along the Bad. You catch up with me this time. Shouldn't be hard, that damn nag I'm riding. If I don't see anything, I'll come back here tonight. That is, if you don't mind us camping with you, Mr. Marsh."

"Not at all!" the professor said. "The hospitality of the camp is yours. Not very elegant, I'm afraid, but we do have fresh elk steak for this evening's supper, which our hunter brought in last night. You know, I'm very fascinated by this business of yours, chasing —"

"We'd best go," Clete said, nodding his head and then starting toward our horses.

Professor Marsh seemed surprised to be cut off and left hanging like that. He was a man who was used to finishing off his ideas to a high polish, I guessed, no matter how long-winded they was. Only Clete was a man who knew when he'd heard enough.

"Just you and I, then, will be going out to the dig, Mr., uh . . ."

"That's right," I told him. "And you can call me Willie."

Clete was already mounted up when we got over there. "If I'm not back by morning, come after me," he said.

"All right, but don't go trying to find his campfire along the river tonight," I warned him.

I didn't notice 'til then that Banty Foote'd climbed up on that little animal of his and here he come along and pulled up right beside Clete, who looked down at him for a minute.

"Where do you think you're going?" Shannon ask him.

"I'm goin' with you," Banty said.

"No, thanks," Clete told him. "I'll look for him by myself."

"Well, I'm goin' anyway," the little man said, looking right up at my pardner. "Free country, ain't it?"

"The sheriff has to go by himself, Banty," Professor Marsh said. "He feels your presence may hinder him in his search, and he may not be coming back here. Is that correct, Mr. Shannon?"

"Close enough," Clete said, spurring that old roan into a trot, the best it would do. I'd intended to trade horses with him, but he rode off before I could offer. Marsh and me and Banty Foote watched him coax his horse up onto the sod table to the south.

"An impetuous man, your Sheriff. Obviously a solitary man of action," the professor said. I didn't know just what to make of him saying that about Clete, but he didn't sound like he was taking my pardner down any, so I let it ride.

"I wouldn't a been in the way," Banty said, almost bawling the words.

"You come with Willie and me, Banty," Marsh said, walking toward the saddled horse his wrangler was bringing over. "We'll need you along if we run into the Sioux."

Well, I didn't see what good a midget without a gun would do if we run into a war party, but then I figured out the professor was only trying to gentle the little fellow. Marsh and me climbed up and the three of us started west. I saw that Foote kept watching Clete ridin' toward the south, and we didn't get more than a hundred yards 'til Banty spurred his pony hard in the flanks and pulled him off sharp to the left, after Clete.

The professor called after him, but that little man was ridin' like thunder, bent low over that pony's neck and he didn't even look back. "Oh, well," Marsh said. "I suppose it will be all right — if he doesn't go too close to your sheriff, and if Mr. Shannon doesn't decide to shoot him."

Chapter Fourteen

Where the White River turns and runs due north, he sat his horse on the eastern shore and scanned the banks in one direction and then the other with his long glass. Upriver, almost a mile off, he spotted a mule wagon on the other side. Even at this distance he could see that it was stuck in the mud. Two men, one in the water and one astride a mule, were heaving and straining, but they were making no headway. Stupid sonsabitches, *he thought, and started across. When the tired paint stopped on her own to drink, he got out his glass again and studied the banks a second time. It wasn't 'til then that he noticed the riding horse tied to the back of the mule wagon. He crossed the swollen current and turned the mare upriver once he cleared the deep mud.*

I was surprised how well Professor Marsh sat his horse, a tall creature with big, swelled-out jaw muscles. Looked like they'd raised him on walnuts. The schoolmaster was less a dude on his horse than off, that was certain, though he still talked as odd as he done before.

"You have been in pursuit of this man how long, Willie?" he ask me after we was up the trail a ways.

"A week, I guess, maybe longer. I sorta lost track of the days."

"And what has this fellow done that you and

155

your sheriff are so intent upon apprehending him?"

I told him about the gun our man'd used to shoot Clete and about the fire that killed Nell Larson and Jesse McLeod. He shook his head and said something about how raw the West was. He wanted to know where I was born, and was surprised when I told him. He asked about my schooling and my folks and everthing like that, no more ashamed about doing so than a prairie dog is of settin' up on his hind feet beside his hole. I could see then what he meant about folks doing things different where he come from. He got even more curious when it come out I'd worked for the Pinkertons a few years back.

"Why on earth did you quit Allan Pinkerton's Detective Agency, Willie? You seem to have had a good position there with a considerable future!"

"I guess it could of been, but it wasn't the kind of a future I wanted, not after that business with the James boys' family," I told him.

"You took part in the attack on Castle James, their stronghold?" he ask, looking real serious.

"Shoot, there wasn't no *stronghold* to it, nor no castle, neither. Just an old country doctor's house was all, and the James boys wasn't even there, as I told Billy Pinkerton at the time."

"I've heard quite a few conflicting stories about that occurrence, and I've read that contradictory evidence was presented on both sides. What really happened?"

"Well, it wasn't like the papers had it, if that's what you mean. And it wasn't no bomb Dave Farley dropped in the window, neither — just an old turpentine flare to make it smoky inside was all it was, so's they'd have to come out. Dave'd never of throwed a bomb at no one, not even the James boys themselves. Still, what Billy Pinkerton did to them James people in Missouri just wasn't right, firing on a house with women and children inside. Never was and never will be."

When Walter Turnbull first saw the man walking his horse up the river, he had a notion to go get his rifle. But when the tall stranger waved, Walt changed his mind and went back to kicking his nigh wheeler in the flanks. But it was no use. They just couldn't budge it.

"Want help?" the scrawny man called from the bank.

"Yeah, if you think you can get these critters pullin' any harder than me and the boy can," the broadbacked muleskinner replied.

The stranger came down the bank, glanced at the tow-headed boy standing in water up to his knees beside the lead pair, and plodded his paint through the eddy out to Turnbull. "Got another whip?" he asked.

"Shore, always carry a spare. Toss the other out, Ellie." The blond-haired woman in the wagon threw the coiled fourteen-foot bullwhip to her husband, who handed it to the scarecrow with rotten teeth.

"Are you certain the James brothers weren't at Doctor Samuels' house when the raid took place?" Professor Marsh ask.

"Am I sure? Why, I was the man *shadowing* Jesse! I had trailed him from his ma's place to Missouri City, and that's where I wired Mr. William Pinkerton from. We was supposed to wire him three times a day — concerning their whereabouts — but damned if I could stay on Jesse James' trail and do that. Even sent a copy to Billy care of the station master in Kearney, in case the train'd left by the time my first telegram got to the Northland Hotel where he was staying. Nosiree, Jesse wasn't even near. Fact is, Mr. Jesse James was havin' his ashes hauled in a cathouse in Missouri City while Billy Pinkerton was leading the noble raid that killed the James boys' kid brother and hurt their ma so that she had to have her arm cut off. And Frank was elsewheres too."

"I see," Marsh said. "Did you ever find out whether or not Mr. Pinkerton received your telegram before he conducted the raid?"

"Indeed he did," I told him. "That was the first thing I checked on afterward. Fact is, he got both of them. A telegraph man in Kansas City delivered the one, put it right in his hand, so he told me. And the other, Billy picked up himself in Kearney. Said so later."

We rode along silent a while after that.

"I been haulin' for ten years," the broadbacked

skinner said, standing on the high bank and offering his hand, "an' I never seen nobody whup mules like that." The boy understood why his father admired the stranger, for under his lash the team had pulled like they never had before. Still, he pitied the beasts as they stood quivering and bleeding and dripping river water on the high bank.

"Oh, you jest got to know where to tech 'em, and how," the skinny man said, giving the man back his whip instead of shaking with him. A bashful smile slid over his narrow face. "I enjoy a good bout with mules now and again, jest to let 'em know how it is."

"Will you stay and eat with us?" Ellie called from the wagon. "Seems the least we can do."

"Why, surely, ma'm. I'd be pleased to."

We come to the steep place I'd saw on the map and we had to go single file, but after we got up on top and took a good look across the valley, the professor wanted to talk some more. "What I can't understand, Mr. Goodwin, was why you felt obligated to resign your position simply because William Pinkerton had done something you considered to be morally reprehensible."

Took me a minute to understand him, and even then I had to ask. "Do you mean to say that you don't agree with what I done or do you really not understand why I done it?"

"Why, the latter, of course! I do not mean to set myself up as a paragon of pragmatic expediency, but I would not have done what you did, under similar circumstances, and I simply wondered what your motives were."

By that, I took it to mean he was just wondering about why I quit, not wanting to tell me I was wrong for doing it, though I wasn't completely sure. Any one of the man's words could make you see double, and strung together like that they'd crack your skull wide open.

I just looked at him, not knowing what to say.

"Let me put it this way," he said. "At Yale, the dean refuses to fund my expeditions to the extent he should, even though my uncle underwrites the entire Scientific School — through which my funds come — as well as the money for the library and the Peabody Museum, named for my dear uncle, of course. Now, my question is this: do you feel I should resign my position, as well as my Chair in Natural History, simply because the dean acts improperly in witholding money that my uncle donates? Is science well served if I resign, letting the knowledge of prehistoric life lie buried in this clay?"

I took off my hat and rubbed my head good. I like a good soft chair myself, and his throwing one into the middle of this thing made it a lot stickier. "See if I got this straight," I told him. "Your uncle gives somebody money and furniture that should go to you, for scratchin' around out here, but the man he gives it to don't turn it all over, the part he should, right?"

"That is essentially correct," he said, nodding his head slow and smiling.

"Why, of *course* you should quit," I told him.

160

"Just take your uncle's money yourself and dig for bones all you want. He trusts you with it, don't he, your uncle, I mean?"

He got a good laugh at that. "Of course."

"Take the money direct and tell that fellow back at Yale College to kiss your ass," I said.

Well, if I thought he'd laughed his hardest before, I was wrong.

Ellie Turnbull spread a tablecloth on the ground beneath a single cottonwood tree growing along the White River, and the scrawny man watched her walk back to the wagon. The second trip, she brought biscuits she had baked that morning beside their breakfast fire, cold sliced venison, and gooseberry jam all the way from Indiana. Walter stood talking of mules and weather and the way to Fort Laramie, but he had to carry most of the weight of the conversation on his own broad shoulders. Before very long, Turnbull noticed that their guest was more interested in his wife's figure than his talk, and it made him fume. Still, the skinny man had helped them through a hard place, and if it got no worse, he would let it slide.

Ellie called the boy up from the river and they all sat down crosslegged to eat.

"And what would happen to a fine institution like Yale, to any civilized institution, for that matter, if the men who were a part of it put their individual principles above the good of the whole? If they all resigned whenever one of their superiors violated a moral precept?"

He gave me no time to answer.

"Another example: the Christian religion has committed heinous crimes in the course of its advancement. Take the Spanish Inquisition, for instance. Does the fact of that atrocity mean we must abandon the Church because it temporarily abrogated one or two of its tenets? Would Western culture be the better for it?"

I turned my horse. "I guess I *didn't* understand you square a while ago," I told Professor Marsh. "You really did want to tell me that I done wrong by quittin' the Pinks, only I wasn't quick enough to see it. I don't know enough about religion to say nothing about what a lot of Spaniards done a long time since. But if Yale College can't get along with just the folks who think it's doing the right thing, then it should either lock its doors or find some new hands. Maybe your uncle could help sign some on, since he seems responsible for nearly everything else around the place. Probably be willing, too, if they'd name some more furniture after him." I spurred my mount and we went down the other side.

Marsh come up after a few yards. "You must excuse me, Mr. Goodwin," he said. "The scholiast and casuist in me want to win a debate at any cost, sometimes. But you can see my point, can't you?"

"Yes, I suppose I can. And I guess I must excuse you, if you say I must, for this is your territory, not mine. All I did was to quit the Pinks because they got things turned around to my way of thinking, important things. They valued a good name in the papers and their pride above folks' lives. And that just ain't right. I'm not saying somebody should step in and shut the Pinks down, that's for others to decide. But if *I'd* a killed a young boy, I'd a swung for it. All I'm saying is that I don't have to be a part of no outfit that acts like the Pinkerton boys do, future or no future, big payday or no payday. That's what a free country's all about, ain't it? Hell, they can get along just fine without me, and I sure as the devil get along better without them, 'specially when it comes to sleeping good at night."

I think maybe the professor was a little ashamed of himself for coming at me about quitting the Pinkertons like he did, for he nodded his head and just kept his mouth shut riding the rest of the way down that little clay mountain, but you could tell it pained him to do it.

Close to the bottom you could see across to where the young fellows was working, though it was still more than a mile off from us, over in some country that was broken up pretty bad. By the time we got to where they was, they'd put their shovels down and lined up for their noontime eats. They was pleased to see Marsh, you could tell by the way they spoke to him. Maybe if I'd a went to a school where I could've rode around in some wild country on a horse, slept in a tent, and camped with a dozen or so of my friends, I would of liked my schoolman pretty good too, a lot better than I did, at any rate.

The man doing the cooking got plates for Marsh and me and we ate too, the young fellows telling their teacher what skeletons they found that morning and what they hadn't — only the names they used for the animals was all strange to me. The stew we ate was good, and it had either buffalo or beef in it, I couldn't tell which. Wasn't as good as Mandy's, though. I got a second plate of it after I seen some others getting theirs.

"Anyone find any horse bones?" I asked, sitting back down.

They all stopped pushing food into their faces and looked at me like I had just farted.

"That's what the students were talking about, Willie," the professor explained. "The scientific name for the kind of horse found here is *Mesohippus,* very different from the *Equus* species that we ride." The boys snickered a little at him saying that.

I didn't mind their having some fun at my expense, but it was hard for me to see how horses could a been much different than they are now, and I wanted to know more about it, even if it did make me the jackass of the herd. Sure, I'd seen horses of all sizes and colors, even heard of some with black and white stripes running wild over in England. But this had to be something more than that, I figured, or they'd of found live ones for their remuda. It'd be silly to have just a few old horse bones when you could have

164

breathing ones that could carry you somewheres. "How was they different?" I ask.

"Let us have a short recitation for Mr.
Goodwin's edification, shall we, gentlemen?"
You could tell from the way they grumbled that
wasn't the kind of fun they had in mind.

*All through the meal, the scrawny man's eyes
crawled over Ellie Turnbull's body, especially her full
breasts. What disturbed Walter even more was that
the stranger didn't even try to hide what he was
staring at, which was only proper.*

*"I don't believe I heard your name, sir," Mrs.
Turnbull said. Perhaps if she engaged the man in
conversation, she reasoned, he would stop looking at
her so hungrily. And maybe Walt wouldn't lose his
temper this time.*

"It's Smith, Mam."

*"Smith what?" Walter asked, chewing a
mouthful of biscuit.*

*"Just Smith," the thin man said flatly. "This
here's your boy, ain't it?" he asked Ellie.*

*"Yes, he is," she said uncomfortably. "Walt's and
mine. Do you have children, Mr. Smith?"*

*The scrawny man spit a piece of gristle into his
hand, examined it, and then flung it toward the
river. "Had one, once. A boy."*

*Jimmy Turnbull knew something was wrong, but
he didn't know what. "Did something happen to
him?" he asked.*

"Jimmy!" Ellie cried. "I declare!"

"I'm sorry," the boy mumbled, though he wasn't

sure what sin he had committed this time.

The scrawny man seemed to pay no attention to the boy and his mother. For several minutes he simply chewed his food and looked into the distance. "Sheriff east of here killed him." He turned quickly to Walter, as though the broad-shouldered man had asked the question that forced him to return to something he did not want to remember. "Shot him down in the street like a goddamned dog."

"We don't curse in front of the boy," Ellie Turnbull said, her cheeks reddening.

But the stranger appeared not to have heard her. He stood up quickly, though there was still food on his plate, Jimmy noticed. "I'm goin' now."

Walter Turnbull stood too. "I thank you for your help, Smith," he said.

The thin man smiled and extended his hand. When the muleskinner took it, DuShane squeezed hard, drew the gun that was strapped to his left hip, and shot Walter Turnbull low in the belly.

The echo of the shot died along the river before the boy realized what had happened. He lunged at the thin man. "You shot my pa! You —"

DuShane smacked him above the ear with the barrel of his revolver and watched the boy slump to the grass like a sack of old shoes.

Ellie Turnbull sat frozen. A dollop of gooseberry jam still clung to her knife blade, and the biscuit-half she had been going to spread it on still lay in her loose hand.

Her eyes glazed over and her jaw dropped. The scrawny man looked at her pretty white teeth and the

166

soft pink tongue that looked to him like a pink frog in a pink pond. And then he thought about how it would feel to shove his cock in there.

"Now, then, gentlemen," Professor Marsh said, clearing his throat. "A short recitation, please. Contrast *Mesohippus* with the contemporary species *Equus*. Would you begin, Mr. Sargeant? And remember, just contrasts. No comparisons, please."

"Shall I stand, sir?" a young fellow wearing a white cap ask.

"Please do," Marsh said. "And clear away your plates, gentlemen."

The young man in the white cap also wore a funny-looking pair of pants that flared out at the thighs and was laced tight to his shins, which I noticed after he got to his feet. "The most obvious difference is in the foot, of course. *Mesohippus* walked on three toes, while *Equus* walks on only one, the other two toes, those of his predecessor, remaining in vestigial form. If one accepts the monophyletic theory, that is."

He sat down, and all the boys laughed, though I didn't know why.

"Mr. Sargeant and I have an intellectual dispute, Willie, and he took this opportunity to poke fun at what he considers to be a folly of mine. Any questions for Mr. Sargeant?"

I looked from the young man to Marsh and back and forth again, not knowing exactly who to talk to. "A horse with three toes? Are you sure it's a horse?" I ask.

"Oh, yes," the young man said. "Most early Paleolithic horses have three toes, except *Eohippus,* which has four. I'll show you a whole skeleton when we're done here, and you'll see it's a horse all right."

"Very good, Mr. Sargeant, very good. You next, Mr. Ballard. Any inaccuracies in Mr. Sargeant's recitation?" It was clear the professor was enjoying himself.

The next young fellow, who was big in the belly and wore specs, stood up. "Basically, what he said was correct, I think, though I'm not so sure that the foot would be the most obvious difference we would notice if a specimen of *Mesohippus* had walked up to us while we were eating Billy's delicious stew."

The boys all clapped their hands and whistled, but the cook looked more embarrassed than pleased.

"No," the chubby fellow said, drawing out the sound of it, "I think we'd notice the difference in size first, and that's the contrast I wanted to talk about. *Mesohippus* stood about sixteen or eighteen inches at the shoulder, about as tall as the coyotes that keep us awake at night. A little higher at the rear, probably." After that he sat down.

"Finish the contrast, Mr. Ballard," the professor said.

The fellow wearing specs looked puzzled for a minute before he spoke. "Oh yes, and *Equus* is,

168

well, as big as a horse!"

We all laughed at that one, even the professor. "Questions, Willie?"

"You mean to say this horse was no bigger than a good-size dog?"

The chubby young man nodded his head.

"Then how could anyone ride him?" I ask.

Everbody chuckled at that, too.

The professor answered that one himself. "That was not a problem, Mr. Goodwin, for there were no men around at that time!"

I never saw folks enjoy themselves any more than those fellows did that afternoon, talking and arguing and joking about a critter that'd been dead for thousands of years — so they said — though I couldn't see how the bones would last that long in the ground. I had dug up a few dead things too in my day. They went around 'til everyone had his turn to say what he knowed, and they knowed a lot. I admit I didn't understand very much of what was said toward the end. Besides not knowing some of the words they used, I kept picturing that little horse with three toes on each foot scampering around and around with no cowboys to rope it, and that kept me from listening to some of it.

He stuck his head out the front of the covered mule wagon and looked both ways before jumping down. Buttoning up his pants, he walked to where the boy lay and poked at him several times with the toe of his boot. Then he rolled Walter Turnbull over on his back.

He mounted the paint, spurred her hard, and no-ticed how tired she was. The tall man reined her in and turned her around. There stood the mule-skinner's horse at the back of the wagon, and he laughed at how forgetful he was getting as he rode back for it.

"Very good, gentlemen, very good," the professor told them. "I'm quite pleased at the progress you're making, and we have about eight tons of fossils to send back to the Museum, which is excellent. But now we have another matter to attend to before you return to your shovels and trowels for the remainder to the day's dig. Mr. Goodwin is an officer of the law in this Territory, and he has come here in search of information concerning a murderer who may be in the vicinity. Just another reminder, gentlemen, that you are no longer in Connecticut. I'll let Mr. Goodwin tell you the rest."

I stood up, like they done before, and told them about the man Clete and me was after, told them what he did, what he looked like and what kind of horse he was mounted on. They thought on it a while, but none of them'd seen him. The fellow with the specs'd seen a muleskinner's wagon to the south a little after dawn, before the rain stopped, he guessed, but none of the rest seen no one else. I thought to ask them about Mandy then, and I told them what *she* looked like and the horse *she* was on, but none of them'd seen her either. From the looks on their faces, though, it was plain they'd of rather run into her than him.

"I want to thank you young men," I said. "I enjoyed your speeches here about them tiny horses you're digging up. And I appreciate you trying to help me find those people I spoke about. Let me give you some advice, now. If you see the man I told you of, stay the hell away from him. Don't try to capture him or nothing like that, 'cause he'll kill you — he's had practice at it. One last piece of advice and then I'll stop. When you're diggin' up the bones of them little horses, be on the lookout for golden crowns. You just might find one or two. Might be worth some money."

They looked at me so queer for a minute, and then they talked quiet among themselves, and finally started to laugh some. I guess they believed I was telling them some kind of a Western joke, but I wasn't.

Chapter Fifteen

Marsh and me started back toward his camp not long after I ask the students about our man and Mandy. The professor give me a lecture all the way along about something he called geology, but it wasn't 'til we'd went a ways that I figured he was talking about why the clay hills and the gullies washed into them was the way they was. Something about an ocean being here once, he said, but I didn't see how that could be. I guessed he could make mistakes like anyone else, Yale College or no. Then he ask me what I was getting to about them golden crowns I had told his students to look out for, but I just winked and said he'd have to wait 'til he got to the end of the Book to figger it out.

We were on top of that high place when I told him that, and when we got near the bottom, his face looked like he still had some chewing left to do on it. In a brushy draw between two buttes, I saw a rider making his way toward us slow. I thought for a minute it was the man Clete and me was chasing — only he wasn't on a paint. But he *was* tall and thin, and I warned the professor to be on his guard. After he looked good, Marsh said he knowed the man and gave him a big wave and a haloo.

We sat and waited for him, and he was in no hurry at all to get to where we was. He was dressed all in buckskin, only it was fringed down the legs and all along the sleeves and at the bottom of his open coat. And everywhere there wasn't fringes there was strips of fur sewed on, over the shoulders, mostly. His light gray hat had a wide floppy brim and eagle feathers hanging off the back of it, tied with rawhide strips to a hat-band of rattlesnake skin, so I thought for a minute he might be a half-breed. But when he got up close, you could see he wasn't, for his skin was pale as a woman's and his eyes blue as a lake.

Though he wore no shirt, he had a red silk scarf, or something fancy like that, tied around his neck. A sash of the same color stuff was wrapped around his middle, and stuck under-neath it was a big old Colt. Looked like an un-comfortable way to carry a revolver, pokin' into your side the least little bit you turned around. His hair, which was dark and wavy with just a few streaks of gray, hung down below his shoul-ders. He had a narrow little chin beard, long as your thumb, and his mustachios was full and waxed and they stuck way out, straight as any-thing, to beyond the sides of his face. More than anything else, he resembled a drawing of Bill Cody on a handbill I seen once, only younger and more rakish.

"Good day, Mr. Crawford!" Marsh called. "What have you found for us?"

The tall man reached around behind himself and held up a string of nearly a dozen grouse, prairie chickens and some other kind I didn't

173

know, tied together at the foot. His saddle, if that was what you could call it, was a strange affair, unlike any I ever saw before. A buffalo robe formed the base of it, and the hide, decorated with wolf tails and porkypine quills where the fur was scraped off, hung over the horse's rump and draped halfway to the ground. It was double cinched, I saw, but I couldn't tell just what was underneath him, or under the hide. Firm enough, I guessed, for he had a piece of the buffalo skin folded over and sewn to form a sheath for his rifle. "Should feed you and the young gentlemen, suh," he said real soft. He was a Son of Dixie, you could tell by his talk. He let the birds dangle back to where they hung behind him and then looked at me square.

Marsh noticed and glanced at me and then back to the man. "This is Mr. Goodwin, Jack. He's an officer of the law."

Jack Crawford stuck his nose a little up in the air. "Is he, indeed? How do you do, suh?" he said, nodding his head low then, but keeping his eyes on me the whole time.

"How do," I said.

"Meet Captain Jack Crawford, Willie," Marsh boomed in that big friendly voice of his. "Jack is our guide, and when he's not leading us, he fills our larder with game. And when he's doing neither, he writes poetry." Marsh turned back to the tall fellow. "Is it three volumes you've published so far, Jack?"

The mention of his poem books seemed to

smooth Crawford's hackles some. He smiled real bashful and patted the neck of his horse, which hadn't calmed yet. "Only two thus far, Professor Marsh. As you well know."

"Well, I'm sure the third will be coming off the presses any day now." He waited for Crawford to speak his mind, but the hunter seemed to have nothing to say — to that or to anything else. "If you are going back to camp, we would be happy to have you escort us, Jack."

Crawford gave another dip of his head and we started off, three abreast, the professor in the middle.

"Mr. Goodwin is searching for a man who killed some people in his jurisdiction," Marsh said after we'd went some distance. "Have you seen anyone?"

"Why, I don't believe I have, Professor Marsh," Crawford drawled, looking at the clouds.

"One of the students saw some folks in a mule wagon. Surprised you didn't see 'em," I said. "That's where we was, up talking to Professor Marsh's gang. Not a bad bunch of fellows — for Yankees."

Crawford leaned forward and looked me over good. "Are you from the South, suh, or do you jest with me?"

The look on O. C. Marsh's face was pretty dark, like he wisht I hadn't stirred up this particlar hornets' nest.

"Yes, I am from the South, though I didn't

grow up in the same parts you did, judging from the way you say your words, Captain Crawford. But I guess you will recall that one of the stars in the Stars and Bars was for Texas." I let him look me good in the eye after I said that, for I wanted him to know that I told the truth.

After a time he decided I had. "I apologize, suh, and pray you will accept it. Indeed, the Texans fought bravely in the recent conflict. Were you in their ranks?"

"Wasn't so recent," I said. "About twelve years since, now."

"Twelve years . . . It seems only yesterday to me." The way he said that, and how he put his hand to his heart while he said it, I could see how he might fancy poems. Professor Marsh looked relieved we wasn't about to go at one another's throats.

"Seems like a lifetime to me," I said.

Crawford sat up straight in that funny saddle he rode. "What was your regiment, Colonel Goodwin?"

"I am sad to say that I was not in the army," I told him. "Some of us was forced to stay in Texas. Chained to our work, you could say. I'd a thousand times rather been in the war than doing what I was doing, though."

"I understand that completely," the tall poet said.

"I appreciate you saying so," I told him.

The sun come out about then, and soon the clouds begun to scatter more than they had before. Where the path got narrower in a gully, Crawford dropped back some, so just Marsh and me was beside each other for a while. Once when I looked back, Crawford motioned with his head for me to drop back with him. I told Marsh I wanted a word with his guide, for directions, and then eased back.

"I am sorry, Mr. Goodwin. I didn't want to say so before, for reasons of my own, but just past midmornin', I saw that mule wagon ovuh toward the rivuh. Seemed to be a family, I believe."

"Not our man," I said. "Fellow we're after's astride a paint. A tall man, like yourself."

Crawford turned his head so sharp, I thought he might snap it off. "Ridin' a paint?"

"That's right."

"What'd he do, this criminal you're chasin' down?" Crawford ask.

I figured right then that he had saw our man. "He ambushed someone, the sheriff I work for."

"A *Yankee*," Crawford said, like he was correcting me. "A *Yankee* sheriff."

"Where was he when you saw him?" I ask, knowing he just might draw that old Colt he wore and shoot me instead of answering. I don't often bluff a hand, but when I do, I give 'er all I got. He looked mad enough to bite my nose off, but I just stared at him.

"I have given my word of honor, suh, to a gentleman of the South that I would not divulge any information about him," Captain Crawford said, drawing himself up real tall and righteous.

"No, you give your word to help protect a backshooting sonofabitch who don't have enough honor to fill a percussion cap, let alone to be called a true Southerner. That's what you done." Crawford started to say something, but I put my hand up to stop him. Can't believe I ever tried anything so foolish, for you could tell he was a man who would not abide an offense of any kind and would shoot *any* man, once he believed he was in the right, and not blink an eye about it. I just kept my hand up to stop him from talking and plowed ahead. "You, sir, are siding with a man who murdered a woman in her sleep by settin' her house afire. A barn-burner, I believe you call them in your part of the South. That's the kind of man you have swore to help — a sniper and a barn-burner."

Captain Jack kept glaring at me like he was measuring my head for a watch fob, but I turned and looked straight down the trail. After a while, he dropped back so that we were riding single file. I was still trying to figure out how I could get him to tell me what he knowed about our man when we got to Marsh's camp. When we pulled up, Professor Marsh's wrangler come out to take his horse, and the professor dismounted and went toward the big tent. I walked the bay in the direction the wrangler took with Marsh's animal, thinking maybe Crawford would do the same, and after a time he did. We climbed off beside the rope corral and I fussed with my bedroll, hoping Crawford would feel inclined to talk. I could see no way to force it out of him, for I suspected I couldn't beat him in a fight. Maybe I would have to wait for Clete to have a word with him.

Crawford eased up close, still lookin' at me like I had stole his last dime. He stood about a head taller than me, and poet or no poet, I didn't look forward to no rolling around in the dirt with him.

"How do I know you're tellin' the truth about his burning down a woman's house?" he ask, them watery blue eyes of his trying to bore inside my head.

"Well, I have no piece of paper that says so, but if you were a captain in the Confederate Infantry, I suppose you've had considerable experience judging men's character by what they say and how they strike you. I'm willing to rely on that, Captain."

Jack Crawford drew himself up to his full height. "I was a lieutenant colonel in the Confederate *Cavalry*, suh. My rank in the Regular Army, before I resigned my commission, was that of captain." He stood studying my face again for such a long time that I begun to feel itchy. "Damn!" he said, and all of a sudden turned and walked off on them long legs of his towards nothing in particlar, and there he just stood.

To tell the truth, I didn't know just what to do next. And when he turned and walked back to me, slower than he'd walked away, I didn't know what was going to happen. But his face was different, more relaxed, I guess. "The woman whose house he burned . . . she . . . died in the fire?"

"Yes, she did," I told him. "The sheriff pulled her clear, but her life give out that night while we sat with her and her home burned. And she was a fine woman. Her name was Nell Larson and she —"

"I don't want to heah it," he yelled, and turned away.

I didn't know what to make of that, but I guessed he was reminded of something or somebody else. That was the best I could see. I'd planned to say that Nell was a Virginia woman, much as she would have hated that, but I never got the chance to tell that lie.

When he turned back, tears streamed down his face and his eyes looked wild, but he didn't appear to be crying otherwise. "I *knew* there was something wrong about that man. I didn't give my word to him, as I said before, Mr. Goodwin, for if I had, I would have to honor it whether I wanted to now or not."

"I understand," I said.

He nodded his head. "Thank you, suh." And then he put his hands up to his face and just bawled out loud, standing there by ourselves, beside that rope corral. Right there in front of me!

I walked a step or two off to give him what space I could, and he went on for some time.

Damned if I didn't feel sorry for that man, though I couldn't see what the matter was, for he could not have knowed Nell Larson. The best I could figure was that he was thinking on something that my saying about Nell made him remember, something that pained him deep as a West Texas well.

After a minute he walked over to his horse and cut loose the birds that was tied there. He brought them over and handed them to me. "Will you give these to the professor and tell him I won't be in camp tonight?"

"Yes, I will," I said, not knowing what else to say.

He went over and climbed into that funny saddle of his. I wanted to ask him about our man before he left, but I felt sure he would talk on his own, if I didn't rush him.

He walked his horse over close to where I stood with the string of grouse. "Your man is from Kentucky," Crawford said. "I think it was Kentucky I heard in his voice, though it may have been Tennessee. I shared my supper with him last night. He rode up in the rain shortly before dahk and I invited him in — the big flat rock overhang. You know where that is?"

"No," I told him.

"About six miles west of here." He looked across the valley then. "Professor Marsh can show you on his map. Good camping place."

"I'll ask him," I said.

"We ate the hare I roasted and some cheese I

had. Then he rode on. Wouldn't stay the night, though I invited him to. I don't think he trusted me. He headed west after he left my camp. At first he went toward the north, but once, when the lightning flashed, I saw that he had turned and was headed west by south. He said he had tried to avenge the death of his younger brother, but that he had made a mess of the job and would have to try it again some other time."

"His brother?" I ask.

Captain Jack nodded his head. "That's what he said. Was it you or the sheriff who killed his kin?"

"I guess it would have to be the sheriff," I told him.

"That's all I know, except that he fought at Chickamauga." Crawford had stopped crying by that time, but when he said that last, more tears come down his face. "I must go now," he said. "I would be very thankful if you would give those birds to Mr. Marsh and tell him I won't be back tonight."

"I will be happy to, Captain. I'm sorry if my —"

"No matter, suh," he said, and turned his horse to go. " 'Til we meet in a bettah world, Mr. Goodwin." He nudged his horse.

"Just one more thing, Captain Crawford," I called after him.

Captain Jack clucked to his horse and stopped.

I walked over to where he was, carrying them damn birds. "I hate to trouble you farther, but I was traveling with a young gal and lost track of her. I mean, we got separated when that sonofabitch we're trailing jumped us. She might be wanderin' around in these cut-up badlands somewheres. She may be dead by now, or maybe she just rode out of here, I don't know. I'd rest a whole lot easier if I knowed a scout and hunter such as yourself, one who knows these parts like you do, was keepin' an eye out for her."

He looked down at me. Every time since then, whenever I hear the word *mournful,* I think of the way his face looked then. "Of course, Mr. Goodwin."

I was going to tell him what she looked like, but then thought better of it when I saw no way around saying that she was partly a Negro lady. "Her name's Mandy. Mandy Bowden, only she says it Frenchy."

Captain Jack arched his back and swung his hand out in front and to the side, tilting his head back. That rangy scout appeared to be frowning at the clouds, only his eyes was glassy, like he didn't rightly see what he was looking at. Looked more like a politician about to give a speech than anything else. And then he spoke like he was in some kind of a dream:

"A lost damosel with a French surname
Met a desperado named DuShane,
She on a steed with a snow white mane,
He on a paint that was going lame."

I knowed then what he was doing. "Won't be

much of a poem," I told him. "Not with a big whopping lie like that right up front. Clete shot Whitey DuShane some time ago."

He looked at me sharp then, like I had just woke him up from a sound sleep.

"How'd you know about Whitey DuShane, anyway?" Soon as I said that, even before he said anything, it hit me.

"I was speakin' of the man you're chasing. He told me his name's DuShane," Crawford said. "Was his younger brother named Whitey?"

Chapter Sixteen

I stood beside the rope corral and watched Captain Jack Crawford lope his horse up the valley. Probably heading back to that camping place he favored under a flat rock, I figured. I couldn't get over a grown man bawling like that in front of me. Naturally, I had shed a tear or two myself, over one damn heartache or another, but never right in front of nobody else, like he done. And then went right on to make up a poem, on the spot, about people he didn't even know!

Professor Marsh was tinkering with his bone pile when I got over to where the tarps was stretched up on poles.

"Captain Crawford wanted me to be sure you got these grouse," I told him. "He also wanted me to say he wouldn't be in camp tonight, though I can't say why. I mean, I would say why if I knowed why, he didn't intend to keep it no secret, I believe, only I don't."

Marsh took the birds and looked them over. "Thank you, Willie. You seemed to be getting along quite well with our scout. After your initial discord, that is."

"Yes, well, he was only trying to do what he thought was right, and after he seen what the right thing was, he told me what he knowed." I went over and looked at that big map he had spread out on a table.

Professor Marsh couldn't of been more surprised if I had all of a sudden turned into one his big dead lizards. "He saw the man you're after?"

"He did," I told him, looking the territory over good on the map, out where Clete'd went. That flat rock place wasn't more'n two miles from where Clete'd strike the river. "But I have no time to talk about it. If you want the story, you can ask Crawford, I suppose. What I want is to tell Clete, soon as I can, what I found out. Could you sell me a horse, Professor? The sheriff is mounted on our pack horse, and it's a poor animal to be chasing anyone on. Hell, it's a sorry excuse for a horse under any circumstances. Only thing worse would be one of those little critters like you're digging up."

"Of course, Mr. Goodwin! But you don't have to pay for it. Three horses wandered in the other day, and my wrangler has been complaining about feeding them ever since. Take whichever one you want. In fact, take all three if you like. Come along, I'll speak to Mr. Sims."

Marsh walked to the rope corral with me, but I didn't listen much to what he was saying, for I kept thinking one of the horses that come in to the professor's remuda might be my old buckskin, and that would mean Mandy was either afoot or dead. I didn't see how my old horse could be there and me not seen it, but then I didn't look his horseflesh over any before. If the buckskin was among 'em, I decided, I was going looking for her, and Clete would just have to wait or go on alone. Only it wasn't.

Marsh spoke to Sims and I picked the best of the three, a dappled gray stallion in nice shape — though I didn't want to take the time to see if he had any speed to him. The wrangler brought a saddle and throwed it up without a blanket.

"I don't need that," I told the man.

"Horse came in with the saddle, it goes out with the saddle. Take the whole shebang or leave it," Sims said.

I looked at Marsh, but he just shrugged. I took the gray and the saddle, of course, though the wrangler's thinking made no sense to me. While I saddled the bay, I got to thinking on the men who worked for the professor — Banty Foote, Captain Jack Crawford, and now this man Sims. I couldn't figure out whether fellows from Yale College had a preference for hiring men who acted crazy or if it was just the luck of the draw.

I mounted up and said goodbye to the professor, thanking him for his help and for the stallion.

"Glad to be of service to the law officers of the Territory," he said, giving me a kind of bow. "If you have a son, Mr. Goodwin, I would be happy to help him gain admission to Yale. I may be able to arrange a scholarship of some sort, too."

"That's awful nice of you, Professor Marsh, and I hope you mean it, 'cause I just might take you up on that some time."

Marsh handed me up the stallion's reins. "Of course I mean it, Willie. Just write to me at the college."

"What if he wasn't entirely white, this boy I don't have yet?" I ask him. "Maybe I'll be the daddy of a child who ain't entirely white, a mixed-breed."

"I believe that our institution has liberality enough to admit a person of . . . mixed racial heritage," Marsh said, a big smile on his face.

"Well, that's good news," I told him. "What about if it's a mixed-breed girl?"

"A young woman?" he said, looking like I'd hit him over the head with a board. "At Yale?"

"Yeah, how would that go?"

O. C. Marsh shook his head. "I doubt we'll live long enough to see the day when women students will matriculate at Yale," he said, starting to shake his head even faster. "I doubt, in fact, that that day will *ever* come."

"Well, it was just an idea," I told him.

He scratched his chin underneath his beard. "If you ever consider changing professions, Willie, let me know. I'm always looking for collectors in this part of the country."

I thanked him for the offer, but I hoped I would never get my brains scrambled enough to see that day roll around.

Clete's trail of that morning was easy to follow, for the ground was still muddy from the damn rain that had soaked my clothes. They was still wet and muddy — and rolled up in my bags, I remembered while I rode out toward the river. Ground had dried a lot from the afternoon sun and the breeze that'd picked up.

It struck me how close I come to lighting out after Mandy, instead of doing what I was doing then. Maybe Clete and me could get this DuShane business over with in a short while, and then I could go looking for her. At least to find out what become of that girl, for I knowed right then I would have little peace 'til I learned how Mandy was — scalped or still curly-headed, dead or alive.

At the river the Professor had called the White, Clete's tracks swung downriver, and looking close I could see that he'd followed another set of tracks, faint and mostly washed away, for they was made while that damn rain was still spittin' some. And they was made by Mandy's paint, too. I sat and looked up and down the banks, for I was sure our man would of went west by south, upriver, the way he'd been traveling before coming into this rough country — and the way toward that flat rock of Crawford's. Instead, Clete's trail turned northeast, downriver. Back toward the higher parts of them badlands again. Sure enough, Clete'd followed him. No way for me to go but after them, but I felt sure we'd be coming back this way before long.

Wasn't more than a mile downstream, here come Clete on that wore-out roan. He was waving his rifle at me, so I sat and waited. Took him a while, for though he spurred hard, the best he could get was a trot.

"This damn horse!" Clete yelled when he neared me, wet up to his shirt and the roan about as muddy as a horse can get.

"Here, try this one on for size," I told him, tugging on the gray's rope.

"Fine-looking animal," he said. "What'd you have to give for him?"

"Nothing. A gift from the Professor," I told him.

"Wish to hell I could give him back his other present," Clete said. I had no idea at all what he was talking about. "That little bastard I had to punch this morning, Banty something-or-other."

"Banty Foote," I reminded him. "I forgot he come out looking for you."

"Yeah, well, he found me, and the little fucker's been on my assend all day. I took a shot at him but he doesn't discourage easy." We got down and he looked the stallion's teeth over good. "This horse have a name?" he ask.

"Not that I know of. Marsh's man didn't say. I guess you can call him whatever you please."

"Whatever You Please? Pretty long name for a horse, don't you think? Put you at a real disadvantage in a race. The other fellow would get too good a start while you was still telling your horse to c'mon. 'Giddap, Whatever You Please!' " Clete had meant it for a joke, pretending he was in a horse race. But it was clear the stallion didn't get it, because he started forward a few steps. Clete and me had a good laugh. "Well, I guess that'll be his name, then, since he already answered to it." Clete patted the gray's neck and

190

you could tell he took to that animal. "Thanks again for the horse, but why did you bring that saddle? The one I got's fine."

"It's a long story, and I'll tell you some time, best I understand it. But right now I got something better to tell you. The man we're after is Whitey DuShane's brother."

He stopped assaying his new horse and turned them wolfish eyes on me. "How do you know that?" he ask.

While he was getting the extra saddle off the stallion and putting his own on it, I told him about Captain Jack Crawford and what he told me. He wanted the details, too.

"We could stand here all night 'til I told you all this," I said. "How about we get on that sonofabitch and I'll fill you in later."

He pushed his hat back. "What the hell has set you on fire?" he ask.

"Nothin' at all. I just want to catch him and end this."

"Me too," he said, putting the spare saddle on the roan and then starting to load it with some of our trap. "Only I lost his trail downstream about three miles, so I was heading back to Marsh's camp to look for you. Hell, I've just been going in circles anyway."

"That's because he's backtracked upstream through the river on you."

"What do you mean?"

"Aw, it's an old trick," I told him. "Only works alongside a muddy river, but then, I ain't seen one hauling any more dirt than that one."

He turned and looked. The White was muddy, all right, only it was the same light gray color as the hills around there, probably why they called it the White, though it wasn't white, entirely. Not brown or red, either, the way a muddy river ought to look.

"He found a hard place down there, I'll bet, rocks or gravel will do, and wiped his tracks out a ways, sort of like he done back at that creek. He's careful, this old boy. He ain't forgot you fired at him yesterday."

"Yeah, there's a rock ledge down where I lost him," Clete said.

"It would take some time to go upriver very far, wading your horse against the current, like he done. I bet we could pick up his sign not too far in that direction. And not too far up beyond where we struck the river, either. May be on the far side, though. Since I seem to be the brains of this outfit now, why don't you do the dirty work and see whether that gray can swim. Hell, you're wet anyway."

He mounted the stallion and that horse danced around some, doing a few crow-hops and looking like he thought about bucking some more, but he give that up after Clete pulled his head sideways and spun him in a tight circle. "At least I got some clothes on to *get* wet," he said.

I didn't know whether he was talking about catching me with Mandy or coming down that hill with just a blanket on. But before I had a chance to ask, he had the stallion down the bank and swimming for the far shore.

I led the pack horse and headed back up the way I'd come down a few minutes before. Wasn't very long before my pardner saw his tracks and called to me from the other side.

"Good, keep your eye on them sign pretty sharp," I warned him.

"Aren't you coming over?" he ask.

"No, not yet. My guess is he'll cross back over here." And half a mile up from where we struck the river, his sign come out of the water on my side and continued upstream.

Clete swum the gray back over to the east bank. "Old Whatever here takes to water like a regular fish," Clete said, and then cocked his head at me. "How'd you know he'd do that, cross back over here?"

"From Marsh's map. Steep banks up ahead on that side. Bluffs come right down to the water, almost, and it'd make the going slower. More important, some streams come in from that side too, between the hills, and he'd probably like to get dry before he beds down. Wouldn't you?"

Clete laughed at that. "Damn you, Willie. Looks like I'm bound to learn something if I'm around you long enough."

"Well, I got *me* an education today, I can tell you, talking to Professor Marsh and them Yale boys. No reason you shouldn't oil your mind a little too."

We moved pretty quick then, the sign clear

and Clete's horse fresh and strong. The bay didn't lag none either, and with the lighter load, even the roan kept up. The sun set in a blaze of yeller and orange ahead and to our right, behind some flat buttes. Those badlands was finally petering out, though they took their own sweet time doing it.

We slowed to a trot to save the horses.

"Why do you figure the Good Lord made this damn cut-up country?" I ask Clete.

"Beats me," he answered. "How about you?"

"It beats me too. Wouldn't be so bad a place if it wasn't for all this damned geology the professor talks so highly of."

He just looked at me after I said that. We rode silent for quite a stretch along the river, but it was getting darker by the minute and the moon not up yet.

"Can you still see the sign?" Clete ask. "Because I sure as hell don't."

"No, I can't see it anymore."

"Don't you want to stop, then? You wanted to stop when it was lighter than this over along the Bad, when you couldn't see the sign. Or was that just the girl being along then?"

I shook my head. "No, not entirely. We was still pretty green on the trail then. Didn't know what he had up his sleeve, either. Besides, he probably thinks he's slipped us. At least bought himself a bushel of time. No doubt he believes we'll have to wait for morning to figure out what he done back there, backtrackin' through the river. No, I'd like to gain some on him."

"Suits me," Clete said, and we spurred the horses to a lope. Of course, it was pitch dark before long and the stars out full.

We kept that pace for nearly an hour, too, 'til the banks started to change from a broad smooth path to a patch of deep mud. We climbed up higher on the shore to get out of the muck, and we was stopped, about to get off and walk the horses for a stretch, when we saw a low fire about a half mile ahead, on the far side.

"How you want to do this?" I ask Clete.

He studied the lay of the land a minute before answering. "You cross here and I'll circle away from the river and cross up above. Tie your horse and the roan well back. Walk in close and wait for me. Give me plenty of time and then fire that goddamn shotgun and keep firing it toward him, fast as you can. I'll rush him. Just ride in and shoot the bastard."

"I'll start it and you'll finish it, is that the way of things?"

"That's it," Clete said. "Just wait twice as long as you think you should. You ready?"

"Ready as I'm gonna be for this. Don't count on me for nothing fancy, my friend."

"No danger of that. I've seen you shoot, remember?" He slapped me on the back and headed the gray away from the river. "C'mon, Whatever," I heard him say quiet to that stallion.

I walked the bay and the roan into the water, and the coldness of it took my breath away for a

195

second when it reached my manly parts. The bay didn't need to swim more than ten yards, so I just kept my seat, though I didn't keep it dry. We come out slow on the other side, for the mud was even deeper over there.

I found a pretty stout sagebrush to tie the horses to, and hoped they wouldn't nicker and give us away. Nothing to do about it if they did, though. After I dumped the water out of my boots, I checked the shells in the shotgun and started to walk in slow. When I could see the fire, I got down and crawled, though I thought about snakes once or twice.

I got to a patch of ass-high grass and from there I could see him sitting beside the fire, his back mostly toward me. That's where I stopped. Out of range for the shotgun. Beyond killing range, anyway, though it would sting him good. I waited. The night wind blowed through that high grass along the river, making it wave and whistle some. Young frogs down below was noisy, too. Don't know how long I waited, but it seemed a long time. After I was sure I'd waited long enough for Clete to get ready, I cut loose with the one barrel and then right away the other. While I was reloading, I heard a wild scream and a horse galloping in toward the fire and three quick pistol shots. Then silence.

"Stand up, you sonofabitch!" I heard Clete yell. "You're not hit!"

I run in fast as I could. Clete was still on his horse, pointing his Remington at two men who was stretched out on the ground.

I poked the one hard in the ribs with the muzzle of the shotgun and rolled him over with it. He let out a howl and started bawling. Wasn't 'til then I saw he was just a boy.

Chapter Seventeen

I sat the boy up on his blankets while Clete looked at the man who was still stretched out.

"Stop cryin', son. You're all right now," I told him. "We thought you was someone else. We didn't mean you no harm. Are you hurt?" He rubbed above his ear. I took his hand away and found a big lump there. I put my arm around his shoulder and give him what comfort I could.

He wouldn't stop bawling, though. Big deep sobs that shook his shoulders.

"Let him alone a while," Clete said. "He'll quiet down in a spell. This one's been shot. Doesn't look like he'll make it, either. Lost a lot of blood and's been gut-shot."

I sat with the boy and Clete tossed the last of their few sticks into the fire. After it caught up good, I saw the white canvas top of a wagon up on the high bank.

"Did you notice the wagon?" I ask Clete.

"Just before you set off that scattergun. I'll go have a look."

"No!" the boy yelled, and then jumped at me, punching and kicking. I wrapped up his arms good and just waited 'til he stopped. He couldn't a been more than ten or twelve, and not very big for his age either. Didn't take him long to tire out and give it up, and when he went back to crying hard again, I let him go. He flopped face down on his blankets and let her out full.

"You suppose there's someone up there?" I ask.

"That'd be my guess," Clete said, taking a gander that way, but making no move. He bent down and looked at the man's face and then turned the boy over enough so's he could see his face too. "Boy's about the right age to be this man's son, and they sort of look alike." He took a pair of burning sticks from the fire and walked up to the wagon. I heard mules nickering, the way they do, and they moved the wagon a few feet when he got close.

"Anyone in there?" Clete hollered, but no one answered. "I'm a law officer and I'm coming in. Hold your fire." He walked up to the back end, raising his sticks high in one hand and laying back the flap with the other when he got there.

The blast from a gun lit up the canvas from the inside at the same time I heard the shot. I grabbed the shotgun quick and scrambled up to the high bank, though it was dark as hell without no light. The glowing sticks were on the ground, their flames out, just back of the wagon.

"You hit, Clete?" I called over there.

He startled the hell out of me, for he was right beside me when he answered. "I'm all right, but whoever's in there ain't gonna be when I get through with him. Gimme that shotgun!" He more grabbed it out of my hands than me giving it to him, and he blasted both barrels into that wagon.

A scream come out of there, one I hope to forget the sound of some day. High and screechy and sounding like someone being branded by devils.

"Jesus, it's a woman," Clete said. He jumped up and ran over while the scream kept up. Clete climbed into the front, over the seat, and the screaming stopped.

It was quiet a long minute after that. Only thing I could hear was the peepers down by the river. "Willie, fetch a light!" Clete hollered, finally.

I run down to the fire and grabbed the biggest stick left, though it wasn't much. The boy and the man was just where they was before, so I went right back toward Clete.

"Everthing all right in there?" I ask when I got close to the back of the wagon.

"Yeah, bring that damned light," Clete said.

When I stuck my head inside and held my burning branch up, there was a woman huddled in a blanket under a big old drop-leaf table. Other furniture was piled around her, too, a rocking chair and such. She was all rolled up in a ball with only her head sticking out. The lady was clutching something and kept rocking her body back and forth and talking low, almost like she was singing.

Clete sat up at the other end on the seat, but with his legs inside. The old muzzle loader she'd shot at him with was in his hands, and his face looked whiter than the wagon cover. After a minute he put the long gun aside and climbed in to where she was, but she still didn't look up. He lifted the blanket from her a little and it was plain she had no clothes on, nothin' at all. The woman held a little baby to her breast, but even from where I stood, you could see that its head was smashed in, and it dead a good while. Blood all over the baby and her and the wagon floor and everything.

Clete dropped the blanket and crawled out the front. I took a lantern that hung just inside the back and lit it with my branch. Pretty soon he come around the back end of the wagon.

"I didn't know there was a baby in there, or a woman either," he said. All of a sudden he turned and walked away from me, back toward the fire.

After a minute, I went around to the front and crawled up over the tongue and the seat. I set the lantern on a little cleared space on the floor and looked at that poor woman. She was rocking and singing low to that little child who would never hear her songs no more. Holding the lantern up high, I saw where the shot from the shotgun had tore through, and it was like I thought before. That baby was dead long before Clete and me come upon this sad camp. I lifted the blanket like Clete'd done, and saw that the blood on her body and her hands was all dried, and still she didn't look up, despite that she was naked and me taken her cover off. I dropped the corner of the blanket and went back outside. She was still singing soft when I started down with the lantern.

Clete sat by the fire, across from the boy, who was awake, but looked dazed. The man was still out. When first I felt for his heartbeat at his wrist, I thought he'd died. But a heartbeat was still there, real faint and slow.

Clete had his knees drawn up and his arms around his legs, hugging them in. I told him where the shot'd gone through the wagon cover, well above where the woman and child was. Then I said about the dried blood, about how the little one would of had to been dead for hours for all that blood to dry. I was telling the truth, too, not just trying to make him feel better, and I think him hearing that in my voice is what calmed him.

He looked at me a second, looked back into the fire, and then nodded slow. "Then DuShane shot this man and knocked the boy alongside his head. God knows what he did to that woman, but it's clear what he did to the child." His eyes bore into the flames.

I started talking to the boy then, telling him who we was and what we was doing there. I asked him a bunch of questions — his name and where he was from and the like — but he wouldn't answer me. Except, when I asked if the man lying beside us was his pa, he nodded his head. Other than that, he just stared into the fire like my pardner was doing. After a while Clete stood up and walked out to where my horse and the roan was. He led them back in and started getting the gear spread out. After hobbling the horses, he took the lantern and gathered a big pile of chips. All the while I kept talking to the boy, but he still hadn't spoke.

Clete went down to the river and come back with a potful of that chalky water. Once he got a good look at it, though, he tossed it away and went up to the wagon and got some from their side barrel. Before long he had peeled a pile of potatoes and set them to boil with bacon frying in the skillet and a pot of coffee going, too. Smelled damn good, I can tell you.

"What about the woman?" Clete ask when we started to eat.

"I don't know," I said. "She'll be all right 'til morning, I suspect. Maybe something'll occur to us by then. I don't know." I dished the boy some of what we had, but he didn't touch it. He laid on his belly beside his pa and stared into the flames.

"It's good food, son, and you're welcome to it," I told him. "I'll bet you're hungry, ain't you? When was the last time you ate?" I guessed that was the wrong thing to ask him, for he begun to whimper again.

About that time we heard a yowl out beyond the edge of the firelight, and Clete stood up and drew his pistol. It was supposed to sound like a coyote, I guess, but any fool could tell it was a man tryin' to sound like a coyote — and doin' the worst job of it.

"Shit," Clete said, holstering his Remington and then sitting back down.

"I'm coming in, now," a voice called to us. "Don't you go shootin' at me again, Sheriff."

Well, of course it was Banty Foote. He marched in on them short little bowed legs and stood beside the fire with his arms crossed. "Pretty chilly night," he said in that real quick way of his. "Fire feels good. Who's this boy?"

I waited for Clete to tell him, but he looked like he was pretending Banty wasn't there, so I told him myself what'd happened.

"I'll be dogged!" he said when I finished, and sat right down in the dirt. "Are we goin' after him now, the man what done this?"

"You're not going anywhere!" Clete yelled, causing the boy to fidget and sniffle again. "Not with us, you're not."

Clete looked at me and I tilted my head toward the boy. My pardner lowered his voice after that. "Why don't you git the hell out of here?" he ask Foote.

Banty dug in the dirt with his finger and looked downhearted. "Just wanted to help is all," he said. I thought for a while we was going to have two fellows crying on us. Clete went back to his food, and I offered Banty the plateful I had put out for the boy, for it was plain he wasn't interested in it.

Banty Foote spooned potatoes into his face and kept his eyes on Clete. That little man smacked his mouth louder while eatin' than Stalking Bear ever did, and that's saying something.

I told them the rest of what Crawford told me. What the Captain guessed of where DuShane was from and all. "He told Marsh's scout that you'd killed his brother and that he set out to get you back for it."

Clete thought on that for a minute. "The girl mentioned something like that too. But didn't she say he'd told her it was his *son* I had shot?"

"Yes, I think she did," I told him.

"I wonder which it is?"

"Beats me, but I guess I'd trust Crawford's recollection more than Mandy's. Her lingo is more French than American, and them damn French get the sex of everthing so turned around, I don't wonder they get confused between brothers and sons, too."

"Crawford's a good man," Banty offered. "Acts strange, but he don't miss much."

Clete shook his head and then we just sat quiet. The boy was still awake, though not stirring at all. Banty belched like a cow, stretched himself out on the ground beside the fire, and in a minute he was asleep. I guess he didn't have no bedroll along anyway.

"Then it was me he was after all along," Clete said of a sudden. "I didn't understand why he burned down Nell's house, but I do now. He must have known I stayed there sometimes, and when he saw Jesse go in that night, he thought it was me. Nell got killed because of me, then." He nodded his head slow and the fire glinted in his eye. When he spoke, his voice was quiet and hard as a spike. "*Que cabrón de mierda.* Wait'll I catch that sonofabitch."

Banty rolled over after Clete said that, and the boy looked more awake than ever. We sat and I listened to the night sounds and smoked my pipe while the fire burned lower. After a while Clete checked the man's breathing and then lay down on his sogans without saying anything, and in a while he was snoring.

I touched the boy's arm and he looked up.

"Ain't you gettin' sleepy yet?" I asked him.

He shook his head.

"Well, I ain't much sleepy myself, but it would be a comfort to hear your voice just once tonight. Want to tell me your name now?"

He shook his head again.

I nodded and rubbed his hair, being careful not to get close to his sore spot. "I know how it is for a young fellow out away from home and a terrible thing like this happens to him, with his family and all. Same thing happened to me when I was about your age." I stopped and relit my pipe.

He looked up again and you could see he was waiting for me to go on.

"Yes, I was coming out from the East with my Ma and Pa and little sister. Just west of the Mississippi River, we was, when a dozen or so Indians jumped us. My Pa killed four or five and I shot one myself. But my little sister must of got scared from all the shooting and run away, for after them braves cleared out, we couldn't find her nowheres. Ma had thought she was under the wagon with my Pa and me, and Pa thought she was inside with Ma. Only, as it turned out, she wasn't neither place. The Indians had took her, for they will do that. We followed them redskins for weeks, long after we knowed we had no chance of catching them, but we kept on after them 'til we got to Texas, and there we stopped.

"That was a long time ago, son, for I ain't no young man anymore. Only thing I can remember about my sister is her name and the color of her hair. It was long and black and hung in ringy curls way down her back. Bright and shiny black in the sunlight, it was. It's hard to lose kin, I know. Often I try to remember what she looked like, my little sister, but all I can recollect is the way her hair looked, black as midnight and shiny as stars. Just that and her name."

The peepers down by the river was raising a ruckus.

"What was her name?" the boy asked.

"Why, it was Amanda, son, but we called her Mandy. Say, your tongue *ain't* broke, is it?"

"My name's Jimmy," he said, and then laid his head down.

I pulled his blanket over his shoulder and he was asleep well before the moon come up.

Chapter Eighteen

Clete shook me awake before dawn, just a little strip of gray showing toward the east.

"We got work to do before we can get after him, so we better get started," he said. "I made a pot of coffee. Get yourself awake and start digging a grave." He hunkered down beside the fire and poured us each a cup. "The man died during the night. Guess one hole will do for him and the baby. Those mules are gonna founder if I don't water and feed them soon."

I sat up and drank my coffee still in my bedroll. The boy stirred and opened his eyes before I spoke to him. "Come on, Jimmy. The sheriff needs your help with the team."

Best to keep him busy, I thought. Banty was up and poking at the fire when I went and washed my face in the river and then found the short-handled shovel.

Diggin' a grave's odd work. And making a final bed for somebody ain't as simple as it looks, either. First you need to find a good place. I went up the bank a piece, up on the last bench before the prairie started right. Still wasn't very light, but I could see well enough. I watched Clete unhitch the mules down below, and not long after, Jimmy come and took the lead team from Clete down to the river.

No trees there where I decided on, of course.

That woulda been nice, and I *could* of buried him right where we'd slept, under the one big cottonwood that was close by the edge of the river. But it was mucky down there, and I figured he wouldn't like lying in mud 'til kingdom come any better than I'd like digging in it for the next hour. Maybe he'd rest better, too, a little distance off from where he was murdered.

After you have a spot picked out, you've got to keep the size of the person you're putting to rest in mind. Sure, you could dig a hole seven feet long and three feet wide, a grave that would fit anyone. But that's a lot of extra diggin' for nothing, the way I figure it.

The strangest part of digging a grave, I guess, is the way it makes you think about your own dyin'. It's funny how, most of the time, you can keep from considering it. But not when you're digging a hole to put a man in, you can't. At least I can't. Always makes me think on how little I done, so far, with this life I got. Always makes me sweat, too, no matter how chilly it is, and it was, that morning. Even after the sun come up bright and clear.

The diggin' was going real easy, but I was only down about two feet when I heard Banty screeching and hollering. "Come and git it now, you men, or I'll throw it to the pigs!"

When I saw Clete and the boy start toward the river to wash up, I dropped the shovel in the hole and went down, too.

"What's this?" Clete ask after we come up and

wiped our hands on our pants and was sitting down to the plates Banty'd filled.

"Why, it's pancakes and bacon. Can't you tell pancakes when you see 'em?" the little man said, his face all scrunched up. "If you don't want 'em, give 'em here. I'll eat 'em."

"No, they look all right," Clete said, taking up his fork. "Smell all right, too. Just surprised me, that's all."

"Well, you had flour and you had sody and salt. That's all you need, sody and salt. And flour, a course. You need flour."

"What's this on top, molasses?" I ask.

"Hell, no. You ain't got no molasses in that pack. We'd have molasses right now if I'd a packed it, only I didn't. No, I scorched some sugar in the bacon fat. That's what my ma always done. She died some time ago. Snake bit her." He was smacking his food so loud, eatin' and talking together, you could hardly think of nothing else.

"I expect I'll feel snake-bit after I finish these," Clete said. "But they taste all right, I'll admit that."

"I'm a good cook. I don't mind cookin'," Banty said, and right away I saw what he was after. "I can handle a gun, too. Shot a man once, but he got away anyhow."

You could tell Clete was thinking something, for just a hint of a smile turned the edges of his mouth up. He didn't say nothing, though. The boy was quiet too, and he was eatin' his pancakes like what he had in mind was to fill up a big hollow space inside, quick as he could.

"I can handle a rifle too," Banty said. "And I can ride fast if I have a good horse." He looked at me and then Clete and then back at me. "Betcha I can ride faster than either of you two," the little man bragged.

"Got no time for a horse race this mornin'," Clete said, finishing his bacon. "But you ride fast enough."

"Then why don'tcha let me go along with you men after this man you're chasin'?" he ask.

I lit my pipe and drank my coffee, watching Clete close to see what he was up to.

He just shook his head.

"Why not?" Banty asked, looking almost tearful.

Clete shook his head again. "No, you ride all right, and I believe you about shooting straight. But I only take on men who know how to follow orders. To the letter and real quick, without any backtalk or argument. I don't think you could handle that."

"What!" Banty yelled, jumping up. "Why, I can take orders better and faster than any man alive. You ask the Perfesser if I can't! Just you gimme an order an I'll show ya right now."

Clete looked like he was considering the matter real careful. "I don't know," he said after a spell, and took a sip of his coffee.

"Try me out is all I'm askin'. Go ahead, gimme an order!"

"And if you don't do it, you'll clear out and

leave us alone, right?" Clete ask.

"Right!" Banty said, sticking his chin up in the air and folding his arms.

"Well, all right," Clete said, slow and deliberate. "I'll give you three, but if you don't do 'em, or can't — or make a fuss about it — you get the hell out of here."

"Yessir, three at a time. Just the way I like 'em."

When Clete stood up he towered over Banty. "Try these on, then. First, wash these dishes and get our gear stowed away good. Then go get that dead child away from that woman in the wagon and wrap it up in a tarp along with that fellow over there. He's the baby's daddy and we're going to bury them together."

Jimmy looked over toward his pa real quick. He must have knowed before then that his daddy'd died, for Clete had covered up his face. Probably knew about his baby brother or sister, too. But maybe it just hadn't sunk in on him yet.

Banty swallowed hard, and his smile fell away. But he didn't complain. "That's only two, ain't it?" he asked.

"That's right," Clete said. "The third one is to take the boy and the woman back to Marsh's camp in that mule wagon, after we get done with the buryin'."

You could see right then that Banty knowed he'd been dealt off the bottom of the deck. There was nothing to do but play the hand he held. "You men are gonna ride out after him before I get back, ain't you?" he asked, his voice real squeaky.

"Yes, we are," Clete said, going back toward the mules with Jimmy following him.

"Then how the hell will I find you?" Banty yelled after him.

"Just track us," Clete called back. "That's what we're doing. If you can't do that, then you're not worth taking."

"All right, Mr. Sheriff," Banty said to himself. "All right, but you ain't seen the last of me!"

By the time I'd finished my digging chores, Banty had made a neat parcel of the man and the child, wrapped up together in the man's blankets and tied with a heavy rope he found someplace. Clete and Jimmy fed the mules and hitched them back up while Banty and me carried the father and his child up to where I had the grave dug. We laid them in gentle. Clete and Jimmy joined us and Clete handed me my old Bible.

"Read us a word, Pardner," he said, taking off his hat. I remembered something about where a man was killed and left his wife a hard lot, in a part called Ruth, and so I read that. It didn't fit, exactly, but it was close enough.

Jimmy stood close to Clete and stared into the hole.

I'd had about as much funeral as I wanted and was just starting to go back down the bank when Banty cleared his throat and started talking quiet, his hands clenched together and him lookin' at the sky. "Lord, I didn't know these

213

folks at all, but they was no doubt good as most. Too late now to do much for the man and this little baby. But you could look out for the momma and this boy standin' here. If you've a mind to. Amen."

Clete appeared a little confused at Banty saying a prayer like that. When he recovered himself, he put his arm around Jimmy's shoulders, turned the boy away, and walked down toward the wagon with him.

Banty picked up the shovel. "I'll finish this," he said. "Diggin's been my trade of late."

DuShane was having a hell of a time with his new horse. He had already figured out that it was a walker, a gentleman's Sunday afternoon mount. It had refused the bit at first and didn't know what to do when DuShane yanked on the old snaffle. It would learn, the bony man vowed, or the sonofabitch would bleed to death from its mouth.

He thought about saddling the paint again, but he didn't want to stop. His trick back at the White must have fooled the man after him, but then again, maybe not.

When he struck the Deadwood road, he turned southeast and slowed his pace. At a stream crossing, where hoofprints clustered as thick as ants around an anthill, he turned and went back the way he'd just come, toward the northwest. Nobody'd ever be able to trail him with all these wagon ruts and tracks.

But when he got back to where the sign from his walker and the paint cut in from the right, he stopped and looked that way for several minutes. The lawman who had killed Whitey was still after him. He could feel it, almost smell it.

DuShane dismounted and hobbled the walker close, then hopped up on the paint bareback and, leaving the walking horse to follow with its eyes, he retraced his tracks away from the road. At a rocky place two hundred yards from where he'd stopped and looked, he turned the paint several times and then trotted her toward the south. After another hundred yards, beside a dense growth of sage, he dismounted, removed the lead rope and slapped the paint hard with his revolver. She took off like a mountain lion was after her.

The scrawny man cut a sagebrush branch with his clasp knife and wiped out his bootprints, walking backwards, and then swept away both horses' tracks from the rocky place to the road. When he had finished, he remounted the walker, stood in the stirrups and looked back toward where he'd set the sheriff off his trail, though he couldn't see the spot from the road. "Let him foller that awhile," he said, and spurred the walker hard.

Banty Foote sat astride the near-wheel mule and held the reins high. His pony was tied behind the wagon and Jimmy stood waiting by the lead pair.

Clete was giving Banty some more orders, and I sat my horse beside the boy. "You'll have to take care of your ma now, Jimmy. She ain't got no one else."

215

"I know," he said, his eyes in the dirt.

"I expect you'll spend a day or two at a camp not far from here, run by some fellows from back East. They're good men, though, friends of Banty's back there. They'll look out for you and your ma. You got any relations in these parts?"

"Just my uncle at Fort Laramie. That's where we was going."

"Well, that's not so awful far. Tell Mr. Foote's friends about your uncle. Tell them Mr. Shannon, the Sheriff of Two Scalp, said for them to take you there. Think you can remember that?"

Jimmy nodded his head. "Yeah, Mr. Shannon says we're to go to Fort Laramie. To my Uncle Caleb's house. Mr. Shannon, he's a real sheriff, ain't he?"

"That's right, son, a real hell-raising *Western* sheriff. Just you don't take no for an answer, the way he don't, and you'll be okay. That, and doing what you think's right."

Clete rode up to me about then and Banty yelled to us. "Don't catch him 'til I git there!"

"Jesus," Clete said. "Let's get the hell outta here!"

"Goodbye, Mr. Shannon," the boy said. "Thanks for rescuing my mom and me."

"Rescue?" Clete glanced at me, but I didn't know what to say so I just shrugged.

"Goodbye, Jimmy," I told the young man.

"Goodbye . . . sir."

Clete spurred that good-looking gray, and the bay and me took after, leading the roan. I often wondered about that boy after that, whether he got to Laramie or not. What happened to his ma, did she ever come back to her senses? I never knowed, but I often got pleasure from thinking about how it might of turned out. How Jimmy's ma began feeling herself again after a while, maybe, and started working for her brother in a dry goods store like John Tate's. How she met a nice businessman, or maybe a deputy or a lawyer, and got Jimmy a daddy, and maybe a baby sister, too. How the youngster grew up strong and straight. Sometimes I see him being a lawman or going off to Yale College, but I never learned exactly what happened to him or his ma.

One thing for sure, though. Jimmy or Banty must of told quite a story about Clete, back at Marsh's camp or somewheres, about how he and his ma was rescued by a sheriff named Shannon. The people Jimmy told must of turned it into a windy the size of a sandstorm, because years afterward, when they got around to making counties in the state of South Dakota, the place where that muleskinner and his baby child was murdered — down there in the southwest corner — they called that Shannon County. Still is today, far as I know. People will have their heroes, no doubt about it. And if they can't find ones that suit, why, they'll just cut them outta whatever cloth they've got. Now, I

217

ain't saying Clete didn't do as much as Bill Hickok. He did, maybe more. But there's another side, too, and I'll get to it fast as I can.

The sign showed clear that our man'd headed upriver on the west bank of the White. But we was no more than half a dozen rods from where I'd buried Jimmy's daddy and his baby child when I noticed another set of hoofprints beside those of Mandy's paint. From the look of it, our man could of been following someone else, for the paint's tracks covered those of the other horse in spots.

"Did the boy say anything about there bein' two men who jumped his family?" I ask Clete.

"No, he didn't. But I see why you asked."

I got down and looked close at the hoofprints. I guessed our man was riding another horse and trailin' Mandy's when he lit outta there, for the paint's tracks looked different than they did yesterday. I don't know how, but they did. Another half mile up the river, where a stream come in, our man cut due west, cross country, no trail at all. Looked like he knowed where he was going, all right.

Easy sign to follow, for it was skimpy new grass, growin' in white sandy soil. We picked up the pace pretty good and stayed at it 'til nearly noon, when we found his campfire ashes from the night before. In another hour we come to a rocky spot where the paint's track took a sharp bend south, and the sign of the other horse just quit. After a quarter mile, I reined in the bay and stepped down. I got low to see the hoofprints good. "We've got to go back," I told Clete.

"Why?" he ask.

" 'Cause he tried getting foxy on us, tried to give us the slip again. No one was riding this horse when it come through here. He's off in the other direction on the other horse is my guess. Let's see that map again."

We was almost to the Deadwood road, according to the map, so we backtracked to where the paint'd turned, and then we cut over and hit the road. No tracks at all to follow.

"North's the way to go here," I told Clete. "Seems like it ought to be the other way, I know, but he went north."

"How can you tell?" Clete ask, sliding out of his saddle and inspecting the sign.

"Nothin' there that will tell you, but I'm sure he went up the road toward Deadwood."

"I was wrong back there close to Marsh's camp when I went north," Clete said, trying to figure out the different tracks. "How come you're so damned sure."

"Well, part of it's the difference between northeast, the way you went, and northwest, the way this road goes. I doubt he'd double back on himself and risk running into us. He must guess we're still after him, or else he wouldn't have turned the paint loose over there to try and throw us off. Not as much as *he* values a spare horse, he wouldn't. And another part of it is having somewhere to go — meaning Deadwood. A fellow who enjoys killing folks, or makes a trade of it, could do a lot worse than Deadwood if its reputation is only half true. And the last part of it, well, you wouldn't believe me if I told you."

Clete stood and put his hands on his hips. "Why don't you let me decide that?"

"All right," I told him after a minute. "Stalking Bear taught me to spirit track. To put yourself in the place of what you're trackin', see with *his* eyes, listen with *his* ears. After you've been chasing an animal or a man for some time, you can get inside the thinking. 'Get in front of the sign' is what that Apache was always saying to me. Our man went north here. I feel it, like Stalking Bear taught me. Sounds farfetched, I know."

"Yeah, it does," Clete said, getting back on the gray. "But you've been right so far and there's no arguing with that. Let's go."

So go we did. All afternoon and into the evening. I knowed Clete didn't like it, traveling up that road without no sign to follow. He'd look at me from time to time, but he didn't say nothing. Near dark we hit a town the map said was Hay Camp, just a few houses and a saloon.

Clete checked the horses there, and then stood a ways off and looked through the window a spell. We looked everyone over good when we went in, but none of the men at the bar or those playing poker at the tables in back was our man. Clete bought us whiskeys and questioned the barman, but he didn't see nobody new all day —

except the folks on a stage that'd passed through.

"What do you think, Willie?" Clete asked after we got our second whiskey. "Still think he's headed for Deadwood?"

"Yes, I do," I said.

"How come he didn't stop here?" Clete ask, taking a sip.

" 'Cause he knew we would. Likely rode all the way around instead of coming through, too. Probably no one even saw him."

"You're still sure, though, aren't you?"

"Yes, I am. I could be wrong, now, you understand, but I feel he's up the road toward Deadwood."

"You up to riding all night, just on the strength of your hunch?" Clete asked. "We could get to Deadwood by late morning."

"It's not just a hunch," I said. "It's a lot more than that. And, yeah, I'll ride at night with you. Might be we'll even stumble onto him this time. But if we're gonna ride long, let's get a little sleep now and get back on him in a couple hours. Moon'll be up shortly past midnight . . . a good-sized slice of it. What my daddy called a horsethief's moon. I say we sleep a while and then start."

"Sounds all right to me," Clete said. "Be better for the horses, too."

We finished our drinks and walked out of there with everone watching. I could have stood a few more. Two would have to do for that night, though. But Deadwood, I decided right then,

221

that would be a different story. We made a cold camp a few miles out of town and slept 'til the moon rose, clear and sharp, like the points on a bull's horns.

Chapter Nineteen

I chewed jerky while we rode along in the dim moonlight. Stars were bright, and while we trotted on up the trail that old star goose flew slow across the night sky, east to nearly overhead and then winging her way toward the west.

The air smelled sweet. A warm, dry wind straight up the flatlands from Texas made you think of summer, though it was only May. Course, it could go back to being March again tomorrow, but I hoped it wouldn't.

To the west, come sunup, we saw the Black Hills, the first real rise on the plains in a thousand miles. From far off they looked like low-hanging storm clouds, but as you got up closer you saw the peaks and ridges. Wasn't hard to see why the first white men in these parts called them black, either. Darkest green you ever saw, though from far off they was smoky-looking too. True, they wasn't nearly so grand as the ranges between here and the Rockies, all of them higher and wilder, but these looked mighty pretty to me. Don't know why I fancy mountains so, I wasn't born near any.

The road bent west and cut up into a valley. A wooden sign pointed us up the trail toward Deadwood and we followed its stiff finger. Every so often I'd look for those hoofprints we first saw over where Jimmy and his folks'd had their troubles, but I didn't see them even once more. Did I go and climb the wrong tree? I asked myself if I was still doing things the way Stalking Bear taught me to do. I figgered I was, so I said nothing to Clete. There was no other way now than to just go on.

As the valley we were in turned and twisted, it also narrowed. The dark-colored pines crowded closer and closer to the snaky road and swooshed in the breeze. The perfume from all those cedary trees, together with the moisture they give off, made it seem like the plains and them badlands we traveled through only days before was on the sun or the moon. It felt like we'd come to a place not even on the same kind of a map. Gradually we climbed up through gully and gulch, the sun finally rising high enough to set the stream and road afire in a blaze of light. Lots of wildflowers, too — red ones. I didn't know what they were, but I tried not to spend much time looking at them, pretty as they was. No matter how nice it was there, it was also ripe country for an ambush.

Lots of fellows along the streams panning and digging after we got into the Hills a ways. None of them very friendly, though. I waved at the first few gangs of men we seen, but few waved back and none of 'em ask us to come on into their camps, so we just rode on. Some miners'd even hired men to sit guard with a rifle, and those sentries watched us *real* close. I guess there must of been quite a few thieves and claim-jumpers working that territory. In places, the ground along the stream was all tore up and bare — big gashes in the hillsides. Timber'd burned off not too long ago, too, in spots, givin' the hills a kind of bare look compared to where the trees was thick as fleas on a dog.

We heard Deadwood before we saw it. We had come down out of a steep gulch and then up and down a gentler one when gunshots echoed through the narrow valley. So many shots fired, it sounded like an Indian raid.

When we got to where we could see Deadwood good, up on a little rise, we just sat and looked. The streets was full of people, hollerin' and runnin' around. Many of 'em, women as well as men, drunker than Billy-be-damned. Even at a distance you could see that. The town was stretched out down the hill from us, but it started off on the uphill again right away — mostly just a single street, following the line of the gulch. Rougher buildings closest to us, mostly log or uneven ripped boards, and the fancier ones with squared-off false fronts up the hill a ways. I had thought there would be more to it, much as I'd heard about Deadwood.

Toward the far end of town, up on the higher ground, a brass band stood in the middle of the street and struck up a march. Three or four men close to us, after we got down to the bottom, kept throwing their hats up into the air, going to fetch them, and then throwing them up again. Three teams of bulls hitched to wagons was

225

stopped any old where, with no bullwhackers near them — one team with twelve animals.

Riders and buggies was all caught in a big snarl. A pile of poles higher than a man's head — pine tree trunks — had slid right off a flat wagon and nearly blocked the street in front of a place called Liebmann's San Francisco Bazaar, so the sign said. I'd have expected that particlar store to be in San Francisco, myself. But there it was. Clete and me rode right through the middle of it all. Half a dozen men bawling out orders and arguing about what should be done about the logs lying there peaceful as liquored-up Irishmen, but nobody was *doing* a thing about 'em.

I saw a man in a beaver hat with three fancy-dressed women — upstairs girls they looked like to me — two on one arm and one on the other. He kissed one gal and then the second and then the third, right in a row and right in the street. And not just little pecks on the cheek, either. A place called the Red Bird caught my eye. Smelled like stale beer and sawdust as we rode past, so I promised myself I'd stop by there before very long. Everywhere people was hoo-raying and cheering, and the band just added to the racket, once we got up toward the fancier end of town. But mostly what you heard was pistols being fired off. I have seen some strange sights in my day, and heard some god-awful noises, but I was not prepared for the likes of Deadwood.

"What happened, did I sleep through the

Fourth of July?" Clete asked.

"Beats me," I said, almost hollering to be heard. "You suppose it's like this all the time?"

Clete didn't answer, but it didn't matter, because just then it was so loud I couldn't of heard him anyway.

When we got up the street a piece it quieted some. Clete rode close to a young man sitting his horse in front of a rail. "What's all the excitement?"

The man tipped his whiskey bottle at us. "Crazy Horse!" He tried to dismount and landed in a heap in the muddy street. He stood up slow, brushed himself off and wobbled into a big hotel. Had the name, Grand Central Hotel, on a sign right over the door, letters high as a man's chest.

"Crazy Horse?" Clete said. "If this is how they get ready for an Indian attack, I'd like to see what they do for Saturday night."

We tied our horses to the rail beside the young fellow's mount and then stood on the board sidewalk. We'd no sooner started to look around to get our bearings than, bam — out through the open door comes the young fellow Clete'd spoke to, ass first. I thought for a minute he was hurt, but I guess he was drunk enough to fall soft, even on them boards, for he picked himself up, found his hat and headed back inside. But not before he smiled and tipped his hat to us real friendly.

Clete and me waited, but after a while it

seemed like he was going to stick. "I'm going up the street to look for the sheriff," Clete said. "Seth Bullock used to carry the badge here." He looked tired and dusty, and I supposed I looked worse. "You can come along or get swilled in one of these places, suit yourself."

All of a sudden, that young feller come sailing out of that hotel door again and made an even bigger thump going down than he did the first time. He was slower standing up, too, but he started for inside again.

Clete took the young fellow by the arm as he was building up steam to charge back in. "You sure you want to try that again?" Clete asked him. "Doesn't seem like they want your business all that bad."

He give Clete and me a crooked grin, and when he finally got around to talkin' he slurred his words pretty good. "Oh, it's all right. My pa don't like me comin' home drunk is all it is, him ownin' the best hotel in town. He'll not throw me out a third time. It was twice I come out now, wan't it?"

"Yep," I told him, "twice in and twice out."

"This'll be it, then. Pa don't usually stay mad enough to throw me out three times." He dusted himself off, set his hat on straight and staggered back in.

We waited a while, but it appeared that young man knowed his daddy pretty well, for though there was a lot of hollering inside, he had wedged himself in for good that time.

"You *want* me to go along to see Bullock?" I asked.

"Makes no difference. If I don't see you up there by the time I'm ready to go, I'll come back down here. Maybe you could look around in the bars for DuShane. He's a tall, lean one, and if he's kin to Whitey, he's a Rebel."

"I'll bear it in mind," I told him.

"And get us a room some place, but be sure there's no whores working there," Clete said, taking a step up the street. "I could stand a night's sleep in a regular bed, and the last thing I want keeping me awake is having to listen to every horny miner in these Hills banging his rocks off."

"I'll see to it," I told him, "though I may have to check out the ones that *might* be whorehouses pretty close."

Clete smiled, shook his head, and walked up the street through all that confusion. I went back down to the even noisier part of town.

People inside the Red Bird was celebrating every bit as much as the people in the street. That beery and sawdust smell hit me in the face as I walked in, and it felt a lot like coming home. Lots of gals in fancy dresses at the bar, not all of 'em with somebody, either.

"You had your free one yet?" the barman asked me soon as I stepped up.

"You mean a free whiskey?" I ask the man.

"Unless you'd rather have beer," the fellow told me, standing there waitin'.

229

"Make it rye, then," I said, and he set 'er up in front of me. Maybe I could get used to a town with lots of confusion.

"Here's to General Clark!" a man standing beside me called out, and everybody cheered and raised their glasses . . . so I drank too.

The man who thought so highly of General Clark gouged me in the ribs with his elbow. "Let me buy you a drink, friend. You don't look properly lubricated for such a historic occasion."

"I wouldn't mind if you did," I told him. "But what's the occasion, anyways?"

"Why, ain't you heard?" the man ask, sounding like I'd just asked who Abraham Lincoln was. "Crazy Horse surrendered this morning! We got it on the telegraph more than an hour ago. That's where I work, the telegraph office, so I was one of the first that heard it."

He acted real proud of himself over that, passing his smile around to everyone that would look his way. He went over and sat at a table with some other men wearing suits. I wondered how come he'd walked away from the telegraph office and who was writing down the messages while he was gone. Maybe Crazy Horse changed his mind and was on his way here now, just to stir things up a little worse. Not that they needed it.

It was only natural that the people who lived in the Hills was celebrating old Crazy Horse giving it up. That Sioux chief had killed a lot of folks and would of killed a lot more, for the army had about as much chance of bringing in him and his bunch as it did of throwing a loop over the moon's horns. Still, I hated to think that the last really wild Indian in these parts was going to settle down on a reservation, eat the white man's beef and buy his shirts in a store somewheres.

I picked up the drink the telegraph man'd bought me and moved down beside a hefty gal in a pink striped dress standing by herself and sippin' a beer. Looking me over, so I thought.

"Well, hello there, stranger," she said in a real loud voice. "Haven't seen you in this hole before. You wanna buy a girl a drink or something?"

"The *something* sounds like what I'd *like* to buy — if I got you pegged right, but I don't mean no offense if I didn't understand you proper."

She threwed her head back and laughed a good loud one. "No, you got me right," she said, taking my arm and still smiling. "Bessie's my name and whorin's my game. You ready to go now?"

It surprised me she said it right out like that for all to hear, but nobody seemed to pay much attention. "Whoa, hold on, Bessie," I told her. "I meant that's what I'd *like* to do, but I ain't got the time right now, so instead I'll just buy you that drink."

She twisted up her smile and slapped me on the back. "Then I'll take whiskey and be glad for that."

Soon as the barman set our drinks down, she tipped hers toward me and put 'er back in one

231

splash, then took a sip of her beer. Never batted an eye. Long time since I saw a gal drink whiskey like that, even a whore.

"Seems everybody's too busy to dip his wick today," she said, free and easy, not caring how she talked.

"Still pretty early for that, ain't it?" I asked. People always like to talk about their trade, man or woman.

"Not for Deadwood. Hell, Sundays I'm wore out before most of the tin shits around here get out of bed the first time. Lots of gals working this town, but there ain't a one of 'em goin' hungry, even the old bags."

"You been around here awhile?" I ask.

"About four months now. That's a long time to stay in one place. For me, anyway." She pawed at her hair and began looking around the Red Bird for something, customers I guessed.

"You know a long, tall Southerner? Maybe just got in the last couple days."

"I know a few men that might be," she said, looking me over a different way than she did before. "What's it worth to you?"

I dug into my pocket, pulled a half-eagle out of the pouch I carry my gold in, and tossed it on the bar in front of her.

Quick as a cat she picked it up and dropped it into her handbag. "You ain't the law, are you?"

"He's not a young fellow," I told her. "Maybe my age or more. Maybe he has a son or a brother who'd be twenty-five or so, but maybe not.

Anyway, his kin is dead — supposin' he had one."

"That's a shit load of help," she said.

"That's all I know. I'd tell you more if I had saw the man I was after, but I didn't. He's tall and skinny, though, that much I'm sure of. And he talks Southern."

"This fellow have a name?" she asked, curling her red-painted mouth funny.

"His name's DuShane, his last name. I don't know his other."

"Well, that's real useful too," Bessie said, putting her hand on her hip. "Men around here don't go by their last names much, don't even tell their partners, usually. Lot of men up here have their faces on a poster someplace else. Say, you ever been in a gold camp before?"

"No, I haven't," I told her. "And from the likes of this one, I don't care if I never go near another."

"Well, I've been in lots, Colorado and everywhere. And at least I have enough sense not to go into a gold strike town and go asking some box hustler to help me find somebody. Hell, you could get killed doing that. Don't you know that?"

"Do you know the man I ask you about or not? Just give me my five dollars worth and then I'll look elsewheres. Any honest whore would do that much."

The barman came and poured us two more whiskeys, and she stopped talking while he was there, just looked around the place. Bessie was still a pretty woman, though a mite fleshy for my tastes, but you could still see how sweet she would have looked a few years back. Her eyes was dark and so was her hair, long and full and clean. The life and the whiskey would soon begin to show a lot more in her face, but just now the years was still kind to her. "Well, I'll see what I can find out," she said after the barman left. "What'd he do, kill somebody?" she ask, making a joke.

When she saw my face, she didn't have to ask a second time. "Oh shit," she said, then took her whiskey in a jolt.

I did the same with mine. Pretty fair whiskey. Didn't feel no worse goin' down your throat than swallowing a nervous cat backwards.

Bessie pulled a hanky out of her sleeve, wiped her mouth, and then tucked it back in just like a lady. "Come back later," she said, kind of careless. "I can't promise nothin', but I'll ask around. What's your name, anyway?"

"Willie," I told her.

"No last name, huh? See what I mean?"

"It's Goodwin. Willie Goodwin. And I'm not running from nobody."

"Well, you watch out for yourself, Willie Goodwin," she said, patting my hand. "And don't go asking every tainted dove in Deadwood about this tall old Southerner you're after, you hear me? You're about the same age as him, I know, but you look like you could still give a gal a pretty good roll in the hay, if you catch my meaning. And I hope you don't get shot up before I have a chance to find out."

She made half a grab at my manly parts. When I pushed her hand away she winked at me, picked up her beer, and then strutted over to the table where the telegraph gent and his friends sat. Pretty soon Bessie walked out the door with the ugliest one of the bunch. She didn't even look back at me.

Chapter Twenty

I had another whiskey and went back outside. Things'd quieted a good bit in the street, but some fool still fired off his pistol every once in a while. I walked uphill toward where we'd left the horses and it was a climb. On the way, I looked over the establishments that might have been hotels. Some was certainly whorehouses, all right, and I couldn't tell for sure which was which. By the time I got up to the Grand Central, I figured I'd try there.

That young fellow that had got hisself throwed back into the street wasn't just braggin' about his daddy's place, either. Maybe it wasn't the showiest hotel west of St. Louis, but it was neat and clean and fancy enough for me. In a room like a parlor, a man sat reading a newspaper on a big stuffed chair and two others at a little table was studying a checker board.

I didn't even bother asking the serious man standing behind the desk, a fellow about my age, if whores lived there. His hair was plastered down enough to withstand a tornado and his beefy face was all business. If this was the daddy of the young fellow who went in and out of here like one of those birds in a clock, then there would be no midnight ruckuses at this place.

I paid him for one night, signed his book, and ask where the livery was. After he told me, I went out and got Clete's things and mine off the pack horse and took them inside. The man I'd rented the room from said he'd carry our trap upstairs for me, so I let him. I went outside again, climbed the bay and led Clete's horse and the roan back down through town, the reverse of the way we come in.

Deadwood smelled like a town, all right. Onions and potatoes frying in some lady's kitchen — horseshit trampled into the mud of the street. You'd catch a whiff of pine pretty strong every once in a while. Wove in with all them smells mixed together was one that meant somebody wasn't throwing lime enough down the hole of his outhouse. Deadwood smelled like people living close together always does, I suppose.

A tall redheaded gal wearing a funny ruffled hat and swingin' her ruffled handbag crossed the thoroughfare right in front of me, smilin' real pretty, and the smell of her was mighty powerful. A lot of it was perfume, of course, but a lot of it wasn't, too.

After I looked over all the horses he had there, recognizing none of them, I gave the livery man my name and Clete's and a brand-new fifty cent piece and walked back up through town. The celebratin' was nearly through with by then, and the hollering and music was coming mostly from the saloons, of which there were a plenty. Some all decorated up with colored paper streamers and paper balls and bells and the like, strung on the walls and behind the bars, most of them you could see into through the swinging doors.

At one saloon that called itself a theatre, a man standing just outside the door grabbed my sleeve and started telling me what-all they had inside. After a while I figured out he wasn't just a fellow trying to show me where to have a good time, but instead, he was a man hired by that saloon to drum up their business. I walked away from him soon as I saw into what he was trying to do.

I was thinking about another whiskey, but the sun'd slipped below the mountain and I wondered what Clete'd found out about DuShane. So I forwent the rye and walked on up the street looking for Bullock's office. Once I found it I saw right away, even from the outside, it was a whole lot nicer than ours back in Two Scalp. Three stories high, made entirely of white-painted boards. Around the top was a fussy balcony and below that, narrow little porches for the rooms on the second floor. I wondered what use a sheriff had for all them rooms.

I started in through the door beside Sheriff Bullock's shingle and run straight into Clete coming out, looking madder than a cornered badger.

"Let's get the hell out of here," he growled at me, and I followed him across the street to a saloon.

Clete smacked the batwing doors open and walked straight through to the bar that stretched all along the back. The baldheaded man behind it saw Clete coming and brought a whiskey right away and then got another after he seen me.

"Yeah, I was here before, while I was cooling my heels waiting to talk to the high-and-mighty Sheriff Seth Bullock," Clete said, his voice sand-dry and his green eyes sharp. I seen Clete heated up a time or two before, so I knowed that him reining himself in so tight and stiff was what happened before he exploded. The next step was knocking somebody down. He killed his whiskey in a gulp and I downed mine.

"The sonofabitch is sitting over there talking to a salesman, deciding whether he wants to add a line of mining equipment to the store he runs here . . . his deputy said he *wouldn't have time* to see me today. Meanwhile, that goddamn DuShane is running around loose in these goddamn Black Hills." He shook his head a couple of times and stared at his empty glass. "An old friend of his wanted me to say hello when I got to Deadwood," he said after a time. "Well, here I am, by God!" He turned around and headed for the door. "C'mon, let's go pay a social call on Mr. Bullock."

By the time we got across the street I had caught up with him. He flung open the door, walked straight up to a tall man sitting at a desk, looked him over a second, and then drew his Remington quick as a snake. Before that fellow could even blink.

"I'll see Sheriff Bullock right now," Clete said. "C'mon, move your ass." He waved the barrel of his gun toward what I guessed was Sheriff Bullock's private office — since that's what was painted on the door in big gold letters.

The fellow stood up, his face angry and red as a brand-new union suit, and he was even taller than I'd guessed. Clete took the man's gun from his holster and it wasn't 'til then that I noticed the deputy badge on the vest of the tall drink of water that my pardner was shoving toward Bullock's door. The deputy knocked once and when he started in, Clete give him a shove that sent him halfway across the room. We walked right in behind him, Clete pointing that big-bore Remington directly into the face of a man wearing a dark-striped suit who sat behind a big desk. I guessed from his look that he would have to be Seth Bullock.

The Sheriff of Deadwood was damn surprised to see someone have the drop on him in his own place, I'll tell you. It was clear he wasn't used to it and even clearer that he didn't like it at all. He was tall and thin, like his deputy, but his face was leaner and hatchety. First thing you noticed when you saw him head-on, though, was the longest, fullest moustache you ever laid eyes on. Seth Bullock's moustache covered his mouth and reached almost to the end of his chin. The tips of it hung down nearly to the points of his stiff white collar.

He had pans and spikes and wooden boxes of bolts and all kinds of hardware spread out on his big oak desk. The drummer sitting in front and to the side of Bullock took one look at Clete's gun, jumped up, and dumped a tray of silvery rings right off his lap onto the wood floor. They clattered and spun away in all directions.

Clete let the last loop roll to a quiver and stop before he spoke. "You're through looking at hardware today, aren't you?" His voice was calm, like he was just talking over a business deal.

Bullock stood up slow, looked at the drummer and nodded toward the door. "I'll see you later, Mr. Lawrence. I'll send Sam here by your hotel room with your wares within the hour."

The salesman appeared damned relieved to be let out of there, but he glanced back at his bag and things. He was a mighty unhappy-looking fellow as he hurried out and closed the door behind him.

Bullock looked Clete over extra careful. "This better be good, Mister, or you'll be sleeping in my jail tonight."

Clete smiled. "Pretty big talk for a man looking down the barrel of my .44," he said, but then uncocked his Remington and holstered it. He took his time sitting down in a leather-covered chair by the door — stretched his legs out and crossed them at the ankles. "Take it easy, Sheriff. This is only a social call, Montana style. I heard you deputied up there awhile so I believe you know what I'm talking about. Matter of fact, an old friend of yours from up that way asked me to look you up and say hello." Clete tossed me the deputy's gun. "Take the cylinder out and give it back to this gentleman. No use boring him with a lot of jawing about mutual friends."

Bullock's eyes narrowed and looked from Clete to me and then at his deputy.

When I give the tall man back his empty gun, he glanced at his boss.

"It's all right, Sam," Bullock said matter-of-fact. "I'll take these men upstairs for a drink and you can return this merchandise to Lawrence." He walked from behind his big oak desk toward some curtains in the corner and moved the heavy drapery aside, showing a fancy carpeted stairway with a carved handrail. "After you, gentlemen," he said, a thin smile on his sharp face. The deputy began banging things into the drummer's bag and Clete walked over toward Bullock.

"You go first, Willie," Clete said. "But I'll ride drag after Mr. Bullock here."

The lean-faced Sheriff of Deadwood chuckled. "I see you're a careful man, Mr., uh . . ."

"Yes I am," Clete told him. "I don't trust everyone wearing a badge, either. And my name's Shannon, Clete Shannon. I'm the sheriff of a little town to the north and east of here, Two Scalp."

Bullock's eyes showed his surprise at that. "I don't know as I've ever heard of it," he said. "And what the hell is a lawman doing breaking into my office at gunpoint?"

"And what the hell is a town sheriff doing posting an armed guard at his door? Keeping everyone out while he spends the afternoon looking at hardware?" Clete asked right back, and then plowed straight ahead. "I needed to see you today. I've been on a man's trail for more'n a week, and I don't intend to wait 'til tomorrow, especially if he's in this town. As I believe he is."

Bullock looked at Clete a little amused. "I have many interests, Mr. Shannon, and each one gets its due. Now then, who are you looking for?"

I started up them stairs about then, since Bullock was still holding the curtain aside and it looked like we still might get that drink he had spoke of. They followed me, Clete coming last, talking about the man we was after. It was pretty dim in the stairway, but once I got to the top, a little light from the west windows lit the room some and a lamp with a ruby shade was already burning on the table in the middle of the room, but nobody was there. The wick was trimmed poor, though, and the smell of kerosene pretty strong.

That was about the fanciest room outside a whorehouse I ever saw. Heavy red drapes on the windows and the tablecloth of the same rich stuff. That room was big, too, and it was nearly filled up with dark, heavy furniture of all kinds — a big desk kind of thing with glassed in book shelves above it, reaching nearly to the tinned ceiling. A fancy little table set between the windows, with big hairy plants and little figurines of angels on it, the whole affair just perfect for spiders to hide in. Sofas and chairs of all description. Two wood pedestals in front of the windows held statues of men's heads, though I didn't reconize who they was of, and a big floor clock ticked out the seconds while I stood watching the brass pendulum swing back and forth.

"Wilson?" I heard Bullock ask when he got to the top of the stairs. "Yes, I've heard of him, but I never met the man." He went straight over and adjusted the lamp 'til the flame stopped fluttering and the smoke cleared away.

Clete stopped at the head of the stairs. "Well, he ran the town before we got there. Ran it at a pretty hefty profit, too, grabbing everybody's land in the bargain." He quit talking and looked around at the fancy place Bullock had for himself there. "Appears you're doing all right, too."

Seth Bullock's squinty eyes narrowed down to just slits. It was plain he didn't like anyone throwing down hints that he run things like Wilson done. "Yes, I'm doing well for myself, Shannon. But I do it honestly. Besides the store, I have a ranch up near Belle Fourche. Next year I'm going to build a sixty-room hotel just down the block. Pretty stupid trying to work both sides of the law, isn't it?"

"That's what a friend of ours from Montana always says. 'One side of the law at a time.' "

"If you're talking about Wilson, I told you I

never knew him," Bullock said, easy and comfortable, though you could see the strain pinching his narrow face. "Have a seat, men," he said, and then went over to a little cupboard and got out a cut glass bottle of whiskey and some fancy glasses to match. He set them on the table with the red cloth on it.

Bullock was about to sit when he seemed to remember something. He walked over to an archway draped in the same red stuff, big tassels hanging down to chase the flies off your hat. "Sarah, would you bring us some water, please?" he called into another room. I guessed he had a servant girl up there.

He come over and poured us each a stiff one and then sat down at the table. Clete sat across from him, but I took one of those cushioned seats by the window so I could look both outside and in. Bullock's deputy Sam was going down the street with the drummer's bag, so I figured no one was about to come bustin' in there and try to throw us out.

"It *was* Wilson you had reference to, wasn't it?" Bullock asked after he took a sip. "Concerning our mutual friend from Montana?"

"Hell, we chased Palmer Wilson out of town before I had a chance to ask him where he hailed from," Clete said. "No, I was talking about old Hank Wormwood from Miles Town. You deputied for him, I understand. Worked for him *before* he was the marshal, too, I believe?"

Bullock kept his voice low, but he sounded excited. "What do you want, Shannon? Money? How much?"

Clete started to shake his head before Bullock even stopped talking. "No, no, it's not like that. I didn't come here to put the squeeze on you. Shit, I'm glad there's at least one lawman in this Territory who's getting rich by doing nothing worse than gouging prices in a store or a hotel."

Bullock looked like he didn't quite believe him.

Clete pushed his hat back. "All I want is what I should have got from you a couple hours ago, your help finding the killer we're chasing. Give us that and we never heard of old long-haired Hank Wormwood and his crew who used to rustle government beef, change the brands, and then sell them back to Uncle Sam for more than he paid for them the first time." Clete kept a straight face for a minute, but then he started laughing.

Bullock was surprised for a second, but then he begun to chuckle and pretty soon he was laughing right along with Clete. "Where'd you ever hear a lie like that?" Bullock asked, laughing and talking together.

Things had got a whole lot more relaxed in that room all of a sudden. You could tell those two men had reached some kind of a understanding.

Clete took a sip of his whiskey. "Straight from the horse's mouth. Hank came to Abilene while I was deputying there for Marshall McKee and

246

him and Wormwood got to swapping yarns about the old days over a bottle. That lazy bastard McKee had spent his share of time in the outlaw trade, too. Hank Wormwood was real proud that one of his boys was doing so well for himself, and he bragged you up good, how you got yourself one of the fattest gold towns in the West." Clete was smiling through all of this, and you could see he wasn't trying to tell Bullock the error of his ways.

"That was a long time ago," Bullock said, still nodding his head. "And I was a lot younger and hell of a lot more foolish in those days."

"Well, hell, who wasn't? But those were wild days right after the War, weren't they? I hate to say it, but I miss them sometimes."

"Goddamned if I do," Bullock said. "Living in the dirt and not knowing who was going to take the next shot at you." They each stopped talking for a while, lost in their memories, I guessed, different as they was. Wasn't uncomfortable, like it is sometimes when men talk and then run out of words. Just quiet. After a minute Bullock looked at Clete real close. "What's the name of this man you're after?"

"It's DuShane, but that's about all we know about him," Clete said.

"Yeah, I know him," Bullock answered. "Mean bastard, enjoys killing. He came here to shoot Hickok, like a lot of men did. Only this one might have done it — beat Hickok, I mean. But he was too late. Jack McCall had put a bullet in

Hickok's back before Whitey got here. Don't know where he is now, though. He cleared out —"

"No, it's not *Whitey* DuShane we're after," Clete said. "I know where *he* is — Two Scalp's bone yard. He came gunning for me last fall, but he didn't get the job done. The man we're after —"

"You shot Whitey DuShane?" Bullock asked, showing surprise and admiration both. "Why was he out for you?"

"Long story," Clete said, waving away the rest of an answer. I guess he didn't want to talk about that mess. "The man we're after is kin to Whitey, but damned if we can figure out how. Some folks we run into tell us he's Whitey's father and others say he's Whitey's brother. Don't know his name — his first name."

Seth Bullock got up and walked over to the window and looked down the street. "Just what I need in Deadwood, another DuShane." I saw then that deputying in this town would be a whole lot different than locking up drunks in Two Scalp.

"I'll be happy to take him off your hands if you help me find him, and I'll save the citizens of Deadwood the expense of a trial and a hanging too."

"Fine, you do that," Bullock said, turning away from the window and toward Clete. "Personally, I don't give a damn how you do it, but the decent people of this town won't stand for another backshooting, even if it's done by a lawman. Gives the town a bad reputation and it's bad enough already. Just make sure he's facing you when you take him."

He caught Clete off guard with that.

"You got no call to be talking that way," I told him straight out. "Clete shot Whitey DuShane in a fair fight. I saw it. Any man who says otherwise is a lying sonofabitch who oughta be gelded."

It was Bullock's turn to be pushed off balance and it was my strong words that done it. I had got to my feet and went over to him, for I ended up talking right into his face. And that's where I was when he looked at me so queer and then started smiling.

Clete chuckled, and I seen that what was so funny to both of them was me. I suppose my face colored up pretty good. I set back down without saying nothing further.

"You've got a loyal deputy there, Mr. Shannon, a rare beast. I doubt many of my men would stand up for me like that. Oh, they'd shoot somebody if I told them to, no questions asked, but . . . I'd value him if I were you."

"Well, I do, mostly," Clete said, looking right at me. "He's got some damn peculiar ideas of how men ought to act, though, especially lawmen, even more especially how they should act towards women. But nobody ever questioned his doing the right —"

I looked around and seen why Clete'd run out

of words so sudden. A tiny woman had come in through the archway carrying a pitcher of water on a silver tray. She walked so slow across the room and her hair was so white, I thought she was an *old* woman for a second. But then you saw how smooth and fair her skin was. She didn't no more than set that silver tray on the table before I seen what a bang-up, well-favored creature she was. Didn't look bleached, either, her hair — the way it was on most women I had already saw in Deadwood — just as blonde as snow. You'd expect a gal as fair as that to have them pale blue eyes you see on Swede girls up Minnesota way, but hers was reddish brown, the color of raw cedarwood. She was young, too. *Couldn't be no older than Mandy*, I said to myself, *maybe even younger.* Maybe I thought her younger than she was.

Seeing us there — me and Clete — her face looked all fluttery and disturbed for just a flicker of a second, 'til she put it back to being empty.

"Thank you, Sarah," Bullock said after she'd set her tray down on the table and stood beside him. Bullock noticed Clete looking her over good and then glanced at me, and I guess he seen I'd been doing about the same thing my pardner still was. Seth Bullock, instead of being mad, though, seemed pleased she interested us so.

She turned to go, but Bullock caught her by the wrist and she stopped, just stood there. She took us each in slow, Clete and me, and then looked down, like she was shutting a door on us in her brain. After that, she kept her eyes glued on that silver tray.

"This is Sarah, gentlemen, my princess," Bullock said, pouring us each a glass of water to go with our whiskey. Reminded me of a man showing off his prize mare. He looked up at her face and then reached behind her and put his hand on the small of her back, but she didn't move when he did it. "She lives here in the castle I built for her and never goes outside. Do you, dear?"

I waited for her to speak, but after a few seconds it was clear she wasn't going to say nothing.

Bullock let his hand slide down her back and it was pretty clear what he was doing there with her, though I couldn't exactly see.

Clete noticed too, and he shifted some in his chair.

"Show the gentlemen your lovely hands, Sarah," Bullock said, and after a time she lifted them from her sides and held them out in front of her, palms down, though her eyes she kept on that silver tray. That girl's hands was something to see, all right, delicate and fine as they was, but I felt uncomfortable looking her parts over, right out in the open like that and she not even paying attention. Some of it was Bullock's way of showing them off, too. Clete glanced at the girl's hands, I saw, but he looked back at Bullock right away. He didn't seem to be enjoying the show no better than me, pretty as it was.

That Sarah girl kept her hands held out in front of her, quivering a little, I noticed, and might of kept them there all night, I had the feeling, if Bullock hadn't of told her she could drop them.

"If you think that's something, look at this." He reached up and unbuttoned the collar of her long blue dress and then worked his way on down the front, unbuttoning those tiny pearl buttons. I couldn't believe what I was seeing, and her standing there so quiet and calm, almost like she was asleep with her eyes open.

"That's far enough," Clete said.

Bullock looked at him real surprised. "Why, I was about to offer you a taste of my choicest —"

"That's enough of that!" Clete yelled, standing up quick and knocking his chair over backwards into the bargain.

Bullock looked froze, his hand still on that girl's buttons. After a minute he smiled and waved her away. She went back through that fancy archway as slow as she come out, fastening herself up as she went. I figured it probably wasn't the first time Bullock'd entertained his guests that way, and it probably wouldn't be the last, either. I just wondered how the show ended. I was just curious, you understand, and I felt about as low as a snake for being so.

"Sit back down, Shannon," Bullock said, that big mustache of his spread out over the lower part of his face, so you couldn't see much what his expression was. "You're making too much out of nothing." He laid his hands flat on the table and waited for my pardner to do as he said.

But Clete just stood there and glared at him.

Chapter Twenty-one

After a minute, Clete pulled out his makings and rolled one, taking his time about it. Then he leaned over the lamp to light up, sucked the smoke in deep, and blew a big tobacco cloud across the table toward Bullock. "I've had about all the entertainment here I have the stomach for. And I've burned all the time I intend to trying to get your help."

Bullock stood up and faced Clete. "Of course, Mr. Shannon. Come downstairs and I'll see what I can do." I wondered how Sheriff Seth Bullock could just forget about that business with that girl Sarah so quick, but he appeared to close his mind on it like a banker slamming shut a big steel vault.

He went to the stairs and we followed him down. At his desk, Bullock pulled a green ledger out of a drawer, flipped the pages 'til he come to the one he wanted and read for a minute. "No, no claim registered under DuShane's name, as I expected. He's no miner — or speculator. This record is pretty accurate," he said, rapping the page with his knuckles, all business. "I could send someone around to check the hotel registrations — this week's. And your man here could read the hotels' books from last week and before, going backwards. A woman who works for me goes around every Friday and collects them. The hotel owners complain like hell because they have to keep two sets, but I just let them. I like to know who's come into my town and who's left." He got a tall stack of bigger books from a cabinet and dropped them on his desk. "These things aren't exactly what you'd call reliable. Some places do pretty well, but others don't keep very good records — even though I threaten to close them down. Still, it's worth a try. I guess you realize how men drift in and out of here. Women too. It's a gold town, you'll recall."

"Yeah, I know," Clete said. "Abilene had a lot of saddle tramps, so I know you can't keep track of everyone."

"Well, most of them I can," Bullock said, and it didn't sound like bragging. "If they stay at a hotel or buy anything, that is." The sheriff put his book away and smiled at Clete. "Have you eaten yet, Mr. Shannon?"

Clete'd looked a little surprised when it appeared Bullock was going to help us, but being asked to dinner was more than he was set for. "If you're buying, I'm eating," he said, sort of testing the water.

"We'll let the Merchant's Association buy your supper," Bullock said, then got his hat from the rack.

He set that hat just so on his head whilst looking in a mirror, such a dandy he was. "I will pay for my own meal, however. The President of the Merchant's Association must set a good example, especially if he has an election coming up." He done a little bow then. "One hand scratches the other, you see? You'll describe the man you're looking for to the merchants and they'll have their clerks keep an eye out for him. Agreed?"

Clete nodded. "Agreed." He looked a long minute at Bullock, rubbing his stubbly, squared-off chin. "I hope you'll excuse me being curious, but how come you changed your mind and decided to help us?"

Bullock looked more pleased with himself than took unawares. "Why, I never decided not to. I thought at first you were trying to blackmail me, but now that I see you're not . . . And I sure as hell don't want another DuShane loose in Deadwood, and neither do the townspeople, the folks who elect me to office." He walked over and opened the door. "Pay attention, Shannon. You might pick up a few pointers on how to run a town like this — at a profit, certainly, but entirely within the law. Shall we go, Sheriff? Supper's not for another half hour, but the drinking generally starts a little earlier. A good time for you to meet the members and tell them about your man."

"All right," Clete said, and then he come over to me. "You have a good time with these hotel books, Willie. I'll be back after we eat and then you can get something. That suit you?"

"Yeah, sure, you go suck oysters with a bunch of bootmakers and habberdashers and let me rustle through these. I'll see what I can find."

They went out the door and I sat at Bullock's big oak desk and looked at all the books lying there. Took me more than two hours to comb back through two weeks of names in the hotel records. Pretty busy town, Deadwood. But DuShane's name was not there. I took the books back over to the cupboard where Bullock'd got them from and found a lot more. Instead of going back any further than two weeks, though, I got the ones from last fall, when Whitey DuShane was here to shoot Hickok, before he come to Two Scalp. And I found something, all right.

Second of October, 1876, last year, somebody who signed the book at a place called the Gem had scribbled a big letter J and then after it a D and S close together. Whoever it was had squiggled lines after them big letters, but it didn't look like any writing I had ever saw. To the right of that chicken scratchin', over in another little square, somebody else had writ the word half. And behind that was wrote $9.50 in clear numbers. Nothing in the space for saying where you was from. Nothing in the room number box, either.

Of course, I figured the name could just as well be that of Whitey DuShane's brother or pa, whichever it was, as that of someone else. Might be, but there was no way I could be sure. Other names in the book had seventeen or sixteen dollars marked down after them, so I thought maybe the one-half was for half rent. Sure enough, six pages earlier, and writ a lot plainer, was Whitey DuShane's name, clear as day. They shared room 12 and took no meals there. On the spot for saying where you hailed from, Whitey DuShane had wrote *Elsewheres*.

I went back and studied a long time on that scratching made by Whitey's kin, the letter J and the wavy lines that followed it, what was supposed to be our man's first name — even got a loupe from Bullock's top desk drawer and looked through that. The longer I looked, the surer I was that the man who'd writ that couldn't read or write — not even his own name. Oh, he knowed his initials all right — them big letters — only the rest of it was pretend writing, such as a kid will do.

When I leaned back in Seth Bullock's stuffed chair, it felt like Stalking Bear was standing across the room watching me, with pleasure in his eyes, like he done the few times I learned something right. The sign wasn't hoofprints in mud, but them ink marks on paper led just as clear to a den DuShane'd holed up in once, one he would likely go back to. And I was on his trail again.

But there was no use tryin' to puzzle out what was never wrote there. I propped my feet up on Bullock's polished oak desk and pulled my hat down over my eyes.

I was just starting to get comfortable when a pair of sheriffs come in the door.

"Damn, Willie, I never saw you sleeping on

the job before," Clete yelled at me, coming over to the desk. "You practicing up being the rich sheriff of a gold town sitting there?" He had some liquor in him. The words spilling out of his mouth wasn't exactly wobbly, but they had the sharp edges wore off them, all right.

"I'm not asleep," I told him. "Just restin' my eyes after finding what I found. Look here." I showed him the names and explained what I put together.

Bullock come behind us and had a look too. "The Gem is where he stayed, huh? I might have guessed that." Bullock looked me up and down then. "That's mighty good work, Deputy. What did you say your name was?"

I told him.

He nodded his head, picked up one of the hotel books and then walked over close to the cupboard where he kept them. He waited a minute and then motioned me over to join him. I thought he was going to have me look at something else over there, but instead he spoke low so Clete, who was still bent over them names, couldn't hear. "I could use a man of your talents, Mr. Goodwin, and the pay is $125 a month. Probably a lot better than you're making up in Two Strike. I could get you a free room, too, and most of your meals."

"Two *Scalp*," I corrected him. I looked over at Clete, but I guess he had drunk a little too much to be paying attention good. "And no thanks, all the same. Deputying is just something I'm doin'

259

for now. I'd have myself shot in a week if I followed the peacekeeping trade in this town. Besides, me and Clete has other plans. Least we did have."

Bullock smiled and patted me on the back. "I understand. Don't want to leave your friend out on a limb, right?"

I didn't know what to say to that.

"Well, I didn't expect you'd be interested, but it was worth a try. Damn hard finding good men these days." Bullock walked back to Clete and looked over his shoulder. "If he's in town now, it's likely he'll go to the Gem again, Shannon. I think you and I ought to walk down there and see Mr. Al Swearington, the current owner and whore master of that establishment."

Bullock sounded pretty uppity when he said that last, but I didn't understand how he could see himself any different than the man he was talking about, only on a smaller scale. Didn't seem to strike him that way, though, for he set his hat back on, using his mirror again, and started for the door like he was on an errand of justice.

"DuShane bunked at a dove cage?" Clete ask.

"Well, it's a hotel, a saloon and a whorehouse all rolled into one," Bullock said, turning back and waiting for Clete. "They have stage acts and other sorts of shows too. Something to suit every vice and human depravity — so I hear tell. So long as no one complains or gets killed, I let them alone."

I stood up and followed them out. Sam, Bullock's deputy, was in the outside of lice, and after he give Clete a hard look, he listened close to what Bullock wanted him to do — to check all the new hotel registration books in town except the one at the Gem. Him and Clete would do that themselves.

It was clear dark by then, but the street was lit up from the windows of all the buildings along it.

I walked beside Clete, told him where our hotel was and give him his key. "While you and Bullock are talking to the man at the whorehouse, I got someone to see myself. Some gal I met today is asking folks she knows about DuShane. I paid her to."

"Yeah, you probably paid her all right, but not to tell you about DuShane, I'll bet," Clete said, a big sloppy grin on his face.

Bullock laughed on that.

"That's not how it is," I told them. "But if the chance for it knocks on the door, I'll be standing there ready to open 'er up wide."

Clete laughed too. "By God, I believe you will be, Willie."

Deadwood had got pretty noisy again, lots of miners in the street hoo-rayin' and singin'. A fat man was sharing a bottle with a couple of his friends, but he put it away when he seen the sheriff come swaggering down the walkway with a couple of mean-looking hombres in tow — meanin' Clete and me. A man wearing a big white apron standing outside a place to eat, he collared Bullock. Clete and me stood in the street and waited for him.

The smells coming out the door made me hungrier than a bear in spring. "Pretty important fellah, this Sheriff Seth Bullock. Quite a man," I observed.

"Yeah, if you don't take into consideration how he likes to pass around his upstairs woman. Probably watches her doing it, too. But from another room, I'd guess."

"I don't know nothing about them things," I told him. "I do know that he offered me a job not more than ten minutes ago — deputy job, I reckon."

Clete looked up at me pretty taken back, then over at Bullock. "Why, that sneaky sonofabitch!" Then he laughed again and turned to me. "Well, are you going to take it?"

I couldn't believe he ask me that. "Why, of *course* I'm going to take it! Hell, next year I'll probably run for mayor of this place."

After a time he turned and said, "You might be better off, my friend." I seen then that he was just looking out for me. "I'd appreciate it if you wouldn't quit me 'til after we get DuShane. You've a better head for this tracking business than I do. I doubt I'd have got this far on my own."

That damn Clete! Why, he could insult a man half crazy one minute and flatter him red-faced the next and never know he done neither.

"Last I heard," I told him, "we was heading

for Texas after locking this DuShane up. Maybe hang around Two Scalp 'til they hang him and then head south. Maybe your being spoke for changes that, I don't know."

Clete shook his head. "I don't know what to say, Willie. One day I'm going to marry her and the next day I just want to take off. Hell, it'd be hot in Texas right now."

"Yeah, and it would be pretty hot in Two Scalp, too, if you was to tell Mary you wasn't marrying her."

Clete shook his head some more.

After a while Bullock come over to us. "Some people can't take a shit without asking me how to," he said. "Are we ready to go, gentlemen?"

"You two go on. I'm going in this here cafe and eat," I said. "And then I'll go talk to that woman at that Red Bird place. After that, I'm turnin' in. Not much sleep last night and I'm about wore down to the nubs."

They went on down the street and I stepped inside and then sat at a little table by myself. I ask the gal for the biggest beefsteak they had and it wasn't long 'til she brought it, overlapping the plate all around, a big mountain of mashed potatoes piled on top of it and everything covered over with gravy.

DuShane stood at the bar in a noisy crowd of miners and whores, sipping his fourth whiskey. He didn't usually like feeling drunk, but tonight he was letting himself go a little. For weeks that goddamn sheriff had been after him, but now DuShane knew he had slipped him. No matter how good a tracker he was, and he was back-home good, DuShane was certain no one could follow him all the way up the Deadwood road. True, he hadn't shot the man who'd killed Whitey, but he was out of danger now, at least. Maybe later he could figure a way to take care of that bastard Shannon.

Towns always sickened him after a while, but tonight it felt good to be where men were getting falling-down, vomiting drunk and women were plying their trade, though none had come up to him as yet. He had been trying to catch the eye of the youngest, smallest whore in the place, but the perky little brunette was already getting more attention than she knew what to do with. She reminded him of his cousin Rachel, and he had always wanted a go-around with her back when he was a sapling.

He had lifted his glass high to drain it when he looked across the room and froze.

He reconized Seth Bullock right away and almost as quickly saw that the tall man with him was Clete Shannon. DuShane stood rigid as a corpse as the two lawmen approached the bar and then spoke to the man behind it. Slowly, he put his glass down and lowered his head, pulling his hat down further over his face. He glanced up and saw that Shannon was looking over everyone in the place, and DuShane knew who he was looking for. Bullock told the barman to go get Al.

DuShane thought about drawing his gun and killing them both where they stood. He might get

Shannon, but then there'd be Bullock. Instead, he turned slow and walked toward the back door. The fear grew big as a mountain as soon as he turned his back. Every second he expected to hear the blast of a heavy handgun and feel the lead ball tear into his spine. But he fought himself to keep from running 'til he was through the door, and then he gimped up the alley as fast as his long, lean legs would carry him, his gun slapping against his thigh.

When he got to a narrow cross street, he turned and looked back, his big Army Colt shaking in his left hand. Nobody had come after him. If Al was going to tell on him, they'd be on him by now. Slowly he went back down the alley and when he got to the Gem, opened the back door just a crack so he could look in. Al was still talking with Bullock and Shannon and it sounded like an argument. DuShane drew his gun and had the barrel through the crack before he changed his mind. He holstered it and went around the side of the building to the front and then walked quickly across the street. He sat on a bench outside the undertaker's, beside two loafers, and waited for Shannon to come out of the Gem.

He'd follow his man, get him alone, and take him when he didn't expect it.

That beefsteak was all I had room for, but I eat a big wedge of apple pie anyway.

When I stepped back outside, everything seemed a lot friendlier than when I had went in. The Red Bird wasn't but a block on down the street. Still a big crowd in there, but I didn't see

Bessie nowheres. The barman come and poured me a rye and I ask him if he'd seen the lady I was looking for. He told me she'd gone out with a customer a little while ago and would probably be back soon. He kept pointing out other gals I might like and couldn't get it through his head that none but Bessie would do. Ten minutes later she come struttin' in, looked around and saw me, and after poking her head toward the door, stepped back outside. I killed the rest of my rye and followed her.

She was off down the sidewalk a piece, standing in the shadows and looking nervous as a long-tailed cat in a room full of rocking chairs.

"You coulda got me killed, you sonofabitch," she said, first words out of her mouth when I come up. "Seeing as who he is and what he's done, I figure you owe me five dollars more for what I found out."

"The way I see it, I already paid," I told her.

"Goddamn you," she said, real pissed off, but after a minute and me not saying anything she calmed down. "All right, he's in Deadwood. Got back yesterday, he was here before. You stay away from this bastard if you know what's good for you, though I doubt you do. He'd sooner slit somebody's throat than fuck, and I'm not messin' in this anymore, I mean it. I don't know where he is right now and I ain't askin' around no more, either, not for all the gold in these Hills."

"Did you get his name, his first name?" I ask.

She looked kinda sideways at me. "I sure did, Sugar, but it'll cost you that other five to find *that* out." She cocked her big hip out to the side, waiting on me to come across.

I fished in my pocket and pulled out my pouch. "This better be right," I told her, handing her the coin.

"Oh, it's right, all right," she said, popping my half eagle into her bag like she done with the one that afternoon. "His name's Jezrael. Jezrael DuShane, and he's one of the meanest sonsabitches you're likely to run into. And don't go calling him Jez or Jess when you catch up to him, either. A friend of mine made that mistake last year, and he cut her face up so bad she hadda get out of the trade and get married. Now I want nothing more to do with either him *or* you," she said. "Unless, of course, you'd like a quick —" She stopped and looked up and down the street.

After a bit she shook her head. "No, I better not," she said. "You're likely to get shot and if I'm with you, I might too. No, I'm going back inside the Bird. And don't you follow me, neither. Nothin' personal, but I don't want to see your face again. And don't go saying who told you about him." She turned on her pretty heel and went back inside.

I just stood there a minute and collected my thoughts. I considered finding that Gem place that Clete and Bullock had went to, but figured they'd probably left there by then. After a time I walked on down the street, just taking in the sights and listening to all the music spilling out of the different saloons. Most of it piano music, but I could hear a banjo twanging away and somewheres else a guitar and a gal singing along with it in a high, sweet voice. It struck me I remembered that song from somewheres. I walked across the street to see where that singing was coming from and right then, even before I stepped inside and saw her up on a little stage they had there, I knowed who it was.

Mandy was all slicked out in a shiny-bright yeller dress with black lace on it, a little yeller hat to match, playing that beat-up old guitar of hers and singing one of them songs she had sung me as we rode double along the Bad.

Chapter Twenty-two

Mandy didn't see me, of course. There was fifty or sixty people, men mostly, listening to her, but some was laughing and talking to women. Lots *was* listening, though, for her voice was sweet as an angel's, and her face, even if some might of thought it too dark, was still the closest I seen to an angel's since I saw her last. You couldn't tell how tall a woman she was, either, for she was sitting on a stool so she could get at her guitar good. Beside her, on a gangly three-legged affair, was a sign with her name painted on it, only they'd spelled it wrong. Her last name they spelled B-o-u-d-o-i-r. I wasn't exactly sure of what the *right* spelling was, but at least I knowed there wasn't no *R* at the end of it. It surprised me she didn't get it fixed.

I sat down in the back and wondered what'd happened to her that night in them Badlands, when it'd started to pour and her just gone and me not able to find her for anything. I listened and thought on that and watched, such a sight she was.

She was looking at the crowd there, singing right to the folks who was paying the most attention to her and after awhile her big dark eyes come on to me. She didn't seem to see who I was at first, though she was looking right at me. The smile on her face slipped a little then and after a few seconds it got even prettier than it was before. She stumbled over the smallest part in her song and for a time she sang without thinking the words, you could tell — just beaming at me from up there on that little stage. My, she was a picture.

She finished her music on a long high note, clear as a hermit thrush, and then the crowd clapped and hollered and stamped their feet, but all the while she looked just at me.

After a minute she raised her hand and they quieted down. "This next song I sing for a good friend of mine who has just come in, Mr. William Goodwin." She nodded at me and everyone turned to gawk. Most was surprised at what they saw when they seen me, from the looks on their kissers.

Mandy began on that rooster song she taught me while we rode double along the river. The first verse she done in American, but for the rest, the parts that was a little bawdy, she sung it in French. Made me remember real clear how nice it was sittin' at the table eating supper with her back at her folks' soddy out on the prairie. And then I remembered the night we had later on down the trail, under all them stars. I guess my face reddened at that and I wondered if she could tell what I was thinking. From time to time some of the men there turned in their seats in order to take me in — most just curious, I guess, but many looked madder than hornets at me, so it seemed like. Damned if I knowed why. I paid 'em little mind and just enjoyed my song and my remembering. When Mandy finished, the clapping wasn't so loud as before, but it was still pretty strong. She put aside her guitar and come down the steps to where the tables was and then straight back towards me.

"Willie!" she called out when she got near. "I have been so worried over you."

"You? Why I was —"

I had stood up and she flung her arms about me and give me a big kiss — right there with everyone watchin'. That whole crowd laughed and cheered and hollered and whistled and made such a ruckus! Mandy turned me loose and hauled me toward the doorway to the bar, where it was a lot quieter and not nearly so full.

"I am so glad to see you, Willie," she said, standing close. "So many times I wondered what had become of you."

"*You* wondered? Why, I searched way into the night to find you. I come back, like I said I would, but you was gone."

She dropped her eyes and looked real mournful, her dark lashes fluttering. "I am sorry, Willie. Truly I am. When you did not come back for so long and the shooting stopped, I thought the killer —" She left off talking of a sudden and looked at me square. "He is here! Here in Deadwood, the man we chased for so far. He was here at the Green Front only last night!"

"Yeah, I already heard he made it to Deadwood. Did he reconize you, do you figger? When he was here last night?"

Mandy shook her head and all that ringy hair of hers jumped around on her shoulders. "No, I don't think so. I was singing, and he looked at my body, like all the men do, but I do not think he remembered me. And he left before I finished. I believe he was looking for someone, because he paid more attention to the men who were here than he did to me."

"Well, that's good. He don't reconize you then." Still, I looked around the bar some, feeling pretty rattlebrained for not doing so before. Then I took Mandy's arm and we stepped back into the room where she'd done her singing. I checked over everone pretty good, and even though I didn't know his face, I doubted that anyone I seen in there was him.

While I was looking that crowd over, a fellow in a checkered suit come out from behind the curtain, spotted Mandy, and charged down the steps and through the crowd. He was mostly bald, but what hair he had, a fringe around his ears and in back, was the same reddish brown color as his thin little moustache. And mad? That fellow was mad from the top of his bald head to the tips of his fingers, huffing and puffing his way toward us.

Mandy leaned close and whispered. "Jacobson, the owner here. I should go back now because —"

By that time he was up to us. "What the hell

are you doing out here socializing with the customers?" he asked Mandy in a loud, sharp voice,
his hands on his hips. Then he barged right
ahead before she could answer. "I pay you to
sing. Not to try and fuck every goddamn
sonabitch with a cock between his legs and a
dollar in his pocket. Now get —"

"Just you hold on there," I told him. "You
might own this here bar but you can't talk to this
lady like that and not get your nose busted."

He looked at me like I just stepped off the
moon. "What did you say to me?"

"You heard me right. You clean up your
mouth, talking to her, or I'll clean it up for you."

He inspected me good, his hands coming off
his hips and making fists at his sides. "Maybe
you don't know who I am, you God-damn idiot,
but I'm gonna have my man beat the shit out of
you. And then maybe you'll remember me the
next time you think about sticking your nose in
my business." He looked toward the door, for
his bouncer I reckoned, but the big fellow there
was jawing with a miner and didn't see Jacobson
waving his arm.

"Whyn't you have a try at doin' it yourself?" I
ask him.

"Willie, leave now!" Mandy said. "I will finish
singing and everything will be all right. Go on!"
She give me a little push and looked awful worried, but I was not going to back away from this
Jacobson fellow, or his hired tough, who seen his
boss by then and was headed our way in a hurry.

A big, bearded, beefy pile of stones he was. Arms like hairy hams and legs the girth of tree trunks.

Jacobson turned and squinted. "We'll see whose nose gets busted now, you sonabitch."

A fellow I didn't notice before, wearing a low-crowned black hat and a black striped coat, took a quick step up close to Jacobson and pushed a snake-eyes derringer into the bar owner's paunch. "Can't this be settled more peaceably, Jacobson?" he asked real low.

Jacobson looked at the stranger's round, smooth face and then down at the weapon shoved into his belly and then back into the man's dark eyes. I looked too, and the derringer fellow had no look on his face at all. He was watching real close to see what would happen next, but there was neither fear nor anger writ on his smooth, even features.

Jacobson got even madder. "Why — why —" He kept sputtering like that, his eyes near to popping out, 'til the bouncer got over near us.

"Bettah tell your man to leave us alone or your funeral will be tomorrah," the fellow said, slow and even as anything.

Jacobson didn't say nothing, so flustered and mad he was, but he waved the bouncer away and stared at the man holding the snake-eyes to his gut.

"That's bettah," the stranger said after a minute. "Now let's just forget about this, shall we? Mandy will go change her dress for her next songs and we'll pretend you're a gentleman."

The even-featured man took a step back from Jacobson and put his little gun back in his vest pocket.

"She's fired!" Jacobson said. "And you get the hell out of my place and don't come back, you bottom-dealing bastard!"

The stranger smiled at Jacobson, but it wasn't what you'd call friendly. "Very well. Several others have already approached us about Mandy singing in their saloons." He turned toward her and his smile changed into a real one. "Come on, Mandy honey, you're about to step up some in the world. I'll send someone back heah later to get your things." He winked at her and she smiled back. Right away I saw there was something between them and I begun to feel tired and heavy in my arms and legs.

"That's a goddamn lie!" Jacobson snarled. "Who'd want her pissy-assed singing in their place? Hell, that nigger bitch doesn't even know any good songs, no dirty ones at all."

I felt bad for Mandy that he would say that with her standing there, about her color, but she didn't seem bothered by it. I guess it wasn't the first time she'd heard that word flung at her. She held her head high and looked like she was enjoying seeing that saloon man brought down a few pegs.

The stranger turned slow back toward Jacobson and eyed him flat. When he spoke his voice was calm and smooth. "If you were even half a man, I'd shoot you for that, but you're not worth the trouble — to her or to me."

That saloonkeeper must of seen then how close he come to dying, for fear flickered bright in his eyes. And being afraid for his life like that galled him worse than before.

"You get out of my place, all three of you!" Jacobson yelled, and the whole room got quiet. I don't think many people'd saw Mandy's friend pull his little snake-eyed pea shooter, or they'd of cleared out already. Jacobson turned and stomped off. Mandy and me and her new fellow headed toward the door. Going out I tipped my hat to the big man, but he just followed us with his eyes.

Outside, I drew a deep breath and tasted the sweet spring air. Mandy put her arms through each of ours and we walked up the street three wide. "This is Justin Thebideaux, Willie," she said real sugary.

"Pleased to meet you," I said to him.

"And this is Willie Goodwin, Justin. The man I told you about who helped me."

He looked over my way and smiled one of his good ones. "I am honored, Mr. Goodwin," he said. "I wish to thank you for the assistance you gave Mandy in crossing the flatlands."

I tipped my hat to him, just like I done to the bouncer — though Thebideaux didn't seem to take notice, and I wondered then if he knowed all the different kinds of *assistance* I give her traveling across that prairie.

"I saw that you came to Mandy's defense this

276

evening, before I had the opportunity to do so. For which I am also grateful." He was a fancy-talking fellow like that, and he said his words deep and slow — even when he wasn't threatening a man's life — in a way that sounded a little like how Mandy spoke hers.

"No trouble," I said. "Just so long as you're looking out for her now."

He threw back his head and laughed, which surprised me some. "Yes, indeed, Mr. Goodwin, I will take good care of her from now on. But she is her own woman, nonetheless, you understand."

Well, I had never heard no one say *nonetheless* like that, right out loud. The truth was I didn't understand — whatever it was he thought I understood, that is. I didn't want to seem stupid by saying so, so I just left it float.

"It was Justin who found me when I was lost," Mandy explained. "I was cold and wet and he got us a place to stay. Then we came here. And after I heard the women singing in the saloons, I wanted to sing in them too. Justin, he got that for me as well, and now we go to a better place, eh Justin?" She seemed cheerful and not at all scared, like she was when I rode off to help Clete.

"Yes, indeed we do, Chere," he said, mixing a chuckle in with his words. He was a smooth one, all right, in both the easy way he spoke and the way he looked. I could see how Mandy might like him.

"Soon we will go to Louisiana, Willie," she said, squeezing my arm and sounding as happy as a schoolgirl with a new dress. "Isn't that wonderful? Justin lived there and he says I will be the toast of New Orleans with my singing. Isn't that so, Justin?"

"Yes, it is," he said, nodding his head.

We had gone up the street a good piece and before long we come to the Grand Central. "This is where I'm staying," I told them. "And I'm ready to turn in for the night."

"Oh, no, Willie!" Mandy pleaded. "I have only just found you."

"Won't you have a drink with us?" Justin ask.

"Thank you, no," I told them. "I was in the saddle all last night and when I get sleepy —"

"Yes, I remember," Mandy said, cocking her head and smiling at me. "Get your sleep then, Willie, and we will see you another time, no?"

"Sure you will," I told them both. I said goodbye to Thebideaux and he shook my hand, thanking me again for helping Mandy — as if I had did it for him. Mandy give me a peck on the cheek and afterwards took her new fellow's arm again. I watched them walk on up the street and then I climbed the stairs to my room, unlocked it, lit the lantern and took off my boots. The hotel man had piled all our stuff on the floor in a big heap, but I decided straightening it out would have to wait 'til morning. The bed was comfortable, but I didn't feel so sleepy as I did before, though I was plenty weary.

I laid on top of the covers with my clothes on and thought about Mandy. It would not be right if I said I didn't envy that Justin fellow she was with a little — maybe even a bucketful. I seen it in myself the minute he looked at her, back at that place she was singing in, and it didn't help none at all that he was friendly and polite to me, treating me like his uncle or something.

But at the same time I seen that she was better off with him. He was more her age and more her background, too. More important, he'd saved her when I went and left her to go help Clete out of a jam . . . just left her out there on her own with night coming down in them Badlands. Truth was, I'd lost her and he'd found her. And then kept her — safer than I ever could. To top it off, he knowed how to find places for her to do her singing in. Lot more than I could do.

Still, as right as it was she should be with him instead of me, I could no more get her face out of my mind than I could sprout wings and fly back to Texas.

Jezrael DuShane sat on a bench across the street from the Gem and waited for his man to come out. The two drunks argued over whose turn it was to buy their next bottle.

"Make tracks!" he snarled.

They turned to him, ready to fight, then glanced at each other and quickly moved off down the street. The bigger one slowed and looked back over his shoulder like a dog in flight to see who it was who had chased him away, but when he saw the tall man in the high peaked hat slide his hand down his pants leg toward his gun, he scurried after his companion.

As the drunks turned a corner, Jezrael DuShane let out a high, squeaky laugh and crossed his long legs. After a minute he planted a sharp elbow on his thigh, cupped his pointy chin in his hand, and made his plans. He decided that if Shannon was alone when he came out, he'd shoot him then and there and be shut of this. But Clete Shannon was right behind Bullock when they stepped out of Swearington's place. DuShane waited 'til they had gone up the street nearly half a block before he rose like a dark ghost and followed them up the street.

I guess I did fall asleep after a while, maybe half asleep and half awake is a better way to put it. For I dreamed of my father a spell, and I hadn't done that in years. A real strange dream it was, for I could see him so clear . . . him sittin' in his chair beside the big green parlor lamp we had back home. And reading a book, probably one of Mr. Cooper's, his favorite, like he liked to do after his chores was done. He was enjoying what he was reading, too, my father, for he chuckled and tapped the page with his finger on the real good ones. I probably wouldn't be trying to tell this today — to explain about Clete and me and Mandy and me — if it hadn't of been for my father reading all his spare minutes away and getting me to do some of the same when I was a boy.

The sound of my father tapping his book changed in that dream and pretty soon it woke me up, for someone was rapping on my door, soft and gentle. It confused me a minute, but then I got up to answer it.

I grabbed my .36 out of its holster before I unlocked the door and opened it a crack. There stood Mandy, pretty as a canary bird.

"Do you mean to shoot me, Willie?" she asked, standing there in the dim hallway. She was giggling while she said it, so I seen it was just a joke.

"What is it?" I ask her. "Did you see DuShane?"

"No, I just wanted to see you again. Can I come inside?"

"Course you can," I told her, opening the door wide and then laying my .36 on the little table. I fussed with the lamp to make it brighter. "Where's your man, Justin what's-his-name." I knowed his name, all right, remembered it good, but for some reason I wanted to pretend I didn't.

"He talks to the man at the saloon where I will sing tomorrow night," she said, coming into the room and looking things over. "Getting me more money than I made before. But he is not my man — not my lover."

I looked her in the eyes after she said that, but I could think of nothing to say.

She sat and bounced on my bed a time or two. "Oh, he is my lover, I guess most people would say. But not the way you mean. We are just friends, really." Her dark eyes watched my face to see the effect of her words.

"Pretty tight friends, it looks like."

She nodded, keeping her eyes on me. "Yes, we are good friends, Justin and me. Good friends like you and I were when we rode your horse together, do you remember?"

"Not likely I'll ever forget that," I said.

She laughed deep in her throat and then stood up, untied her hat and tossed it on the bed. Then she kicked off her shoes, come over to me and put her arms around my neck. "I *could* have two friends at the same time. You do care for me, don't you, Willie?"

"Yes I do. Of course I do." Seemed strange to be saying that to her after she so much as told me she was sleeping with someone else now, let alone her being young enough to be my niece. "But I got no right to feel that way towards you. Never did." I put my arms around her middle, but we stayed a little distance apart.

"Right? What do you mean, *right?*" she ask. I thought for a minute it was another of her jokes, but the way she set a little line on her forehead, between her eyes too, I seen she really didn't know. "What right do you need to love me, Willie?"

I thought on it for a minute, but I could see no better way to tell her exactly what I meant, but I tried anyway. "Maybe another way to say it is that it wouldn't be right for me to love you."

"I cannot understand that," she said, laying

her head on my shoulder.

The perfume in her hair made me think of lilacs and I held her close. "I'm surprised the man downstairs told you my room number, let you come up here. This don't seem like that kind of a place."

"Oh, he knows me," Mandy said. "He comes to hear me sing. He knows I am not a whore." She moved her body a little against me, so as not to let me forget she was there.

As if I could.

I didn't know what to say then, so I just held her close. It was quiet in that hotel.

She yawned against my neck and then giggled for doing so, even though it didn't seem to me like a real yawn. "I believe I am sleepy too, Willie. Are you going to take me to bed?"

It stunned me she would say that, especially after I'd just explained things to her. I studied on how to make it plain why we couldn't do this while I unbuttoned her fancy yeller dress and she was taking off my shirt.

Chapter Twenty-three

Jezrael DuShane stood in the shadows across the street from Bullock's office and waited. After a while he stole to the rear of the building, trying to see inside. Bullock was a careful man, DuShane reasoned after he had circled the place twice: all the windows were draped.

When he reached the front of the building a second time, Jezrael crossed the street again and leaned beside the doorway to a saloon, more in line with Bullock's entrance than he had been before. Once, at an upstairs window, someone moved the drapery. Though the light had flickered for only a second on the heavy red velvet, DuShane stood rigidly erect, his steely gray eyes fastened to that window.

He was still watching it nearly an hour later when the saloon closed and the men piled out, laughing and talking loudly as they passed him. When the man he guessed was the owner or the bartender came out and started to lock the door behind him, DuShane grudgingly moved off a dozen yards. As the street grew quiet again, he sidled back and stood in the shadows once more, his left hand nervously fingering his holstered pistol.

He was beginning to think that Shannon was going to spend the night in there when the front door opened with a creak and his man came out, lantern light silhouetting him in the door frame. DuShane quickly drew his pistol and aimed, but Shannon stepped out of the light and the Sheriff of Deadwood walked right into the notch of his sights. DuShane's anger flared bright and he almost shot Bullock for meddling in his business.

The two lawmen walked down the other side of the darkened street, a little unsteadily, it seemed to the watchful man in the high peaked hat, and he followed them on his side at a safe distance.

Mandy lay close against me, warm and sweet-smelling. I thought for a minute she'd gone to sleep, so slow and regular her breathing was.

"What it is, Willie?" she ask.

"Just thinking on you, girl. How you ain't like nobody else I ever knew."

She kissed me on the neck and then squeezed me tighter with her legs. We was just getting back to what we had started when I heard footsteps in the hall. Of course I knowed right away it was Clete, and just as soon it struck me that he'd be coming in here to sleep. Don't know why I didn't think of that before then, but I didn't.

I heard his key scratching for the lock and I almost had my pants pulled up when he opened the door and stuck his head in and looked around. The lantern was lit and he had a pretty good view of what was going on, but it seemed he didn't understand what he saw for a pretty long minute, looking at me and then seeing Mandy. He still had his hand on the knob when he backed out, though he didn't pull the door closed the whole way.

"Willie?" he said in the hallway.

"Yeah, this is the right room." I glanced at Mandy and she was sitting up with the covers pulled high. "What'll I do?" I asked her.

She seemed pretty amused. "Tell him to come in. It's not the first time he . . . found us like this."

"You're right, it's not. Only he's going to start thinking we got poor imaginations and can't think of nothing else to do with ourselves, is all," I told her.

She laughed loud at that. "Come in, Mr. Shannon!" she called to Clete.

Well, the door swung open, but he didn't step inside right away. The look on his face said he wasn't sure it was her, and then he was sure, and then he wasn't. Finally, he was. He was also drunker than he was earlier, not that he showed it that much.

"Evening, Miss Mandy," Clete said, tipping his hat as he come in the room, wobbling some on his boot heels. "Nice to see you again, though I'm damn surprised to. What — ?" Then he turned to me, his face a blank. "I thought you'd be asleep, Willie. I didn't mean to sneak up on you." He let out a big yawn after he said that.

"Oh, we heard you coming." I looked at Mandy and she smiled at me and then at Clete. It was a awkward, quiet minute. "Guess Mandy and me will get another room so you can get your sleep," I told Clete. "Looks like you need it."

"Yes, I surely do," he said, and then yawned again. "But I'll get the other room. You two just go back to —" He stopped and shook his head. "I mean . . . aw, hell, you know what I mean."

Clete looked kind of stupid, Mandy giggled, which didn't help at all, and I just sort of stood there with my nose hanging on my face.

"I'll see you tomorrow, you old fart," Clete said, taking his saddle bags off the heap on the floor and then heading toward the door. "Bullock and I are going out in the Hills in the morning. He thinks —" Clete waved off the rest of whatever he was going to say. "Never mind. I'll tell you about it after I get up. G'night, you two."

He was part way down the hall by the time Mandy called goodnight after him. I heard him stumble down the stairs and then ring the bell down at the desk to wake up the night man. Mandy flung back the covers by way of inviting me to join her there and I could see no good reason why not to. I got back into bed and after a few minutes I heard Clete come back up, go into the room beside us and flop down loud on the bed.

Mandy and me picked up close to where we left off and it didn't take long to get far beyond that. Somewhere about then I heard Clete laughing over in his room, and of a sudden I knowed what he found so funny. It was me he'd told to pick a hotel where he wouldn't be kept awake by a bunch of yahoos thumping around in their beds, and now here it was me keeping him from his sleep by being the one doing the thumping.

287

Of course Mandy wanted to know what Clete was laughing at, and after I said what it was, she started laughing too. And I guess Clete must of heard her and figured out that I'd told her, and then he started laughing all the harder. Naturally, with the two of them going on like that, I couldn't keep but from joining in too.

About that time some deep-voiced fellow down the hall hollered out to *Shut the hell up!* and that made it all the worse. Trying to keep that laughter inside made it want to come out all the more, and pretty soon the whole floor was awake and either yelling or laughing, though we three was the only ones who saw anything funny about it.

Took a while for that ruckus to end, I'll tell you, but after a time I heard Clete doing that deep loud snore of his. Mandy didn't seem sleepy at all, and I knowed I wasn't, late as it was and as long as it'd been since I'd slept. At one point I was aware of the lamp flame fluttering, running out of oil. But I wasn't at all interested in getting up and blowing it out, even though it was smelling up the room pretty bad. Neither was Mandy, and finally it sputtered out.

Once, while we was taking a little breather, I heard someone in the hall, moving slow and walking soft. At first I figured it was Clete, maybe having to go piss or throw up from all the whiskey he'd drunk or something. I didn't know why I had thought it was him, after I thought it over, for it sure didn't seem like his walk. Maybe

I was paying more attention to other things. Anyhow, I sat up in bed and, dim as it was, I saw the knob turn, first one way and then the other. Well, I had locked that door after Clete'd left, so I knowed no one was going to walk in on us again. And I also knowed for certain right then that whoever was turning that knob surely wasn't Clete.

I slid out of bed and grabbed my .36, but by the time I got the door open, he'd skedaddled. Oddest part is I didn't even hear him go. Since I didn't have my pants on, or nothing else neither, I give up the idea of chasing whoever'd tried to get in.

"Who was it?" Mandy ask.

"Probably just some drunk got the wrong room," I told her, but I didn't believe that, not entirely I didn't. I felt pretty bashful standing there in the open doorway in the altogether, so I closed and locked the door again.

It was not so dark in the room as it was before, I noticed then. Our windows faced the east, and I was surprised to see a pretty healthy red glow climbing above the ridge out that way. Mandy got up and come over to the table, after I put my gun down, bare naked as me, only she seemed nakeder, strange as that seems. She took my hand and laid it gentle on her breast. Mandy looked right into the center of me, her clear brown eyes awful bright and dead-level with mine.

"What is it?" I asked.

Her face, in that soft and rosy morning light, was about the prettiest thing I'd ever saw. "This is the way I want to remember you, Willie, remember us together. Standing here like this and your hand on me here."

"That sounds a lot like a goodbye," I told her.

"Yes, it is. I don't want to be here when people wake up."

I touched that black curly hair of hers with my other hand and expected it to be crackly with sparks, like when you pet a cat in the winter, so glossy and wiry it looked. Instead, it was soft as a beaver pelt. "Sounded like a more permanent goodbye than that."

She shook her head the least little bit and dropped her eyes. "I don't know, Willie. I hope it is not. But we had no goodbye at all the last time, and I thought . . ." She didn't finish her words, but instead put her head on my shoulder and then, after taking herself a deep breath and letting it out in a long sigh, turned and started gathering up her underthings. Funny, but she seemed a little angry about something. Not much, but she frowned and fussed, though when she saw me looking at her she smiled.

I got back into bed and watched her dress herself the rest of the way. Mandy looked to me that early morning like a statue that'd come alive and decided to clothe herself, so smooth her skin was, like a fine brown marble, and so graceful she moved, the way a well-bred young filly does after she really learns how to run good. Considering all that love we had done, you'd a thought I'd of had enough of the smell and sight of her, but I didn't. Must be how some men feel about whiskey, I remember thinking, like they just can't get enough no matter how much they get.

After she pulled her shawl over her shoulders, she come over and sat on the edge of the bed and stroked my hair and then my cheek. "I must go now," she said real low. "Goodbye, Willie."

"You're going over to that Justin fellow's room and crawl into bed with him now, ain't you?" I ask.

"Please, Willie, do not spoil it."

I felt the fool for acting jealous like that, and jealous was what it was, plain and clear. "I don't want to lose you again, gal," I told her. "And I don't mean just the bedding down together, either, though . . . well, you know how I feel about that by now, I reckon. No, the way I feel about you is a whole —"

"Don't, Willie, please . . ." Mandy said, laying her fingers on my lips and cutting me off before I could make an even bigger fool of myself. "You are my friend, Willie, and I am yours. Please do not try to make me be anything else than that, I ask you. You will not lose this friend, eh? Even if I go away again?"

I begun to see then how it was with her, how she looked at things.

Mandy took the key off the table, walked to the door and unlocked and opened it. When she turned back and looked at me, I was surprised, for tears was rolling down her cheeks.

I thought for a minute she'd changed her mind, as women will do. Maybe if I could find the right words she wouldn't go out the door, and keep right on going, which I knowed she was going to do anyway, no matter what I said or did. But I was determined to give it a try, because if I didn't, I knowed I'd be kicking my ass a long, long time. Only, when I drew in a breath to tell her I had to have her be more than just my friend, she must of read my mind, or at least figured out what I was going to say, for she put two fingers to her lips so as to stop my talking and ruining it for her.

Maybe her being young and pretty like she was was a piece of it, part of why I felt like I did about that girl. But a big part of it had something to do with her just being her, too — being free like a deer and doing what she believed was right for herself, not what other people thought you ought to do. That girl called to something in me, called loud and clear, and it's not likely I'll ever hear that wind rustle the grass no more.

It was like she was taking my picture there — not with one of those camera things — but with her eyes and her memory. A picture of me sitting up in that old hotel bed, under that crazy quilt we had warmed up good. Almost like she didn't want me to go moving so as to spoil it. I can tell you how I knowed what she was doing, for I done the very same thing a few days later, and that was when I realized what was going on in her mind back then that morning, not that I knowed it then. Then, it seemed just painful and jealous as fire.

She kissed those two fingers she had up to her lips and then blew that kiss at me. "Goodbye, my friend," she said, that pretty smile back on her face, and then went out the door.

"Goodbye, my lovely," I said in that empty old hotel room.

I knowed I could not sleep after her leaving me like that. Feeling that miserable and lonely, and missing her already, I would probably not sleep for weeks, maybe months. Funny to think of it now, but soon after I heard her go down the steps I dropped straight off. Slept like a baby.

Chapter Twenty-four

I come out of a deep sleep hearing someone yelling and walloping a door down the hall and the first thing I thought of was them people we had woke up last night. But sunlight poured in my windows, and I finally reconized who it was screeching like that.

"Sheriff Shannon! Sheriff Shannon! Open up!"

After I drug myself up out of bed, I unlocked my door and looked down the hall. Sure enough, there stood that damn little Banty Foote banging on Clete's door and raising hell.

"He ain't there," I called. "He was leaving with Sheriff Bullock pretty early. What time is it, anyway?"

Banty stopped his pounding and looked me over good, then took out a big pocket watch. "Why, it's nearly eleven. Ten minutes of eleven, in fact. Most men has been up for hours. Looks like you're just gettin' up now. I'd be ashamed to be getting up now if it was me. Nosir, the sun don't catch me lyin' in bed. I been up all night. Rode in from —"

"Come in here if you got more to say, though I don't see how any more talk could come out of a fellow your size." He followed me into my room and I started to get dressed while he walked around the room looking everthing over careful and running his mouth.

"Like I said, I rode in from Hay Camp. Rode all night. Almost no moon at all. Man in a saloon there told me he seen you men. I figgered Deadwood and I figgered right. Took that woman and that boy to Marsh's and left right away. Where's that sheriff?" He put his hands on his hips and glared at me like I was hiding Clete somewheres.

"I already told you," I said, buttoning up a clean shirt. "He went out with Bullock to look for the man we're after." My head was aching pretty good, and I had heard about all I wanted to of his loud, fast talking.

"Good!" Banty yelled, starting to strut around the room again. "I was worried you might of caught him. Strung him up before I got here." He spun around to face me again. "How come you ain't with that sheriff? You was with him before, back at the Perfessor's dig. How come you ain't —"

"Because he don't need me right now. He's off with Bullock. Sometimes sheriffs like to spook around on their own together, don't you know that?"

Banty moved his head quick side to side, like the rooster he was named for, while he frowned and thought that over. "Of course they do, everbody knows that," he said after a minute. "Say, what's this on the floor?" He went over beside the door, bent over and picked up a little piece of paper and started to read it out loud, a lot slower than he talked. "Dear — Willie, I —

went — with — Sheriff — Bullock to — Eliza —
Elizabeth —"

"Give me that!" I told him. "Can't you see it's
got my name on it and not yours?" I figgered
Clete'd slipped it under the door that morning
before he left.

Banty held that note to his vest and it looked
like he wasn't going to give it up for a minute.
Finally he did, but not before he tried to sneak a
peek at the rest of it.

Clete's note said that he would be back around
dark if they didn't find DuShane in Elizabeth
and that I should stick around Deadwood and
keep my eyes peeled for our man and find out
what I could.

Banty ask me what the rest of it said and after a
while I told him because I knowed he would not
leave me alone about it 'til I did.

"Who's this Elizabeth gal he's goin' to see?"
Banty wanted to know.

"It ain't a gal," I told him. "It's a town a ways
from here."

"How'd ya git there? Which way is it? How —"

"Hold on," I told him. "You go up there and
Clete will be mad as hell. He's with Bullock and
he don't need you around, getting in his way."

He looked kind of disappointed, but then he
nodded his head. "What're you gonna do?"

"Why, I'm going to do just like Clete said,
stick around Deadwood and see what I can see.
Only first I'm going to get some breakfast."

"Good," Banty snapped. "I could eat too. I

missed breakfas', ridin' all night."

Well, I didn't mean to invite him along, but I could see no way out of it so we went down the street to where I'd ate my dinner the night before, Banty asking me a string of questions the whole way, sometimes two or three on top of one another.

The place was nearly empty. I had a pair of eggs and some bread and coffee, but Banty ate the same meal I did the night before — beefsteak and mashed potatoes and gravy. He ate almost as fast as he talked, which he did both at the same time, and he was done with that big plate of food before I even finished my eggs. He waved his arm at the woman there and told her to bring him the same thing again. She stood and looked at him a minute, then shrugged her shoulders and went to get it.

"You going to eat a whole 'nother meal?" I ask him.

"A course," he said, acting like I was a fool for not knowing why. "I said I missed my breakfas'. A man has to eat. Can't work if you don't eat."

I couldn't see what work he had to do that required all that food, but I didn't say so. I waited 'til the woman brought his second plate and took away his first. "I'm going to walk around town and have a look," I told him.

"Where'll you be?" Banty ask.

"In the saloons, mostly," I told him, heading for the door.

"I'll eat this and then find you," Banty hollered across the room at me. "After I eat me some pie I'll —"

"All right," I said, and went out the door.

I don't know whether it was especial quiet in Deadwood that noon or if it just seemed like it after listening to him for almost an hour. The sun was bright and the day warm, but I felt tired out already and walked down to the Red Bird for a rye to settle my nerves. Bessie wasn't there and the barman didn't know where she was so I went out in the street again.

I stood on the board walk outside Herrmann and Treber's wholesale liquor emporium and looked in at a case of Kentucky sour mash bourbon and thought maybe I would just go in there, buy it, take it back to my room and drink it all. But I didn't.

Instead, I walked into the Green Front and had another shot of rye. The piano player there knowed Mandy but he didn't see her at all that day. He did talk to Justin Thebideaux early in the morning, though, and he thought Mandy and Thebideaux had plans to go somewheres together, but he didn't know where. Course, I'd already heard them talk about New Orleans. I asked him to play any old song he knowed about Texas and I sat down at a table to listen. I had give up on the rye and was sipping a beer when Banty walked in, blinking the sunlight out of his eyes. I pulled my hat down some and slid down in my chair, but Banty spotted me anyways.

"Here you are, Deputy. I was looking all over

for you. I already looked in three —"

"Well, sit down and have a beer if you have room for one," I offered, trying to hear one of the Texas songs the man was playing. "Texas Sunsets," I think it was.

"Nosir, don't drink no beer," Banty said, shaking his head fast enough to rattle his brains. "No beer for me. I could sleep, though. I'm sleepy. That beefsteak musta made me sleepy. I was up all night. Rode in from Hay —"

"You can sleep in my room if you want to," I told him, more to get rid of him than anything else. "Ask the man at the desk for a key. Tell him I said it was all right."

Banty stood there scratching his stubby little chin and thought that over awhile. "All right," he said, nodding a couple of times. "All right. I could sure sleep." He yawned a big one so fast I almost missed it. I reckoned he even slept fast.

"Just sleep on top of the blankets if you keep your boots on," I said.

"Where'll you be?" he ask.

"Probably right here," I told him, slapping the table and propping my feet up on a chair.

"All right," he said again. "But, mind now, if you see that killer, you come and git me. Don't you take him yourself. Come git me, you hear?"

"Hell, I don't even know what he looks like, but if he should walk up and interduce himself, I'll just say 'Excuse me a minute, Mr. DuShane, but I got orders to go get Banty Foote before I shoot you,' and then I'll come get you. Is that what you had in mind?"

Banty thought that one over a minute too. "I doubt he'd do that," he said. He shuffled toward the door, turned around and waved, and then walked out before I could even wave back. He could of thanked me for the use of my room, I thought, but I wasn't mad about it because that stinking old saloon went back to peaceful so fast you could almost hear it.

That piano player at the Green Front was good at his work, and he knowed even more songs about Texas, or that had Texas in them somewheres, than I even did. I got to buying him drinks and thinking of Mandy, how maybe she would want to go along to Texas with Clete and me. Two big ranches side by side, Clete's and Mary's and mine and Mandy's. Course, that was only a drunk having himself a pipe dream, I see now, but it seemed real enough at the time. He played all them Texas songs, some of them twice when I ask him to, and I must have drunk more beer than I thought I did. When I stood up, I knowed how much though.

I was just coming back from the little house out behind the saloon for the third or fourth time when that boy from the National — the one whose daddy kept throwing him back out the door — he come up to me and grabbed my arm before I could sit back down. "You're Mr. Goodwin, ain't you?" he ask.

"Yes, I am," I told him, feeling pretty woozy and wobbly on my feet.

It was then I noticed how worried that young fellow looked. "My Pa says for you to come quick. That sheriff you was with, he's been killed."

"Sheriff Bullock, you mean?"

"No sir, the other one. The one you rode in with."

Chapter Twenty-five

I walked up the street with that young man from the National feeling miserable, and with every step I got a little more sober. You should of went with him, I kept telling myself. If you wasn't more interested in that girl than in catching that killer, you would have.

"Who found him?" I ask.

"I did," the young fellow said. "I was walking down the hall and I saw his door open and him dead."

I wouldn't say I was all the way sober by the time we went in and walked by the desk, a big crowd of people gawking at me as we started up the steps, but I was all right. From the top of the stairs I seen that my door was open and a lot of people there too, instead of by Clete's room like I expected.

I'd guessed how it was before we got down there. Banty Foote was stretched out in my bed, his throat cut. The whole front of his shirt soaked with blood and him lying in a pool of it where his weight made a hollow in the middle of the mattress. It's something how much blood a man has in him — especially when you see it out of him. Banty's arms and legs was spread out, and while it was clear he'd crawled under the covers, he still had all his clothes and his boots on. I got mad at him for a second before I remembered he was dead. Funny how someone being dead don't hit you all at once. His eyes was wide open and it looked like he was staring at something on the ceiling 'til you noticed he wasn't breathing no more and that a fly was walking across his mouth.

I chased it away, closed his eyes, and pulled the blankets up over his face. That's when I seen where someone'd wiped his hands on the bedspread — used it like a towel. One bloody hand print was pretty clear and I laid my hand over it. Longer than mine, it was, and not so wide at the palm. *DuShane,* I told myself.

I quick pulled the covers down off Banty's face, but not below where he was slashed on the neck. "He's still alive!" I yelled and then turned to the young fellow who fetched me. "Get everone out of here. Then send for the Doc and that deputy of Bullock's."

"I'm right here," Bullock's man said, stepping toward me. "And if he's alive, I'm a —"

"Don't argue with me," I told him, and then pushed everone else out of the room myself, including the young fellow, telling him again to go get the Doc. He looked at me like I was crazy when I closed the door in his face.

"Are you crazy?" Bullock's deputy asked me, cocking his head.

"I hope not," I said. "Do you know who this is?"

"No, I don't. But he came in the office this morning, after Bullock and Shannon left, and asked where Shannon was. I said he was staying in town somewhere, but since I never got the man's name — he was in and out so fast — I didn't tell him Shannon was out of town with Bullock, and I didn't tell him which hotel, either, so this ain't my fault. He ain't who I was told was killed, though."

"Me neither. I was told it was Clete Shannon who was dead. How about you?"

"The same," he answered, turning his head a little and looking at me kind of sideways. "Say, what are you up to?"

"Just one more question and I'll let you in on it. Who else knows this ain't Clete who's dead?"

He stopped and thought it over. "Just Potato Creek Johnny, I believe. I straightened him out. And whoever else he told. Hell, even the hotel people think this sawed-off little runt is Clete Shannon."

"Best to have some respect for the dead," I said, and that startled him. "Go find this Potato fellow and tell him to keep his mouth shut. The man who killed him will try and finish the job if he thinks Shannon's still alive."

He shifted from one foot to the other, confused as a hoot owl in a twister. "But Shannon still *is* alive! Ain't he?"

"As far as I know," I told him.

He started getting a little mad about then. "Look, mister, I know you're Shannon's deputy, but if you don't start making sense soon, I'm gonna lock you up and let Bullock untangle this knot."

"There's no time for me to explain it right now. Go find the man you told and tell him to keep his mouth shut. Is there a newspaper in this damn town?"

"Yeah, sure, two of 'em. The *Pioneer* and —"

"Good, stop by the office of both of them and say Sheriff Shannon was cut, but is going to be all right. Go tell it to that red-haired man at the telegraph office, too. Spread that same story to some other people, only tell it a little different each time, ending up with the idea that Clete is okay. Then come back here and I'll tell you what's going on. I'm going to wait for the Doc and tell him. Now g'on."

I wasn't sure for a minute he would, but he opened the door and went part way out. "Mister, this better make *damn* good sense when I come back, 'cause it sure as the Devil don't right now."

He closed the door behind him and I waited. Banty's vest was on the floor by the bed and another room key laid on the night stand. I figgered he didn't lock the door, maybe because he wanted to make sure I could get in to wake him up if I found DuShane. Instead, DuShane'd found him.

I wondered if that killer knowed it wasn't Clete's throat he cut. Banty's hat was beside his head on the piller, so maybe his face was covered up with it and DuShane'd sliced before he

305

looked good. Though he was a born killer, I doubted if he'd of slit a man's throat if he seen his mistake, for that would of just give him away, give Clete and me warning he was here in Deadwood. Hard to say. Unless, a course, he thought Banty was me, and that idea give me the shivers a while. No way to see to the end of it, but I decided I would have my try at him and hope for the best. I looked at Banty's face there a minute and wished I'd been friendlier to him while he was alive.

I answered the knock at the door and let the doc in.

"Doc Sayles," the white haired gent said. "I was told I was needed here." He pulled the covers down past Banty's opened-up neck. "Jesus!" he said, and then pulled them back up over Banty's face again. Doc Sayles looked me over. "Something wrong with your eyes?"

"No, but I need your help . . . in catching the man who did this."

"What shall I do?" he asked.

"Just have a seat 'til Bullock's deputy gets back. What's his name, anyway?"

The Doc sat, wrinkled his brow and stared at the floor. "Sam something-or-other . . . Hayes, I think. This better not take too long. I have a miner sitting over there in my office waiting for me to set the bones in his foot. Dropped a goddamn rock hammer on his metatarsals and broke three of them." He started explaining to me about how a man's foot was put together, and I

306

listened, though I didn't understand it much. Helped him pass the time, I figgered.

Before he was all done, Sam knocked and come in the room and then they both looked at me. "Well, this is what I aim to do. . . . Doc, you have a sick room? Where men stay when they're hurt?"

"Yes," he said, nodding his head.

"I want to take this dead man — Banty Foote was his name — over to your sick room, pretending it's Clete Shannon, the man who the killer was really after. Also pretending he's still alive. Could you go along with that, Doc?"

"Certainly," he said.

"Well then you lay him out in a bed over at your place like he's just hurt, maybe bandage up his neck some. The man who killed Banty was really trying to kill Clete, and if he thinks Clete's alive, it's my guess he'll try 'er again, try and do the job right. And when he does, Sam and me, we'll be waiting for him."

"I don't know," Sam said, shaking his head. "If I'd a cut a man's throat, the way that man's is, I don't think I'd fall for it."

"It's worth a try, though," Doc said, standing up. "Goddamn lawless town, anyway. I'll go over and get a stretcher and some men to carry him. You two walk beside his head so nobody can see his face very well. Talk to him, too. That'll help make folks think he's still alive."

And that's what we done. Sam got someone to sit in Bullock's office for him and then snuck into the woodshed of the house next door to Doc's after the sun went behind the ridge. The miner with the broke foot was going to spend the night there already, so Doc give him a gun to put under his covers. He didn't fancy going to sleep in the same room with a dead man anyway. Doc put a lamp beside the only window of his sick room and then sat at the desk in his office room with a pocket revolver in his lap. I walked out to Doc's outhouse, no more than fifty feet from the lit-up window, trying to look like I was just doing the regular thing, in case DuShane was watching from somewheres. It stunk some in there, of course, and I would rather of had my scattergun, but how can you walk into an outhouse with a scattergun and have it look like you're only going in there to do your business?

It was a small two-holer with no lids, like in fancy outhouses. Which meant I had to sit on one of the holes or stand up. I could see through the cracks between the boards pretty good, and the door also had a slice of moon cut out of it that I could get the barrel of my .36 through, though it was a little high for aiming. It was a long wait, I remember, probably seemed longer than it really was, but after a while it started getting dark. I wondered what'd become of Clete and what he'd have to say about me trying this, worrying if it was the right thing to do or not.

At least I was in the proper place to answer nature's call, and I was no more than halfway done when I looked through a crack in the door and saw a tall man in a high crowned black hat up close to Doc's window, looking in. He brought his gun up all of a sudden to shoot inside. There was nothing for me to do but stand up and let my pants fall to the floor, take aim through the moon hole and fire.

I missed him. He pulled up and put a ball through that old outhouse, right by my ear. I heard Sam shoot and then I pulled up my pants and stepped out. DuShane was running into the alley, but he turned and threw off a shot that hit Sam as he was coming around the woodshed and put him down.

I took off after DuShane. He was more a shadow than a man, but I saw him crouched down, close to some lady's kitchen window, and I squeezed off three shots. A dog was barking at me and some men were yelling and I burned a chunk of time crawling up there on my hands and knees. I saw then what I'd sneaked up on was only a barrel full of garbage.

I run on down the alley and was about to give it up when his gun fired pretty close in front, the blast lighting up the alley for a second. Rolling to the side, I come up shooting. I could hear from his footsteps he was running down the street so I took after him again. A hundred yards ahead of me, I seen him turn left into Deadwood's main street, heading downhill past the Redbird and the Green Front both. Lots of people was out on the street when I run down it after him. Some yelled and some laughed, but none of them men would help me get after him.

I come to the livery just as DuShane was hurrying his horse out the gate. I held with two hands on my gun, aimed careful, and missed him again.

He dropped the reins, ducked behind a trough and let one fly at me. I shot back and then stepped behind a shed, keeping an eye on where he was hid. My gun was empty then, but I'd remembered to put my spare cylinder in my coat pocket before this whole mess started. While I had him cornered, I yanked the pin that released the barrel of my .36 and then pulled off the empty cylinder. I was watching for him the whole time I reloaded, waiting for him to break for his horse and hurrying to be ready. I slid the full cylinder in and put the barrel back on just as he jumped up and run. I stepped around the corner of that shed and aimed as best I could at a shadow moving fast in the dark.

When I squeezed the trigger, the whole night exploded at the end of my arm. Next thing I knowed, I was on my ass with bells ringing in my ears and dots of light that looked like pink beans dancing around in front of my eyes. I heard a horse run off and tried to stand, but fell back down again, so dizzy I was.

After a while some men from the livery helped me up and walked me over to Doc Sayles', but I was only about half with 'em. I kept trying to tell them men I had lost my hat, but I couldn't get it out. It was like the idea was in my head, all right, but all the words I knowed was locked in another room somewheres and I couldn't find the damn key.

Doc was putting a bandage on Sam's knee when we walked in. "What happened to you, for God's sake?"

"I don't know," I told him, the words coming back to me in little bunches. "I'm not hit nowheres, but something happened to my gun, I think." I was still holding onto it and held it up then. Nothing was left but the grip, the back of the frame and the trigger and trigger guard. The barrel and the cylinder both was missing. What I was holding onto was only about half a gun. I knowed then what I done. When I was hurrying so to reload I must of forgot to push the pin back in — the one that holds the barrel and cylinder in place. I must of flung that barrel and about half a dozen balls at him all at the same time, what you might call a Texas shotgun.

Doc come over and stood in front of me. "What happened to your forehead?"

I reached up and touched it, and it was swelled way out but not bleeding. "I don't know," I told him, kind of surprised myself.

Doc sat me down and put a wet cloth across it and leaned me back. "Gun came up and hit you," he said, looking in my eyes, one then the other. "I've seen it before. I'm surprised you're still walking around."

That was the strangest bang on the head I ever got. It didn't hurt much, except if I pressed on it,

311

and I didn't remember nothing hitting me at all. At the same time, I didn't feel entirely right, either. Sort of like I was standing outside myself watching things happen to me. Doc made me sit there while he fussed around some with his heart-listener and what-all.

He was still fussing over me when Clete opened the door without knocking and walked right up, looking at me as worried as a mother hen missing a chick. "Damn, Willie, are you all right?"

"I think so," I told him.

"Bad bump on the head," Doc said, putting his gear away. "He'll be fine in a day or two."

"You able to ride?" Clete ask.

"Yeah, I guess. Where are we going?"

He looked at me mighty peculiar, but damned if I could figger out where he wanted to go. "He'd be better off not to," Doc said, going back to work on Sam. Bullock come in then and wanted to know what'd happened, so Sam and me and Doc pieced it together between us.

"He's dead? That little runt who followed me back at Marsh's? Banty Foote?" Clete looked like he couldn't believe it and was maybe wondering if I'd been seeing things that wasn't there.

I explained how Banty'd showed up that morning, wanting to help us some more.

"That sonofabitch," Clete said, meaning DuShane, though I thought at first he meant Banty, that's how addled I was. "I'm going after him. Can you trail him with a lantern, Willie?"

"I don't know, I never done it. I'll give it a try."

"Like hell you will!" Doc Sayles said. "You're staying here tonight so I can keep an eye on you. This man has probably bruised his brain, Sheriff. Time enough to get after your killer tomorrow."

"Maybe not," Clete said, and then set his jaw.

"Let's go take a look," I said, "down at the — the, uh . . . What the hell's that word?"

"What do you mean?" Clete ask, looking at me strange.

"Aw, you know, where they keep the horses. I could use some air, anyway." Damned if I could remember that word.

"Don't you go off anywhere," Doc Sayles yelled after us.

Bullock got us a lantern and then went back to talk to Sam. Clete and me walked down to where my gun'd haywired. I found the cylinder nearby and my hat too, but the barrel was way over beside the livery fence.

I stood and tried to put my .36 back together, but the pieces didn't seem to want to fit.

After a while Clete handed me the lantern, put my gun together himself, and give it back to me. "You all right, Willie?"

"Yeah, I'm okay. I almost forgot, though. I found out DuShane's first name. It's Jezrael. Woman at the Red Bird told me." Then I spelled it for him, best I could.

"*Jezrael?* What the hell kind of name is that?"

313

"Damned if I know, but that's what it is." I looked at Jezrael DuShane's tracks beside the trough. A spot of blood the size of a silver dollar was soaked into the dust almost where he'd got on his horse. He had fell down first, though, before he rode off, for I seen the same handprints as was on Banty's bedspread and where he was on his knees a minute.

"Yeah, you hit him," Clete said. "Put a groove in him, it looks like. Think you could ride?"

"I believe I could, but we'd best wait 'til morning."

Clete twisted his mouth up, but then relaxed it some before he spoke. "You feeling that bad, huh?"

"No, I'm all right, and it ain't because the doc said not to. Remember, it'll be damn slow going for us and fast for him. We'll get tired out sooner than him too, because we'll be walking and he'll be riding. I might be able to trail him carrying a light, but not riding my horse I couldn't. Besides that, if he was to lie in wait for us somewheres, we couldn't be no better targets, holding a damn lantern. He'll have to sleep some time, and we can catch up to him when we can see good. We'd be smarter to sleep now and start at first light."

Clete pushed his hat back. "I guess you're not as brain-scrambled as I thought."

Chapter Twenty-six

Clete and me walked back towards Doc Sayles' place, where I was going to spend the night. Suited me all right, because I didn't think I'd get much sleep upstairs at the hotel anyway, where Banty Foote'd got his throat cut. When we walked in, I seen somebody'd moved Banty's body out of the sick room. Clete said he'd get our things together tonight and come around for me early. I tossed and turned some in one of Doc's narrow little cots after he left, but at least that miner with the busted foot didn't snore much.

Seemed like I'd hardly fell asleep when Clete was shaking me awake.

"What time is it?" I ask him.

"After four," he said, turning the lamp up some. "You better now?"

"Yeah, I'm all right." I felt pretty stiff getting up and into my clothes but my head didn't hurt none.

When we went outside I seen it was still pitch dark, the stars shining bright and rolled way over toward summer. Clete'd brought our horses up to the rail there, all saddled and loaded and ready to go. "I thought we'd travel light and do without a pack horse," he said, untying the gray. "We'll make better time. That all right with you?"

"Sure, but it's still too early to read the sign."

"I know," Clete said, leading Whatever away from the rail and starting up the street. "We've got something to attend to before we go."

I untied my bay and followed him, no idea at all where we was going. That was the quietest I heard Deadwood since we rode in. Wasn't but about three or four saloons still open, and I thought about getting a wake-up shot of rye before we left.

We went up the street a block or two, and I seen lots of horses tied outside one place and it all lit up inside. I thought at first it was another saloon, but when we got closer and I read the sign over the door, I seen it was an undertaker's parlor. I knowed then what we was attending to.

We tied up and went inside. Seven or eight men stood there, yawning and shuffling their feet and looking half asleep. Bullock was there too, so I thought maybe they worked for him. "Strange time for a funeral," Bullock said. "We're all ready except to load him."

Three men stood aside and there lay Banty Foote in a wooden box, his face all sober.

Clete and me walked up and looked him over. In the button hole of the new coat they had on him was a big red flower. Dressed in a dark striped suit, he was, his neck still bandaged, and laid out in the fanciest silk-lined coffin I ever seen. Only it was also the biggest coffin I ever seen, too, both width and length.

"Seems a little large for him, don't it?" I ask.

A fellow I took to be the undertaker sidled up

to us. "I'm dreadful sorry for that," he said, twisting at a big diamond ring. "It was the only one we had on hand at such short notice. God knows what I'll do with Mr. Thompkins now, and his funeral's at ten." He glanced at Bullock, worked on his ring some more and shook his head a couple of times. "Does he look all right, gents?" he ask.

"Yeah, I guess he looks about as good as a dead man can," I told him, which was true and seemed to make him a good deal more comfortable.

"Well, let's get this done with so I can get the rest of my sleep," Bullock said.

The undertaker and his man nailed the lid of the coffin down tight and then some of Bullock's men carried it out the back door. I followed Clete out the front and pretty soon a glass-sided hearse come around the building pulled by a matched pair of blacks with black plumes sticking up between their ears, its four lamps at the corners all lit and flickery.

Another of Bullock's men was handing out lanterns for everyone to carry as they rode and then we started off after the hearse two abreast. Up the street and then off to the left and then up a long steep hill. That hill kept going up and up and getting steeper and steeper. After a while I thought maybe we was going to deliver Banty right up to the Pearly Gates.

When we got to the top I seen two men digging by lantern light. They said they wasn't quite done, but Bullock decided it was deep enough. Clete and me helped the four men carry Banty's coffin. But when we went to put it down in the hole with ropes, we seen right away the hole was too short. First we tried putting the foot end in and slanting it up, but the head end was nearly up to the sod. And then we all heard Banty slide down that slick silk and go thump against the footboard, and that surely wouldn't do.

"Take it out and dig it longer, down at the narrow end," Clete said after a minute, so that's what they done.

While they was digging, I took my lantern and read what was carved on a tall marble gravestone nearby. I was surprised to see a name I reconized and pointed it out to Clete.

"James Butler Hickok," he read out loud. "Yeah, I forgot he was buried up here. Banty'd probably like the idea of being planted close to Wild Bill, wouldn't he?"

"I suspect he would," I told him.

When the gravediggers finished, we lowered Banty in again, all the way down this time. The undertaker said a few words and then handed Clete a spade. He pitched a shovelful of dirt in and then I done the same. We left the rest of that work for the men who'd dug the hole in the first place and then we all rode down the hill just as it was starting to get gray toward the east, Clete dropping back with Bullock.

When we was almost in town a young fellow brought his horse up beside mine. "Are you

Sheriff Goodwin?" he ask me.

"No, I'm just a deputy," I said, "but my name's Goodwin. Who's askin'?"

"Bret Roth," he said, lifting his derby hat. "Please excuse me, Mr. Goodwin. I work for the *Pioneer*. Did you know the man who was buried?"

"Yes, I did," I told him.

"Was he a lawman, Mr. Goodwin? Mr. Foote, I mean. The reason I'm asking is that I'm writing up the killing and the funeral for the *Pioneer*. It's my first story and I'd like to get it right."

"Yes, he was a lawman," I said. "One of the best damn deputy sheriffs in the West. You write it up that way and you'll have it correct. Most men, the only name they make for themself is the one on their tombstone. But he was something, was Banty Foote. And spell his name right. Be sure to put an *e* on the end of it. Nothing worse than a man's name spelled wrong in his own obituary."

"I will, sir," he said, tipping his hat to me again. He rode off quick — to write his story while it was still fresh in his head, I guess.

We got back to the undertaker's and Clete had a word with Bullock, handed him some money, and then we mounted back up.

"Thanks again for your help, Seth," Clete said.

"No trouble," Bullock said, and then yawned. "Won't change your mind about taking more men?" he ask. "It's probably against the law, as you said, but nobody would care much."

"No, we can handle this," Clete said.

"Well, good luck. Remember what I told you, Goodwin," Bullock called as we went down the street, headed toward the livery stable.

As it turned out, I *did* read sign by lantern light, since it was still too dark to see good from up on my horse. But I walked little more than a mile 'til it was light enough to read and ride. DuShane'd climbed the ridge right above town and then followed the spine up the opposite way, eventually coming back to the big gulch Deadwood was in, but further up. We surely would of got lost in the dark trailing him, even with a light. His track went on up that vee and then turned left, up the ravine of another gulch, higher than the one Deadwood sat in, mining camps spread out wherever there was water. That gulch petered out close to the top of what you could almost call a mountain and at the peak his tracks turned south, heading downhill, following ridge and valley through some pretty rough country, all of it covered with pine and smelling as fresh and sweet as the second week after creation.

We rode all morning and a good chunk of the afternoon without stopping, eating jerky and bread, drinking from our canteens as we went, and gaining on him a little with every hour. We come onto a couple places where his horse had just stopped and stood a piece, and I couldn't figger it out for a while.

"I think he fell asleep riding and let his horse

pick the way," I told Clete. "This here's one of the places his horse must of just stopped 'til DuShane woke up and nudged him on again." Wasn't far beyond that we come to where he'd built a fire and slept on the ground. Where his head had laid was quite a few spots where he'd bled into the dirt.

Clete stirred the ashes with a stick and found a few little red coals. "Three, maybe four hours."

"Maybe less, since he was burning pine," I said.

We started right off again, but gained no more on him than we did before, though we pushed pretty hard. By sundown I was tired and raw in the seat, and I seen Clete nod off a time or two. He give me no argument when I said I couldn't see the sign clear no more. We camped in a grassy little clearing up from the stream a ways, so the mosquitoes wouldn't get at us. Clete boiled coffee and we ate some more jerky and bread after we spread out our bedrolls.

When we finished our meal, I took the last of the coffee, lit my pipe and sat watching the fire, just as Clete was doing. The wind stirred the pines some and you could hear the creek from down below, but that was all.

"Shit!" Clete yelled.

I looked around quick, but nothing had moved and Clete sat just where he was before, still looking into the flames. "What is it?" I ask him.

He looked up. "I just figured out where that

money is, the gold and cash Wilson stole from the Two Scalp Bank, and I'm a fool for not thinking of it sooner. His horse came back, so he *had* to have froze out there. Since he rode out toward the south, that's the direction I looked. But he didn't go south. If you were shot and freezing and discovered you were riding in a circle, what would *you* do?"

"Why, I'd take some cover if I could," I said. "And try to build a fire."

"Sure," Clete said. "Only I didn't think of him riding in a circle. First place I'm going to look when we get back is those rocks east of Nell's ranch."

"I think you're onto something there," I told him. "Too damn often we look for what we expect to find and forget to just look."

"That's it, Willie," he said, his eyes deep into the flames. "And I figured something else out too — Mary. I'm going to marry her like I planned."

"Good woman is Mary McLeod, smart too. Yes, marry a woman with brains enough for two and you'll come out about even. Though what she sees in you is still a puzzlement." Of course I didn't say nothing about our plans for Texas.

It was like Clete'd heard my thoughts. "Any complaints about the three of us heading out together?"

I looked at him then, but he was still staring into the fire. "You think that'd be all right with her? Last thing most married women want is their husband's old friends hanging around, reminding him he ain't entirely free to do what he pleases no more."

Clete laughed at me. "Damn, Willie, for someone who's never been married, you sure have a lot of ideas about it. No, Mary's not like that. Fact is, I talked to her about the three of us going together after her daddy's funeral. And I don't see what she sees in you, either."

Well, there it was. What I'd worried about'd all been in my head. I'd figgered if Clete married Mary, him and me and Texas was quits. And all along he had it straightened out with her about the three of us going together. Why, that damn Clete!

More I thought of it, the better I liked it, for Mary would help keep a lid on Clete's temper, bring out the best in him, as a good woman often does. And I liked her, too, even if she was a little stiff and proper sometimes. Funny how getting something like that off your mind makes you feel better right off.

He offered his hand and I took it. He shook it once. After a time he laid down and covered up. The peepers started in down by the creek. "I hope we get him tomorrow," my pardner said. "I had about enough of this."

I stretched out too and was nearly asleep when I heard him sit up sudden. "I wonder whether . . ." Clete said.

I waited a minute for him to finish before I ask him, "What's that?"

323

"Never mind, Willie. Never mind." He laid back down and soon was snoring. I never thought no more about it 'til later.

Chapter Twenty-seven

We got a good start in the morning and covered a bunch of miles before the sun come up above the ridge. By noon we passed where he'd camped again and not long after we come to where the road forked, one branch following the bigger stream down out of the hills and the other heading up along a creek into a valley slim as six o'clock.

His tracks led up into that skinny hollow. I didn't see blood anymore, but they were his sign, all right, pressed deep into the rich black soil and the few patches of gravelly sand along the creek — no more than two hours old, either, if that. Me and Clete headed on up into that piney trough, into some of the nicest-looking country you could ever hope to find — especially if you was looking for a good place for an ambush. Them tall, straight pines come all the way down to the stream on both sides. Which meant you couldn't see very far. I felt more exposed than if I was caught stark naked by a whole flock of Sunday school picnickers smack-dab in the middle of the prairie.

Less than a stone's throw from the creek the land angled up on both sides, steeper than you'd want to ride a horse up. No paths led off up these slopes, either, except a few game trails. Maybe a deer could get up them, but I knowed I couldn't. DuShane had to be somewhere in this almost-closed bear trap, straight ahead of us.

About a mile into that V-shaped little valley we come to a flatter place where the trees on one side of the stream was cleared out, maybe a hundred yards long and thirty wide, where it looked like someone, probably a gold prospector, decided to build a cabin and then changed his mind. He finished a rough little dam, though, and below it he panned some gravel by the look of things. Done enough felling of trees so that you could see the rocky places that formed peaks up on those side ridges in spots. High up there, the rock looked like it was cut into twisted church steeples and darning needles for giants, or the legs of the giants themselves. The trail had a good slope to it already, and you could see it was going to get a lot steeper from here, heading up into no more than a ravine, and that going right toward the tallest of those rocks that wind and water had been whittling on since Moses was a pup. Right here, though, it was all brushy and cut-over.

"Feels pretty naked, don't you think?" I ask Clete.

"Yeah, I had about the same idea myself," he answered. "How about walking this stretch."

We was both just stepping out of our saddles when something exploded right between us and a rifle boomed in the distance. Like two thunder claps almost on top of one another.

I knowed before I smacked the ground that it was one of those musket-shell things.

"You hit?" I yelled over at Clete, who had

rolled onto his belly against a felled tree trunk, his hat knocked off and his forearm covering up his neck and jaw, where he'd been hit before with one of them things. Both horses run off, of course, but I could see the bay a little ways downstream, back in the trees.

Clete didn't move for a minute, and I was just starting to crawl toward him when he stuck his eyes up above the log, his Remington cocked and ready. "You see where it came from?" Clete asked, cool as creek water.

"Right up where we was headed, I think. Up at the end of this cleared space." About that time I heard a horse moving out over some rocks at a pretty good clip from up that way. "Stay low," I yelled at Clete when he lit out of there. "Might be a trick, sending his horse off to make us think —"

Clete waved me back toward our horses and then, running bent over, he got into the trees and headed on up. Clete's horse was close to the bay I seen when I got back there, both chomping grass at the edge of the stream like nothing at all'd happened. But they both got nervous when I took their reins and walked them to the edge of the clearing. I couldn't see nor hear Clete, so I waited. I hated doing it, but I knowed waiting was the right thing for there. *They also serve who only just stand around waiting,* my pa always said, and hard as that was to do sometimes, it was true. Up high on the ridge to the left, a white-breasted sparrow give his mournful tune a couple or three times and then all was quiet. I thought of Mandy then, that night she had come to my hotel room, mostly.

A pistol shot cracked in the thick of all that silence and echoed on down the valley below. I was pretty sure it was Clete's Remington, but even if it wasn't, it didn't matter because I couldn't stand there minding the horses no longer. I led them up along the edge of the trees with my .36 drawn. Toward the middle, here come Clete at a half-run down through the clearing. I stepped out and he headed my way.

"You were right," Clete said, a little out of breath. "He went off far enough to give us the sound of his horse and then came back, sitting it and waiting for us to charge on up there. I got a shot off, but I don't think I hit him, goddamnit. Jesus, I want that bastard!" Clete mounted so I did too. "His shirt looked bloody as hell, Pardner. Looked like you got him good."

We rode further up into the ravine part of the valley, me following behind and feeling like we was going into the mouth of hell, big boulders like broken-off teeth tumbled all through the pines and they not near as thick as before. I saw a picture once, in a book, of a place near Gettysburg, where Clete was wounded. Some reb sharpshooters got themselves killed in a pile of outhouse-sized rocks that looked a lot like these.

Within a quarter mile it got steep as the devil, and the horses blowing so hard we got off to walk them. It was almost like climbing a mountain straight on for a while — more than I wanted, I'll admit. Just when it started getting a little easier, we turned a bend and there lay DuShane's horse dead as a board. The saddle still on it, the rifle boot empty and the bags gone, supposing he had some, which I guessed he would.

"That was real smart," Clete said, looking further up the path. "Ran his horse up that grade 'til it died on him." He took off his hat and rubbed his sleeve across his forehead.

I was plenty hot, too, even with the breeze that was blowing up there, so I took me a little squat-sit facing downhill, and I was surprised at how much country was spread out below us. Hills and ridges and gullies all growed full of pine, wherever it wasn't too stony. Across the way, on another rocky peak like the one we was coming to, only lower, there lay a big wooly mountain goat, white as a patch of snow, which I thought it was at first. He had made hisself comfortable in a hollow place close to the top and was just stretched out, watching me. A good half mile off he was, but I knowed I was what he was looking at, maybe Clete too. Maybe keeping an eye on DuShane as well, and wondering what the hell we men was up to, hunting each other instead of his kind.

My knees let me know it when I stood back up, I remember. I showed that mountain billy to Clete, but the only thing that interested him much was straight ahead. We walked the horses right up to a wall of rock, the face of it rising straight above us, the first edge topping off in a row of stomach teeth fifty feet up and other jaws rising behind them. After I found DuShane's bootprints leading into a little washed-out crevice, Clete and me both looked up at where we had to go. We both stepped back under the pines together, too, when we figured out how good a targets we'd be from up there. But that's where we was going to if we was going to take him. Only, he could be looking down on us from a hundred different places, hid good 'til we showed ourselves.

Clete got his Henry and I took out my coat and that old scattergun he had brought me. He checked our canteens and put some other stuff in the jerky bag while I tended the horses, which I ended up tying in a little level spot down from the rocks and into the pines a few rods.

Clete handed me an extra bag of shotgun shells and then spun the cylinder of his Remington. "Don't be stupid up there, Willie. If you see him, shoot him. He's not going to surrender, and I'm not very interested in taking him back to Two Scalp even if he would."

That didn't set well with me at all, but I said nothing for I figured it was just anger talking, that and him wanting our man so bad. We was as armed as we could be and still walk upright, so we started climbing in the same spot where DuShane did.

It was scrabble and stretch, hands and feet, for

330

the most part, and I hoped it wouldn't get no worse up above. That rock was awful rough, too, and it scraped up my fingers pretty good, but there was no help for it. Clete reached down and yanked me up into a little pocket where we could both almost stand up straight without showing ourselves, though I sat as soon as I caught my breath about half.

"How high —" I started to ask, but a gun exploded somewhere up above us and chips of rock from where his slug hit stung my face like birdshot, though only one or two brought blood. And right away, DuShane up above give a scream that might of come out of the Devil's own mouth.

"That sonofabitch!" Clete said through his teeth, looking upward through a notch in the rocks like a wolf eyeing his prey. He snapped off a shot toward where the smoke was rising, but it was mostly anger shooting.

I was just glad none of them pieces of rock'd hit me in the eye.

"You all right?" he asked after a while, talking quiet.

I wiped at my face. "Yeah, just scratches," I said, keeping my voice down like him.

"Was that a pistol he fired?" Clete ask.

"Yes, I think it was. Wonder why he didn't use that cannon of his?" Soon as I ask it, I knowed the answer.

And so did Clete. "Yeah," he said, an ugly smile smeared all over his face. "The sonofabitch is out of ammunition for it, or nearly so. Probably has to make it himself, and it's been a long old ride."

"Why do you suppose he hollered like that?" I ask him.

He come over beside where I was watching through a crack in the rocks, cocked his head and looked at me crooked. "That was a Rebel yell, Willie. Shit, didn't you ever hear a goddamn Rebel yell before? I thought you said you were from Texas."

"I am, damnit! Lived there most of my life, anyways, but I never heard nothing the like of *that* before."

"Well, that was your honest-to-God, genuine, nickel-plated Rebel yell, Pardner," Clete said, then slid down and sat, leaning back against the shady side of a rock. He was quiet a minute, getting his breath and looking at his boots stretched out in front of him. "I heard it plenty during the War." He took off his hat and put his head back against that hard stone. "All up and down the Shenandoah Valley and everywhere else we fought 'em. But I never thought I'd hear it again, not out here." He shook his head and then put his hat back on. "Lot of my friends died with that goddamn screaming in their ears, the last thing they heard." He stood up as straight as he could there, snapped off another shot, and then looked me square in the eye. "Let's get on that sonofabitch."

"All right," I said. "What do you want me to do?"

"You stay here at this crack and keep a sharp look out for him. I'm going to try and get around over there to the right and see if there's a good way up or another way down. I'll be damned if I want him crawling down off of here while we're waiting for a shot. I want this goddamn thing ended right here and as soon as possible — and him dead."

It surprised me he talked that way, for I'd knowed him some time and never had I heard him say a thing like that before.

Clete set his hat on tighter. "If you see him or if he shoots at either you or me, fire once and then wait a couple seconds and fire again. You won't do much damage with the shotgun at this range, but it might give me a crack at him."

I nodded and he slapped me on the shoulder and then started down the way we come up, but he inched toward our right, over the point of one of them stomach teeth we seen from down below and no hand holds at all. The drop behind him was a good seventy feet, too high to fall off of and live to tell about it. I hate to admit it, but I was glad it wasn't me making that climb. I saw then he was taking on the hard jobs himself, like he always done. But he made it across all right and soon was out of sight.

The sun was high and pretty warm by then; the sky blue as a Texas girl's eyes and no clouds nowhere. Everthing was quiet except a warm wind that whistled through the pines down below. I looked for that white mountain billy over on the other rocks, but he must of found something better to do than watch us. Maybe had his nannies somewheres nearby.

A shot cracked up above. I knowed right away it wasn't aimed at me but I fired one barrel of that scattergun from my looking notch, waited a second, stood, and let go with the other. Almost on top of my second blast I heard Clete's Henry speaking out. I couldn't see him over to the right or DuShane up above through the notch, so I didn't know *what* was going on, just doing like Clete'd told me.

After a while I begun to think over that ungodly hollering of DuShane's. The idea of a man riding fast and straight towards the hay doors to hell never give me much pleasure before. But I have to admit that picturing that murdering bastard in them straits, tied onto a big black stallion and galloping headlong toward the Devil, who was holding open wide a red hot iron gate, that tasted sweet as horehound candy in my mouth. But it was sickly sweet after I sucked on it for a minute . . . no matter what he done, to Clete or Nell or them folks back by the White River — Jimmy's family — he was a still a man. A man's a man no matter what, even if he's more snake than human. And DuShane was on this old Earth for a purpose, one that I couldn't see, of course, and neither would he, the murdering bastard.

Wasn't but five minutes 'til DuShane fired his pistol again and I heard it zing off a rock over in

Clete's direction. I fired through the crack, stood and touched off another round before I ducked back down. But that time, he didn't return my fire and Clete didn't shoot either.

The sun was hot and turning that pocket where I watched and waited into a granite oven . . . the only shade under my hat. I took a drink from my canteen and noticed a hawk riding the wind above the peak where that billy was before. After a while he drifted over and circled slow around our pile of rocks. He was a good ways up but not so far I couldn't see how slick and shiny his brown feathers was. He craned his neck back and forth, looking down, getting a gander at what was moving below him . . . which was us. He sailed back over toward them other rocks, where he was before, caught himself a careless sparrow, and settled down over there to eat it.

I stopped watching that hawk and was about to look through my opening again when directly above me a shadow dark as night and tall as a horse reared up against the sun. All I could see of his face was his pale eyes staring crazy at me. I was trying to bring the muzzle of that scattergun up, but he swung the stock of his heavy rifle over his head like a club and it come down at me like lightning. All I had time to do was put my hand up, and all I had time to think was *I'm gone, I'm gone.* And then it thundered and everthing went black as swamp water.

Chapter Twenty-eight

Only I wasn't gone. I swum hard back up to the light on the surface of that black pool. I come to myself gazing straight into the sun and wondering how long I'd been out. It didn't feel like a long time, but maybe that's how it always seemed. Much practice as I was getting, being knocked on the head, you'd think I'd know. Blood run down my face from a gash above where my hair started, and the knot raising there felt big as a turkey egg. Little finger of my left hand was out of joint at the knuckle, too. Soon as I snapped it back in place it swole up tight. I almost passed out again when I stood up.

I found my scattergun, checked the shells and'd just pulled up to fire it, meaning to warn Clete, when I glanced down the way we come up. DuShane was just about to the bottom. I fired one barrel and he jumped the rest of the way. I fired the other at him while he was sprawled on the ground after his fall. Last I saw of him, he'd gathered himself up and was ducking under the trees, heading downhill.

I reloaded and fired again, into the air this time, both barrels. "Clete!" I yelled. "He got behind me and is down below!"

Nothing happened. The bleeding stopped sometime about then, but I couldn't see DuShane nor Clete and no noise from neither.

After wiping some of the blood off my face, I set my hat back on, which I guess had saved me a busted head, pulling it front some to keep it off the swelling. Maybe I did pass out again then, I'm not sure. Everthing seemed to melt and run together and I throwed up worse than I ever remember doing before. When I felt a little better, I reloaded and fired both barrels again, not knowing what else to do.

Clete showed himself partly, way over to the right and halfway to the top from where I was. I pointed so as to be sure he could see where I meant. "He's down there now!" I yelled. Clete stood up the rest of the way and looked up toward the top and then back at me. I seen him shake his head before he turned and headed my way.

I didn't wait for him. Instead, I gathered up the canteens and jerky bag to start down and that's when I saw the long heavy rifle with the tube on top that DuShane'd hit me with, the stock splintered some and broke completely off the rest. I was surprised he left it there, but with no more bullets and it in two pieces like that, maybe it was more trouble carrying than it was worth.

My head hurt plenty going down over them rocks. Damn if I didn't feel stupid and shamed for letting him get away, and that hurt worse. I don't much remember climbing down, it seemed a real short time 'til I was at the bottom and looking at his tracks. I couldn't see Clete up above yet, so I followed DuShane's sign for a piece.

He'd started off running downhill, back the way we come here, but he'd slowed to a long-strided walk after only a few rods. It surprised me he didn't think to look for our horses, but he didn't — easy as it would of been to find them. Maybe my shooting at him done some good after all, even though I was pretty sure I didn't hit him. I went and untied the horses and brought them back up to the base of the cliff. Clete was nearly halfway down by then. I sat my horse and watched him come the rest of the way.

"What the hell happened?" he ask.

"I don't know," I lied. "I looked up and there he was all of a sudden." If it would of done any good to tell him I was watching a hawk instead of our man, I like to think I'd have mentioned it, but I didn't.

"I can't see how —" He got a good look at me once he was in the saddle and the mad went right off his face. "Jesus, you're a mess. Are you shot?"

"No," I told him. "He banged me on the head with that rifle of his. Broke it in two on my head, but I'm still walking around, I think. Hurts a little is all."

"The bleeding stopped?"

I lifted my hat to show him and then said that I was all right, though I wasn't sure I was.

"You're lucky," he said. "Most men aren't blessed with a skull as thick as yours."

I nodded my head a time or two, which made

it hurt all the worse, and then saw he was ribbing at me.

"He must've headed back down the valley," Clete said.

I showed him where the tracks went and we started after DuShane again, me behind Clete. I kept my eyes peeled sharp to both sides of us, leaving up front to him. Down where DuShane's horse lay dead, I thought I saw something off to the left and yelled to Clete, but it turned out to be a squirrel or something.

The more I thought it over, the less I believed he'd try and ambush us again. He was running now, trying with all he had to put distance between him and us.

When we got to the edge of the prospector's clearing, Clete threw his hand out sudden to the side, palm back. "There he is!" he said quiet. He grabbed his Henry and jumped off just inside the trees. DuShane was running hard, though kind of limping too, his long brown coat flapping in the breeze, and him about to make the woods at the far end.

I watched Clete drop to one knee and draw a fine bead on his running target. "Stop!" I yelled, and even right then I didn't know if I meant Clete or DuShane.

Clete was so surprised he turned to me quick and just looked.

DuShane must of heard me too for he stopped, all right. Only then he drew his pistol and fired a shot at us that whistled through the branches overhead. Missed us by yards, but it was enough to get Clete's mad up again. "You sonofabitch!" he yelled. Then he sighted level down the Henry's barrel, squeezed the trigger, and hit DuShane before he took a third step from where he'd shot at us. The slug spun that tall man around twice and he lost hold of his gun, which sailed lazy into the air. He corkscrewed beneath the top layer of brush so I couldn't see where he lay.

Clete stood and tried to get sight of him too, but he couldn't see him either. He mounted then, walked the gray into the clearing and after steadying it good, stood on his saddle for a look-see.

"Is he down?" I ask.

"If he is, it's no fault of yours," Clete answered pretty sharp, still facing the lower end of the clearing. He dismounted and walked closer, keeping low. I stayed a little behind and off to the left, walking my horse like Clete was doing, my scattergun ready. Five yards from the end of the clearing I found DuShane's Colt, spent cartridges in every chamber. Close by a puddle of blood was already starting to seep into the ground. We both seen the direction he'd crawled off.

"He's headed for the creek," Clete said, kind of excited. "C'mon, he can't be far and he's not armed now." We went into the trees at a slow run, and twenty yards in front of us, there was DuShane on the ground, dragging his one leg —

crawling on both hands and one knee. Clete's slug had took him low in the hip and his whole pants leg was soaked with blood. His left leg and foot was turned nearly sideways to his body, dragging useless behind him, but still he crawled along pretty fast, 'specially after he seen us. Clete dropped his reins and started to run hard. He caught up to DuShane just where he'd crawled into the creek a little ways.

Clete was right beside him, his Remington pointed directly at DuShane's head, but that lanky fool kept crawling toward deeper water, so Clete kicked one arm out from under him. DuShane's face splashed into the stream and he come out sputtering and screeching and yelling loud, shouting something I couldn't under-stand, though it sounded more like cursing than anything else. I could see Clete was getting madder and madder that the man wouldn't give it up and face the idea that he was beat, but he wouldn't. When DuShane started crawling away again, Clete put a boot behind the man's scrawny neck, put enough weight on him so he went under, and then held him there.

I stood on the bank holding the horses and watched. "What'd he say?" I ask Clete.

"I didn't catch it, but I didn't like the sound of it." He had to jump around and dance some to keep DuShane down.

I watched Jezrael DuShane's floppy black hat float downstream a little ways and then sink. "Don't you think you could let him up now?" I ask. "Seems like the fight's all out of him."

Clete turned to me, his face a blank, and then looked down at DuShane. "Let him get a taste of how it feels. Besides, drowning is a sure cure for bad habits, so they say."

"You better stop now or you'll kill him!" I yelled, but Clete didn't answer or even turn my way. DuShane'd stopped flailing his arms around and laid like a waterlogged plank in the knee-deep water, Clete's boot still pressing hard on the back of his neck.

Chapter Twenty-nine

I dropped the reins and splashed toward Clete through the creek. I didn't know I was going to crash into him 'til I done it. He stumbled across DuShane, twisting himself around so that when he fell, he hit the water ass first, both feet flying high, but taking care to keep his gun up out of the stream.

I went to pull DuShane up, to keep him from drowning, but his head was already above the surface, water pouring from his mouth and long stringy hair. I took his shoulders to set him up better and when he turned toward me, his eyes wild, in his hand was a little hideout gun, already cocked. I spun backwards just as the shot blasted into my face, stinging like red ant bites.

I cracked my head on a stone, I guess, under water for a second, the shot ringing in my ear like a fire bell. But even then I knowed the ball missed me. I sat up in time to see DuShane start to crawl on across the stream and Clete, still sitting, reach over and rap him on the head with the barrel of his Remington.

To tell the truth, I don't know what happened for a while after that. Everthing got blurry and slow. I must of set there in the creek dazed a long time because when I waded up on the bank DuShane was stretched out, passed out, and facing the sky with his hands tied behind his back, underneath him.

Clete was breaking sticks and feeding them to a little fire he'd built, his hat off and drying on a stone nearby. He glanced at me when I sat down beside his fire but he didn't say nothing.

"Go on," I told him. "Tell me how stupid I was."

He didn't even look up. Instead, he took off his shirt and his boots and set them to dry in front of the fire on sticks he poked into the ground. It had clouded up and was a lot cooler under them trees than it'd been up above in the rocks, and before long I was shivering like an aspen in the wind, my head hurting worse than ever and a ringing in my left ear like a bad hangover. I stripped down to my long johns and set my clothes to drying too. I unpacked my bed roll, laid it even and stretched out on top of it. I remember pulling a blanket over myself, but nothing else for a while.

First thing I knowed, Clete was shaking me awake. When I sat up he put a dish of bacon and beans in my lap and then went to eating his. It was still pretty bright, so I guessed I didn't sleep but about an hour. My head was pounding less, but the ringing in my ear made it hard to hear anything on that side. Damn, but that food tasted good, though, and I had mine about half wolfed down before I noticed that DuShane was sitting up too, his face turned away from us.

"You going to feed him?" I ask Clete.

"No sense in that — wasting good food. Soon

as we're done here I'm going to hang him." Clete spoke real matter-of-fact, like he was telling you the time of day.

DuShane's head snapped around and he looked at us, his pale gray eyes flashing fire. Though I'd been studying his sign for weeks, that was the first good look I got at his face, which was long and skinny like the rest of him. His nose was more like the beak of a hawk than a regular nose, and his teeth, the few he had, was yellow as piss. A big ugly scab stretched above one eye, probably where the barrel of my .36 hit him. The whole front of his shirt was dried brown blood. His dark hair was streaked with gray, thin in front and long, and it was plastered to his face and red buzzardy neck and down into his eyes. To say it plain, he looked like hell. Fresh blood'd oozed from the wound all down his muddy pants, and his foot there laid right out to the side — out of joint at the hip. Must have hurt him bad, but his face didn't show it. What it did show was what he'd a liked to do to us.

Of course I was surprised at what Clete said, about hanging him. It was something an Indian or a Pinkerton would say, tell you what he was going to do to you before he done it, just to watch you squirm, but it wasn't like Clete to act that way. I thought on it some more while I pulled on my boots. Somehow, I just couldn't believe he would take it that far, even after I thought it over good. "Why you going to hang him?" I ask.

He sopped up the last of his bean and bacon juice with a bite of bread, then chewed and swallowed before he answered. "Well," he said, smacking his lips some, making me think of Banty Foote. "Partly because it's a waste of time not to. And partly because I don't feel like nursing him all the way back to Two Scalp, where they'd just hang him anyway. Mostly, though, I'm going to hang the bastard because I feel like it. On top of that, I asked him something and the sonofabitch won't answer me." Clete tossed his tin plate next to the fire and poured us both a cup of coffee. When he handed me mine, I seen just the hint of a sly smile on his face.

Well, of course I understood then. I seen that Clete was just throwing a scare into DuShane to get him to talk, trying to find out whatever it was he wanted to know. After he finished his coffee Clete stood up, fished some paper out of his saddle bags and walked off into the brush.

DuShane sat and stared at me.

"What'd he ask you?" I ask him.

"None of your gawdamn bidness!" he spit out. You could hear the rebel clear through his talk, the surly way they like to draw out their words when they're mad.

I had a sip of my coffee and lit my pipe. "Well, it's your funeral," I told him. "But it'll cost you your life, of course, not telling him what he wants to know. Clete Shannon is not a man to trifle with, as you have already found out once today. You better understand. He'll really do it

346

— hang you, that is. Course, it's your life, and if you want to toss 'er away this afternoon, you found the certain-sure way to do 'er. I seen him hang men for less cause." Naturally, that was a lie. I never even seen Clete so much as shoot at someone who wasn't trying to kill him, let alone take a man's life in cold blood.

But that old boy didn't even blink an eye.

Clete come back and just stood there a minute before he spoke. "Let's get this over with. Help me boost him into my saddle."

I led his horse up close, and then Clete took his rope and tied a noose while DuShane sat there and watched him do it. Clete got on one side of him and me the other. DuShane started to squirm when we begun to lift him, and his hurt leg, which was on my side, twisted more out to the side and he let out a terrible howl and then went limp, which made it easier to set him square into Clete's old McClellan. As tall as he was, he didn't seem to weigh nothing at all.

He come to with a start and didn't appear to reconize us for a minute, but he seen the fix he was in, all right. "Help me, Lord, help me!" he shouted, trying to look up through the pines to the sky.

"You'd be better off praying to the Devil, you sonofabitch," Clete said. He put a foot in the near stirrup, put the noose over DuShane's head and then tightened it on his neck before stepping back down. "You earned this when you set that old woman's house on fire." He handed me the

347

end of the rope and walked downstream a ways, looking up.

DuShane watched him and then turned to me and spoke, looking and sounding a little nervous both. "What's he doin'?"

I took off my hat and rubbed the different sore spots on my head. "Why, I suspect he's looking for a stout limb to hang you from. If I was you and wanted to live 'til sundown, I'd tell him what he wants to know. What was it, anyhow?"

"Go to hell, you damn Yankee! I ain't answerin' to him or you or *nobody!*"

I figgered it would do no good to explain to that cracker I was a Texan.

"Bring him down here," Clete yelled.

When DuShane and me got there, maybe sixty yards and up from the stream a piece, Clete took the end of his rope and tried to throw it over a high, thick limb of a dead pine, one that'd shed about all its lower branches. After missing a second time, he found a stone the size of his fist, tied that to the free end, and finally got his rope up and over the branch he'd picked out. That done, he yanked it tight so that DuShane had to sit up high in the saddle just to draw his breath. Keeping his line taut, Clete walked out behind his horse a short ways and then throwed a couple hitches around a smaller pine, pretty high up, for he was at the end of his rope.

When Clete come back, he drew his Remington, cocked it, and held it high. "I hope you burn in hell," he said, his voice just above a whisper.

"He was my *boy,* my only *boy* you killed!" DuShane hollered, twisting his head around as best he could so as to see Clete. He had kept himself together up 'til then, but now his face was twisted up with fear and I saw the piss darken his pants and some of it drip from his boot heel onto the dead pine needles.

"Then why the hell did you tell people that Whitey was your brother?!" Clete demanded.

I remember it struck me as odd right then that Clete was going through all this just to find out whether Whitey was this man's son or his brother. I couldn't see how it could be so important to him so as to give DuShane the pain of putting him in the saddle — though after I thought on it, I realized we'd of had to set him up anyway, for he surely could not walk. But at the same time it also struck me odd that Clete was so mad as he was — and he was, for the veins was standing out on his neck. Then again, maybe it was just that DuShane wouldn't answer him for so long. Nosir, Clete Shannon was not a man to be took lightly.

DuShane turned his face front again, more in my direction, and got hisself more under control. "He was my brother. Don't hang me, Sheriff. Don't do it!" And then he lowered his head and started to cry, big sobs that shook him all over.

I thought for a minute he was saying whatever he figgered Clete wanted to hear, anything at all just to save his life. What he said made not a bit of sense until I chewed it up in my mind a minute, but what I come up with, that just couldn't be. "How could — ?" I started to ask him before it hit me the way it was. "Well I'll be damned," I said.

"Yeah, and so will he," Clete said, flat as Kansas.

"It was all Ma's fault!" Jezrael DuShane hollered, the tears running down his face. "Climbing into the loft with me, her clothes all off. I wasn't more'n a boy, an' she *made* me do it with her. Pa woulda *kilt* me if he found out Whitey was my boy and not his'n!"

I glanced at Clete and he was nodding his head, a smirky smile darkening his face and making him look mean as Satan. I knowed then what he'd wondered about last night, that he'd figgered this all out, mostly. He knowed for sure now. "Goodbye, mother fucker," he said, and then slapped his horse hard with the flat of his hand and fired his pistol at the same time.

It happened so fast I just stood there froze to the spot. DuShane must of had his good foot in the stirrup on the other side, for when that big strong gray took out, his foot stuck there and I saw the man angled out and stretched out between horse and rope so that he appeared to get longer than he already was, right in front of my eyes. And then his neck snapped with a crack like a splintered oak limb.

Still I stood there glued to the ground. His boot come off and the horse run off and

DuShane swung back and forth like the pendulum of a big grandfather clock. The toe of the other boot, his bad leg, twisted right out behind him, scraping little furrows into the deep pine needles on every swing. And while he swung he also spun, facing me and then away and then back toward me again, a startled look on his twisted-up face, his eyes popping out like a fish's and his tongue lolling to below his pointy chin, dripping spit and bloody froth. Already his face was the color of ashes.

It was like I woke up right in the middle of a nightmare, and I run back toward where Clete'd tied his rope. But as I passed him, he reached out and give me a short, square punch to the chin and I went down like twenty pounds of steer liver.

"I figured you'd try that," Clete said, holstering his Remington and then rubbing his knuckles while I was still on the ground looking up at him. "Let him alone. He's dead, if you didn't know it already. And don't cut him down. When I hang a man, he stays hung." He started downstream after his horse. After a while I heard him down below, giving his loud whistle as he went, trying to call Whatever in.

I stood up and looked at that tall, bony man twirling at the end of Clete's rope. He didn't swing no more, but he still spun slow, dragging his toes. Looking at that man's awful face and broke up body, something turned in me. Something changed right then, even though I didn't exactly know what it was. It felt like the morning you wake up and it dawns on you that summer's over, that from then on it's all shorter days and getting colder.

Chapter Thirty

I took out my clasp knife and cut Clete's rope close to where it was tied to the tree. DuShane hit the ground with a thump. I walked back up to my horse to get the folding shovel and saw my hat and clothes there beside the remains of our fire. I had forgot I was still in my union suit and put them on. Then I took the shovel and went back down to where DuShane lay in a heap.

I had the grave about half dug by the time Clete rode in. "I thought I told you —" but he didn't finish it. I didn't look up at him, either, just kept digging. After a minute he rode on up to the fire.

It was hard digging there, I recall. Weren't many stones, but the roots of them pines criss-crossed all over the place and I wisht I had an axe. When the hole was deep enough to suit me, I took the noose off his neck and pushed him in with my foot. He was a man and deserved burying, but I didn't straighten him out comfortable in his grave and I didn't do no praying over him either after I covered him up.

Clete had everything packed by the time I got up to the fire and all I needed to do was put up the shovel. I handed him his rope.

"Well, you feel better now?" Clete asked.

"No, I don't," I told him, mounting the bay.

Clete got up on his horse and we headed down

the valley, him in front. We just rode quiet, the sun coming through the clouds every so often, angled over to the west. Going along, I saw a bird I had never saw before, up high in a big pine. Orangy yeller, he was, with some black on his wings and head. White on the wings, too. An oriole, I figgered, but not a kind that I'd ever saw. He chattered at us and then piped a pair of notes, so as to say goodbye, after we passed, and I thought of Mandy then.

Where the trail got wider, after the valley spread out some, Clete dropped back beside me. "Look, I'm sorry I punched you. There was no call for me to do that. You were right. Burying him was the right thing to do."

I didn't say nothing.

"If it will make you any happier," Clete said, smiling at me, "we can step down and you can punch me."

I shook my head. "No, it don't bother me that much being punched. I've been punched plenty before, harder than that."

"What the hell's eating you, then?" His face looked like he was tasting something not to his liking.

"Was it fun fooling me like that?" I ask him.

"Whadda you mean?"

"What do *I mean?* You know damn *well* what I mean! You knowed you were going to hang him the whole time, whether he answered you or not!"

"Of course I did," Clete said. "I told you I was

going to hang him. Didn't you hear me say that?"

"Yes, I heard you. But the way you acted, I thought it was all just to make him talk. I didn't even know what you ask him. I figgered it was something important, something . . . I don't know what. Let's hear you say you didn't try to make me think you was just throwing a scare into him. Go on, let me hear you say it!"

"Ahh, this is bullshit. You're acting like a god-damned old woman." He spurred his horse ahead and we traveled another mile, saying nothing to each other, before he dropped back beside me again.

"You're right, Willie. I needed your help, at least I didn't want to fight you over doing it, not in front of him, and I knew you wouldn't go along with it." He looked at me square and offered his hand.

"No, thanks," I told him. "I don't shake hands with no murderers."

He dropped his hand and looked at me like I'd slapped him hard in the face. "Murderer? I think you're a little confused, aren't you? It was DuShane who killed Banty and those people back by the White and Nell Larson. Remember Nell, Willie? Remember that night she died, all burnt up?"

"Of course I do, and I'll remember this day just as long."

"Well, that's the law business, son. Executing horse thieves and killers is a part of it."

I pulled the bay up sharp and after a couple steps, Clete done the same with his horse and looked back at me.

"No," I told him, "*Executing* is what a judge and jury and a hangman does after a man's had *his* say, tells *his* side of it. What you done, stringing a man up for spite and vengeance and God-knows-what-all, that's lynchin'. And lynchin' is murder. Just the same as if you laid in wait for him in the dark and shot him off his horse when he rode by. Just the same as DuShane. No different."

Clete just sat and looked at me and after awhile he shook his head and then rode on. I waited and after a minute I followed him. It had clouded up pretty solid by then and before long the rain started. Nothin' heavy, just a steady drizzle that drenched everthing. I stopped and searched for my slicker, but then I remembered it was still back in Two Scalp. So I just got wet. I kept waiting for Clete to drop back beside me again, to say that he seen what I said was so, that about lynching and murder, but he didn't do it.

When we come down out of that valley to where the road forked, it was starting to get dark.

Clete got out his map and studied it. "This way should take us to Hay Camp," he said, tilting his head to the right. "I see no sense going back to Deadwood. I can wire Bullock to tell him what happened when we get to Two Scalp.

Should save us half a day going this way, maybe more."

"I'm not going back to Two Scalp," I told him. "So I guess this here is where we part company."

Chapter Thirty-one

Clete sat his horse and looked at me real curious, smiling almost. "You mean that? You sure you want to split up now? That's what you want?"

"Yes it is. I ain't so hot on Deadwood, but I can think of nowheres else to go, and I ain't going back to Two Scalp with you, *that's* for sure."

Clete looked angry for a minute right after I said that, but then he drew a deep breath and let it out slow. "You're making a mistake, Willie. Chances are good I can find the $30,000 Wilson stole. We could have a nice spread down in Texas on that . . . two nice spreads . . . fifty-fifty. You better think on it."

He waited for me to say something, but I just shook my head no.

The rain commenced to drip off Clete's hat brim and it was getting colder by the minute. Night was coming on. "You're not so young anymore, Pardner. Before too long you'll be getting too old to just drift around like you've been doing."

"I know."

He pulled the collar of his slicker up and inspected the sky. "It's not that mixed-blood girl, is it? Mandy?"

"Oh, I hope to see her again, though she don't

want me. I know that. No, that's no part of it, I don't guess."

"Well, that's smart of you, anyway. She's little better than a whore, you know. Jumped right in my bedroll with me the night after I caught up with you two. I didn't even ask her. In bed with you one night, me the next."

I couldn't see his face real good, dark as it was getting. I thought for a minute he might be lying to me, just to get me to go along. But after I thought on it a minute, remembering how she was with that Thebideaux fellow, I figgered he was probably telling the truth, much as it pained me to think so.

"Well, it's getting dark," Clete said. "No sense sitting here jawing all night. Sure you won't change your mind?"

"No, I'll be going my own way from here." I rode my horse up close and offered him my hand.

He took it and give a hard shake. "You're a strange one, Willie, and probably the best friend I ever had."

"Thank you kindly," I said. It was a dumb thing to say, I see now, but it just come out of my mouth.

Clete backed the gray up a few steps and started off. "If you change your mind, I'll be in Two Scalp for a month or so and then down along the Rio Grande. Hear that's some of the best cattle country there is."

"I'll remember if I do, though I don't think I

will." I sat the bay and watched him walk his horse part way up a little hill on the trail. He stopped and turned back, just looking at me. I burned him into my memory right then, just like Mandy done with me a few days before, him sitting there on that big gray stallion and smiling at me in the rain.

"Goodbye, my friend," I called to him.

"Goodbye, you old fart," he yelled back. He nudged Whatever, topped the hill and was gone.

Chapter Thirty-two

I sat there a minute getting rained on and trying to figure out what I was going to do. The only thing I could think of was to head on up the road towards Deadwood, like I told Clete I was going to. After awhile that's what I done. To tell it short, I rode all night in the rain, wetter'n a frog in a bog, sleeping and being awake and miserable by turns. Just as I was coming down the hill into Deadwood, the clouds to the east raised up some. The sun clumb over the ridge and lit the whole sky and the town up like a fairy-tale city, the buildings all orange and rosy, the windows in them glittery like flames. I almost didn't mind I was wet and cold seeing that sight.

But as pretty as it was, it was all kind of sour to me at the same time — like I was only about half there. I figured it was only on account of being tired as hell and up all night again and being whacked on the head so often of late.

After seeing to my horse I got a room at the Grand, that beefy-faced owner up and about his business already. He ask me if I wanted my old room back. After I remembered as how Banty'd been killed in it I told him no, to give me another. I just flopped down on the bed and slept in my damp clothes 'til past noon.

I woke up feeling lower than a skunk's belly, but hungry too, so I went back and had another steak at that place I had eat before. After that I looked for where the fellow knew all them Texas songs. Damned if I could remember which place it was, so I had to have a drink in a lot of different saloons before I found it, which I eventually did. Of course, by then I had a pretty good load on and things still didn't look no brighter than when I had woke up. I fooled with the idea of gathering up my things and heading over toward the Grand River country, but I couldn't work up the gumption for it.

I was sitting there minding my own business, trying to figure out what I was going to do with myself, just sipping a rye and listening to them Texas songs again, when who should tap me on the shoulder but Sheriff Seth Bullock.

"Didn't expect to see you again so soon, Willie," he said. "Where's Shannon?"

"More than I can tell you," I told him. "Might be on his way back to Two Scalp if a bunch of Sioux ain't scalped him by now. Or maybe he's took off in the other direction, toward Texas or someplace else."

Bullock sat down and looked at me close. "You two give up on DuShane?"

"*Hell* no," I said. "We're all through with that business. And Jezrael DuShane won't be coming back to Deadwood to stir things up no more, you can count on that."

"What happened?" Bullock wanted to know.

For a minute I thought of telling him the whole story, of how Clete had almost drowned

DuShane — maybe would have if I hadn't of stopped him — of how Clete had finally hung him after pulling that dirty trick on me, making me think he was only trying to scare him. Before I even opened up my mouth to say it, I changed my mind. "DuShane got shot trying to get away from us," I said. I don't know why I said that, but that's what I told him. It wasn't a lie, exactly. DuShane *did* get shot running through that clearing.

Bullock tipped his hat up and looked kind of surprised. "He's dead then, DuShane?"

"Well, he damn well better be," I said. "I buried him yesterday — or was it the day before?"

He got a chuckle out of that, but then he cocked his head kind of odd at me. "What are you doing here, then?"

"Good a place as any to get a drink," I said, looking around at the room. "And the feller here knows even more Texas songs than I do."

"How come you're not with Shannon is what I meant," Bullock said.

I sat and chewed it over for a minute. I thought again of telling him the whole thing, only it just didn't set right. "Difference of opinion, as the man says," I told him, but then didn't say no more.

"Difference of opinion," Bullock repeated after a while, nodding his head. The piano player started on "Texas Sunsets" again.

"Difference of opinion," I said a second time,

nodding right along with him, and then just let her go at that.

After a time Bullock stood up. "Well, I don't get it." He waited for me to talk, but I had nothing more to say. "If you want that deputy job I spoke of, stop around later. Just be sober when you do. I've got no jobs for drunks." The way he said it put me in mind of Clete.

"Thanks all the same," I told him. "But if I ain't deputying for Clete, then I don't suspect I'll be deputying for nobody — and what a man drinks is his own affair."

"Indeed it is, Goodwin. Indeed it is," he said, slapping me on the back. "But what a deputy of mine drinks is also my affair. You can understand that."

"Sure, I understand," I told him. I have to admit my mind was off someplace else — up along the Bad where Mandy and Clete and me had trailed DuShane, I think.

I don't know exactly when he left, but by the time I thought to turn around and look, Bullock was gone.

I gathered up my change, polished off the last few drops of my liquor, and turned my glass over. Going up the street to my hotel, even then I guess I knowed what I was going to do.

That red-faced man at the Grand was still behind the desk, and I told him I was leaving — which I did as soon as I collected the few things I had left in my room. I stopped in a grocery and bought a big hunk of bacon and some tinned goods they had there, including some peaches, though the price was high as hell. The man put everything in a feed sack for me. A bright yeller slicker in the window of a dry goods store caught my eye, and I went in and bought that, too. I decided I'd had enough of riding wet for a while. The boy at the livery got my horse pretty quick and I rode out of Deadwood at a walking trot.

Up and down through the gulches and gullies I went and come out onto the plain by the time it was starting to get dark. I rode all that night, I guess, passing through Hay Camp sometime early the next morning. Rode all the next day, too, and toward evening made a cold camp way the hell out in the middle of nowhere, going back just the way we had come, just like Clete's tracks showed me he was doing, too.

In a way, I couldn't believe I was trying to catch up to Clete. Several times the next few days I stopped my horse and just sat there, thinking I would go some other direction than back towards Two Scalp. Then I'd just keep going on like I was before.

I made good time, sleeping little and riding long. That bay was the finest animal I ever had, and I hated to trade him off to some drovers with fresh mounts, but I had to, for he was even more wore out than I was. Wasn't 'til about ten miles later it come to me I could have trailed the bay and made as good a time. I could have kicked myself for not thinking of it back there. Maybe my brain was tired too.

The new horse was strong, though, and I was putting the miles behind me again at a good clip. *What am I doing this for?* I kept asking myself. *Ain't I got no pride? Wasn't I right in the first place about splitting off from Clete over what he done, hanging DuShane like that and fooling me?* And even though I knowed I was right, that Clete *shouldn't* have done like that, it made no difference. For he was my friend, you see, and even if he was wrong as hell and the devil lumped together, he was still my friend. I could no more say a permanent goodbye to him than I could sprout wings and fly up to heaven. Hell, maybe he even needed me, despite himself, just like he needed Mary to smooth him out in other ways.

Five or six days straight I rode hard, hard as I ever did in my life. Professor Marsh and his boys offered me supper at their camp in them miserable, cut-up Badlands and I didn't refuse. One of the young men had saw Clete earlier that day and though I felt like sleeping there after we ate, I pushed on.

Toward sundown I was up on that big ledge where Clete had camped that night, and then on up where I had slept in the mud. Even that looked good to me then. About dark I was sleeping in the saddle about as much as I was awake, but I kept going. Godamighty, I felt like climbing down and sleeping 'til I couldn't sleep no more. I kept going anyway.

I don't know how much farther it was, but coming awake once I thought I saw a fire up ahead. I looked again and then I was sure. Clete had a big fire built up for me, that's what it had to be. All those days on the trail and he was still building big fires at night for me to see, supposing I might be along. Why, that damned Clete! I snapped off three quick shots and he fired back almost right away. That horse sure didn't want to run, but after I give my whistle I hurried him along as fast as he would go.

There stood Clete in front of a bonfire big enough for the whole Sioux Nation to see, waving his hat slow back and forth over his head, as if I couldn't see him already easy as pie, outlined as he was against them flames. Of course, I couldn't see his face, but I knowed he would be wearing a smile as broad as Texas. I just knowed it.